Green Valentine

Lili Wilkinson

ALLEN&UNWIN
SYDNEY·MELBOURNE·AUCKLAND·LONDON

First published by Allen & Unwin in 2015

Allen & Unwin – Australia
83 Alexander Street, Crows Nest NSW 2065, Australia
Phone: (61 2) 8425 0100
Email: info@allenandunwin.com
Web: www.allenandunwin.com

Allen & Unwin – UK
c/o Murdoch Books, Erico House, 93–99 Upper Richmond Road, London SW15 2TG, UK
Phone: (44 20) 8785 5995
Email: info@murdochbooks.co.uk
Web: www.allenandunwin.com
Murdoch Books is a wholly owned division of Allen & Unwin Pty Ltd

A Cataloguing-in-Publication entry is available from the National Library of Australia
www.trove.nla.gov.au
A catalogue record for this book is available from the British Library

ISBN (AUS) 978 1 76011 027 7
ISBN (UK) 978 1 74336 752 0

Cover and text design by Design by Committee
Set in 11 pt Electra by Midland Typesetters
Printed and bound in Australia by Griffin Press

10 9 8 7 6 5 4 3 2

For my parents, who care about the planet.
And everyone else fighting the good fight.

1

You want to save the world? Here's a piece of advice for you. Don't try to do it dressed as a giant lobster.

The shopping centre was packed – full of people mindlessly wheeling groaning trolleys of useless junk and processed food. Nobody had time to stop and listen to my spiel about the plight of the Margaret River Hairy Marron. They didn't even take a fact sheet or sign my petition. In fact, the only people who spoke to me were the ones who thought I was spruiking the new seafood place that had opened up next to the deli. People just didn't *care*. I bet they wouldn't be so concerned about the two-packets-of-Tim-Tams-for-the-price-of-one deal once the polar ice-caps melted and we all died. *Then* they might listen to what I had to say about the importance of biodiversity, and the conservation of endangered species.

Admittedly, my Margaret River Hairy Marron costume *did* look a lot like a lobster.

Okay, it *was* a lobster costume. The costume-hire place didn't have any marron costumes. So although the Margaret River Hairy Marron is brown with blueish-black claws, I was in a bright-red lobster suit, with a massive headdress thing with curly red antennae and one enormous red foam claw (I left the other one at home – I needed one normal hand to hold my fact sheets and clipboard). I'd also added red face-paint so the whole outfit would hang together. And also because I didn't want anyone to recognise me.

If I was a more shallow, uncaring human being, I'd be hanging out with my friends right now. They were probably at Valentine's only decent café, sipping single-origin lattes and planning their day. They'd probably go into the city later for lunch. Do a little shopping. Maybe see a movie.

Not me. I was too busy saving the world.

I shifted from one foot to the other. The shopping centre PA was piping out an endless stream of tinny pop music, and I felt like my eardrums were being rubbed against a cheese grater. Christmas decorations were already up, even though it was only October. Got to get in early for the planet's most appalling display of mindless consumerism.

An angry-looking woman sailed past, barking into a diamante-encrusted phone. She was wearing Italian designer sunglasses and carrying some kind of dead-animal-skin handbag that would have cost a fortune, and used a tonne of energy to get shipped over here. There was a bottle of French water poking out of the handbag.* I didn't even bother offering her a fact sheet.

---

* What's the deal with imported water? I mean, I know we have a water problem in this country, but importing it in little 200ml bottles isn't exactly the solution. Get it out of the tap like a normal person! Did you know that bottled water costs 2500 times more than just tap water? Not to mention the fact that Australians produce 60,000 tonnes of greenhouse gas emissions just from buying bottled water. Disgusting.

A guy pushing an enormous stack of supermarket trolleys blocked my view. He was like a glacier*, slow but implacable. The guy was cute in a scruffy, Asian way, with skinny jeans, black hoodie, earbuds and angular haircut. I was pretty sure he went to my school – one of those lame stoners who was always in detention or skulking up the back of the classroom.

I watched with dawning horror as, like a car crash in slow motion, the stack of trolleys drifted towards an old lady with a walker. The cute guy didn't notice, too busy off in his own world of whatever rubbish music he listened to. I nearly called out, until I noticed that the old lady was the one who'd pretended to be deaf when I'd tried to talk to her about the top ten endangered species list. She noticed just in time, and scurried out of the way with surprising lightness of foot. The guy didn't stop to apologise or anything, he just scowled and kept pushing.

'Excuse me?' It was a harassed-looking man with two toddlers in tow.

I turned to him with a beaming smile.

'Are you handing out samples? The boys love prawns.'

'It's not a prawn costume, it's a *lob*—' I closed my eyes and took a deep breath. 'A critically endangered *Hairy Marron*.'

The man looked confused, and dragged his kids off towards the supermarket.

---

* For those of you reading this in the future – a glacier was a giant mountain of ice that formed where the accumulation of snow exceeded its ablation over centuries. You've never heard of them because a bunch of idiots known as the human race thought that double-bagging groceries was more important than the melting of our polar ice-caps.

I lasted another forty minutes or so, with no success. I was thirsty, hot, itchy from the lobster suit, and I needed to pee. One of the perks of being a registered volunteer is that I get to use the shopping centre's break room, so I dragged myself down the poky little corridor to the staff toilets, and struggled through a ridiculous dance in a tiny cubicle to squeeze out of the lobster costume so I could pee. The suit was damp and sweaty, and I kicked myself for not bringing along a change of clothes. It was also starting to smell pretty ripe, and I tried not to think about the fact that it had come from a hire company, and that in all likelihood, plenty of other people had sweated inside it before me. Ugh. I pulled it back on with a shudder.

Shopping Trolley Guy was in the break room, his feet up on the table, reading a comic book. He didn't look up when I shuffled in.

I fumbled with the giant foam lobster claw, and eventually pulled it off and dumped it on the table. I then dug through the dirty dishes in the sink to find a glass.

'Gross,' I muttered. Nearly everything in the sink was covered in brown coffee sludge.

'Why don't you just use the water cooler?' the guy asked. 'It has disposable cups.'

'Do you know how many resources are used to make a plastic cup?' I asked. 'Those things aren't recyclable, and take up to a thousand years to biodegrade.'

The guy blinked, and turned back to his comic. I found the least-scungy glass and rinsed it clean before filling it with tap water and downing it in one gulp. I filled my glass again and did some sneaky checking-out of Shopping Trolley Guy.

He had lovely dark brown eyes and just the faintest smattering of freckles across his nose, barely visible against his olive skin. He chewed thoughtfully on his lower lip as he slowly turned the pages of his comic.

'What's with the lobster outfit?' he asked at last, still not really looking up. 'Do you work for the new fish-and-chip place on the corner?'

I groaned inwardly, and explained to him about the Margaret River Hairy Marron. He raised an eyebrow.

'Doesn't seem like the best creature for raising awareness, does it?' he said, laying the book on the table. 'I mean, it's not cuddly, or genetically interesting, or rare. The only thing most people know about marron is that it tastes awesome drizzled with lemon and dipped in tartare sauce.'

'That's the problem with conservation awareness programs,' I said. 'They only ever talk about the cute, cuddly endangered animals. The media is only interested in the ones that make good news stories. Just because the Hairy Marron isn't cute doesn't mean it's not important.'

'And that's why you chose it. Because you feel nobody is telling the Hairy Marron's story.'

'Exactly.'

'And you're dressed as a lobster to get people's attention.'

'Right.'

'Is it working?'

I sighed. 'No. Everyone keeps asking me for free samples.'

Shopping Trolley Guy chuckled, and turned back to his comic.

'What are you reading?' I asked.

5

The guy held up his comic so I could see the cover, without taking his eyes off the page.

'*Blue Beetle*,' I read. 'Is it good?'

'Amazing.' He put the comic down and narrowed his eyes at me. 'So why the environment?'

'What do you mean?'

'Why not starving children in Africa, or marriage equality, or equal opportunities for Indigenous Australians? Why is the environment your thing?'

Kind of a dumb question. 'Because nothing else matters if we don't have a planet,' I said. 'If we don't fix our overconsumption of fossil fuels and fresh water, we'll all die. And not just humans – every living thing on the planet will die. I don't want to be responsible for that kind of omnicide.'

'Omnicide?'

'Like genocide, except it's for everything.'

Shopping Trolley Guy nodded slowly. 'Fair enough. So you've taken on saving the planet as a personal crusade.'

'It's my responsibility as a human being. It's the responsibility of every single human being. But not everyone is willing to step up.'

'Hmm.' Shopping Trolley Guy looked uncomfortable. 'I'm not sure that's fair. I mean, there are plenty of people out there who don't have the time or resources or education or skills to be able to hand out flyers at shopping centres, or buy Priuses and recycled toilet paper.'

I shrugged. 'There are plenty of people out there who *could* do those things. But they don't.'

'Have you considered doing the awareness-raising *without* the lobster costume? At least then people wouldn't think you were promoting the Hairy Marron as a delicious and healthy snack.'

'Yeah,' I said. 'Tried that. Didn't work.'

I'd spent two weekends wearing normal clothes and handing out fact sheets. The results had been dismal.*

'So why do you think it's not working? Your crusade?'

My answer was only one word. 'Valentine.'

Shopping Trolley Guy rolled his eyes and nodded. 'Valentine,' he said, his mouth puckering as if he'd eaten something disgusting.

The problem with living in Valentine, was everything. Valentine was one of those in-between suburbs. It wasn't old enough to be urban and interesting and full of artsy people wanting to reinvent it. And it wasn't new enough to have had actual town planning with parks and wetlands and curvy streets lined with native trees. It was an ugly grey expanse of concrete, too far from the city to be convenient, and too far from the country to be pretty. The houses were all built in the sixties and seventies from asbestos, fibro and concrete. Most of the local shops had closed down after the big shopping mall opened – an enormous box filled with multinational brands and soul-sucking fluorescent lights.

It was awful. Living in Valentine was like living in a bleak dystopian wasteland. The most colourful thing was the signs

---

* Old ladies who asked me for directions to the chemist: 3
People who tried to convince me to become a Mormon: 1
Girls who thought I was handing out free cosmetics samples: 4
Guys my age who asked me out: 7
Guys old enough to be my father who asked me out: 2
Fact sheets taken: 0
Signatures obtained for petition: 0

outside fast-food restaurants. The only greenery in the entire suburb was the football oval. Everything else was grey and dry and dusty. Our local council had distinguished itself by managing to achieve nothing in ten years other than embezzling a truckload of public funds, and had recently been impeached. So despite my endless petitions and letters, we had no bike paths, no electronic waste recycling scheme, no community gardens and no sustainability awareness programs. I'd heard rumours that our new mayor was more proactive, but I wasn't holding out any hope.

'It seems like nothing I do gets through,' I said. 'I'm so tired of shouting when nobody seems to listen. People don't want to *hear* what I have to say, because then they'll have to acknowledge that there's all this stuff going on outside their tiny little universes.'

'I know what you mean,' Shopping Trolley Guy said, leaning forward in his chair. 'It's like the world is designed for these plastic Lego people, going about their plastic boring lives – wake up, go to work, slave at a desk all day making money for some evil corporation, come home, eat something out of a plastic package that's full of fake colours and numbers, and then turn into a zombie watching whichever dumb reality TV show is hot right now. And if you're interested in living and seeing things differently, then you don't fit anywhere. You can't exist.'

I nodded. 'Nobody ever wants to go outside anymore, or imagine different ways of *being*,' I said. 'Nobody wants to believe there's something *more important* than who wins the latest football game or singing competition.'

Shopping Trolley Guy held my gaze for a moment too

long. I felt my cheeks flush. Lucky they were already covered in red face-paint, so he'd never know. There was fierceness in his eyes, and a joy at recognising a kindred soul. A soft smile spread across his face.

'It's cool that you understand,' he said. 'Nobody understands. Certainly nobody at school, anyway.'

I felt the blush drain away. School. Shopping Trolley Guy seemed nice, and was *very* cute in a brooding, scruffy way, but we were *not* in the same league at school. Not even close.

'School doesn't *get* people like us,' he went on. 'School is designed for the Missolinis.'

'The what now?'

'The Missolinis. You know, those alpha popular girls at school who think they're better than everyone else.'

Oh.

'Like, Benito Mussolini? Italian fascist dictator? Same like those girls. They decide who's popular, and what music we're supposed to listen to, and what stupid shit we should be caring about this week.'

I didn't say anything.

'I know it's lame,' said Shopping Trolley Guy. 'And I know school doesn't really work the way it does on TV – with the jocks and the stoners and the populars all in their separate cliquey ghettos. People are more interesting and complicated than that. But school is designed for a certain kind of person. Someone who wants to be part of the system. Get good marks and get into a good university. Join clubs and societies and go on dates and pass notes and *giggle all the freaking time*. And there's a certain kind of teenage girl who slides into that mould. School is designed for her, not for me. You know?'

9

I did know, but before I could figure out how to respond, a skinny weasel-faced man wearing a supermarket uniform stuck his head around the door. 'Are you planning on joining us any time soon?' he said to Shopping Trolley Guy, who scowled and rolled his eyes at me.

'Coming,' he muttered, slipping the comic into his back pocket. He got up and hunched his shoulders, sending a resentful look in the direction of Weaselface. Then he turned back to me and his face changed, the scowl replaced with a hopeful smile. 'Maybe I'll see you here next week?'

I knew I should probably have told him that I, Astrid Katy Smythe, *was* a Missolini. But he was nice, and funny, and talking to him had been the high point of what had otherwise been a decidedly average day. So instead I smiled.

'Maybe,' I said.

It wasn't until he'd left that I realised I should have asked him to sign my petition.

2

Paige and Dev sailed into form assembly on Monday with their usual bubbly panache.

'You will not *believe* what happened yesterday morning,' said Dev, as Paige slid me a take-away coffee.

I stared at the shiny paper cup. 'What is this?' I said.

Paige shrugged. 'Non-fat single-origin organic soy latte?'

I tapped the plastic lid on the cup. 'Where's my keep-cup?'

Paige lived near the only decent café in Valentine, so she picked up the coffee every morning. I had bought her three ceramic keep-cups, and a little holder-tray thing so she could easily carry them to school.

'Oh,' Paige shrugged. 'Sorry. I didn't get around to washing them last night. I thought just once wouldn't matter.'

I shook my head in mock (well, mostly mock) disappointment. Of course I wasn't truly mad at her. If I was *actually* telling Paige off, the other students of Valentine would probably have me flayed alive.

'The cups are made from recycled paper,' said Paige, as if that made everything okay.

I couldn't help myself. 'Sure,' I said. 'But the paper is now plastic-coated, so it can't be recycled again.' As I said it, I had a flashback to the break room at the shopping centre and Shopping Trolley Guy asking why I wasn't drinking from the water cooler. The thought of those dark, intelligent eyes sent a thrill through me. Was I going crazy? Grungy emo stoner was *so* not my type.

'Sorry,' said Paige again, but I was too busy thinking about Shopping Trolley Guy to reply.

'*Anyway*,' said Dev pointedly. 'Yesterday morning.'

'Right,' I said. 'Yesterday morning. What happened?'

'I met him,' said Dev. 'The One.'

Paige let her head thump down on her desk. 'Snore,' she said. 'You meet The One at least once a week.'

Dev shook his head. 'This is different. I'm in love.'

Paige was right. Dev was *obsessed* with meeting The One. He'd seen way too many romantic comedies, and had totally deluded ideas about how relationships were supposed to work. The stupid thing was, he never *dated* anyone. I mean, our school wasn't exactly overflowing with eligible gay guys, but the handful that we did have would have done *anything* to be seen on Dev's arm. He had slightly curling black hair and rich dark skin and enormous brown eyes. Guys at our school had been known to come out just so they could ask him on a date. But Dev swore he'd never date anyone from Valentine, so instead he kept falling in love with random unattainable guys he met in the city. Last time it was a barista in a laneway café.

'Well?' I asked. 'Who is it this time? A busker? A librarian?'

Dev bit his lip. 'It's my new music teacher,' he said in a soft voice. 'He's *amazing*.'

Dev was a ridiculously talented singer, and he also played the flute, guitar, piano, harpsichord and violin.

Paige lifted her head from her desk. 'Are you serious? That doesn't sound good.'

'Why not?' Dev tossed his head. 'You're dating your aikido instructor.'

'That's totally different! We didn't get together until my black belt graduation party, so he isn't technically my *sensei* anymore.'

'How old is this music teacher?' I asked.

Dev shrugged delicately. 'Twenty-something.'

Paige narrowed her eyes. 'Twenty-something as in twenty-*one*? Or twenty-something as in *nearly thirty*?'

'Does it matter?' Dev had a dreamy, faraway look that spelled trouble. 'His name is Sanasar and he lives in the city in this amazing warehouse apartment.'

'Um,' said Paige. 'How do you know where he lives?'

Dev chose not to answer her. 'He's Armenian and plays eleven different instruments. He has the most delicate hands. Our babies will be so beautiful.'

'You know you can't have babies with a guy, right?' said Paige. 'You're missing some requisite parts.'

Dev waved a hand. 'There are ways around that,' he said vaguely. 'You know, science.'

'Is he gay?' I asked.

Dev grinned. 'My gaydar pretty much exploded.'

'But you don't have any actual proof he's gay.'

'I don't need proof. I *know*.'

I sighed. 'Just don't *say* anything to him about it,' I told Dev. 'Not yet, anyway. Wait for a couple of weeks.'

'Yeah,' said Paige. 'In two weeks you'll be over him, and head over heels for the garbage man or someone.'

Dev laughed a low, husky laugh. 'You're funny,' he said with another happy sigh. 'But this time I know. This is it. I will never love another. My heart is steadfast.'

Ms Whitfield entered the classroom. 'Good morning,' she said, smiling at the three of us and completely ignoring everyone else. She then proceeded to give Chris Bateman a detention for bringing an energy drink into class, but pretended not to notice that Paige, Dev and I were all sipping from take-away coffee cups.

Yes, I got special treatment from the teachers.

Yes, I found school very easy.

Yes, I pretty much got everything I wanted.

Yes, I was a Missolini.

A lot of it was because of Paige. Paige was *the* Missolini. Old Benito herself. Everyone wanted to be Paige, or be with her. Or both. Paige was beautiful and confident. She was one of those people who just seemed effortless, in everything she did. You couldn't help but love her. If it wasn't for Paige, I probably wouldn't have the social standing that I do. I'm a shade too academic, and I'm aware the whole environmentalist thing isn't exactly a popularity-booster. But I was bathed in Paige's aura, so none of that mattered. There was no doubt about my Missolini status. I was popular and smart and pretty. Teachers loved me. Guys wanted to date me. Girls would fall over themselves to be nice to me, so that they might have a chance of getting close to Paige.

It wasn't that we were so wonderful. Once again, the reason was Valentine. Ours was the only local school, except for a snooty private girls' school just over the freeway in leafy Cambridge Hills. Valentine High wasn't great. The school had one ugly brick building with no heating, and twenty demountable classrooms that acted as ovens on hot days. There were no fancy electronic whiteboards, no state-of-the-art laptop stations, no wifi. Running water and electricity were considered luxuries at Valentine High. So all the best and brightest students went elsewhere – either shipped off to boarding school, or sent to other, faraway private schools. I'd had the option, of course. Dad's a dentist, so I could have gone to posh St Catherine's or somewhere. But I didn't want to. I figured I'd do more good at the local high school. Plus Dev and Paige would be at Valentine High, and the three of us had been friends since kindergarten.

So at a school with no facilities and no really outstanding students, it was easy to rise to the top. Teachers were grateful that the three of us listened to them and handed in our homework on time. On the whole, if we wanted something, we could have it.

Unless that thing was, you know, getting people to care about the future of our planet.

But yeah, I could see where Shopping Trolley Guy was coming from. School was super easy for people like Paige and Dev and me.* We were generally allowed to do what we wanted. If I needed to skip PE in order to set up the school hall for a lamington drive, then I could. If I didn't turn up to

---

* I know it's not exactly fair to call Dev a Missolini, given that he isn't a Miss. But Paige and I have been friends with him since he wore a cravat to the first day of kindergarten, and he carries nearly as much popularity clout as Paige, so he's a Missolini in reputation, if not in, you know, bits.

class one day, my teachers would assume I was doing something important and necessary, and no questions would be asked. I found the study pretty easy, and if I did struggle, my teachers were more than happy to sit down with me for half an hour and explain the intricacies of logarithms. Teen angst was something that happened to people on TV. For me, adolescence was a breeze.

And it wasn't like I was abusing my powers. Quite the opposite! I had a social conscience, and made sure that I used my visibility and popularity to spread the message about climate change and the environment. Kind of like Bono, I guess.

But less effective.

'So we have *got* to talk about what happened on *Mom vs Mom* last night,' said Paige, leaning over and giving me a very serious look.

Now don't get me wrong. I loved Paige as much as anyone else does. I loved living under her benevolent reign. I loved being a Missolini. But sometimes I had to admit that she struggled to focus on what was truly important.

The bell rang for assembly, and I joined the streams of students spilling into the school hall. I made my way up to the front, as I was giving a talk about the school's new compost bins. I'd raised the money for them myself, and had posted signs all over the school reminding students to use them for food scraps. But a talk at assembly would really bring it home.

After we'd limped through the school song and the national anthem, and the principal, Mr Webber, had made his usual boring speech about appropriate behaviour and community expectations, I stepped up to the podium and spread out my notes.

'Hi everyone,' I said.

A few people whooped in response, and I grinned out into the audience. I quite like public speaking. No, that's not true. I love it. I love it because people pay attention to me. I knew that if it wasn't for Paige, nobody would be listening. Students would be gossiping and fighting and climbing the walls. But there was Paige, front and centre, sitting up straight and listening attentively, her head cocked to one side. I knew she didn't care about the benefits of composting food scraps the way I did – she'd heard it all before from me anyway. But she knew it was important to me, so she pretended to listen, and everyone else followed suit. The auditorium was full of attentive faces casting sneaky sideways glances at her, to see if she noticed how good they were being.

The only exceptions to this rule were the stonery losers up the back. They were unaffected by the Missolini aura in all respects. If anything, it was an incentive for bad behaviour. They sniggered and chatted, their feet on the backs of the crumbling vinyl seats in front of them. I could barely make them out from my position at the front of the hall, but I knew they were there. They were a black hole of indifference, sucking away my energy and cheer.

Luckily for me, one of them set a student's bag on fire, and they were all kicked out of assembly within the first few minutes of my talk. Unluckily for me, the smoking bag set off the fire alarm, and we all had to evacuate, cutting my speech short.

This kind of thing is a regular occurrence in Valentine.

After the fire department had arrived and declared the school once more safe to enter, I was on my way to English when Mr Webber came puffing up behind me. 'Astrid. Glad I caught you. Good speech.'

Mr Webber was the only teacher at Valentine High who didn't love me.

'I've found you an after-school helper for the rest of term. In the garden.'

This was new. Mr Webber hated my kitchen garden project. I was quite certain he hated *me*, but was too scared of me to do anything about it.

'Hiro Silvestri. The teachers are all far too busy marking, they can't take detention. So I'm sending him to you.'

I nodded and tried to look pleased, although I knew that Mr Webber wasn't actually doing me a favour. In fact, I was kind of doing his job for him.

'What did he do?' I asked.

'Who?' Mr Webber was reading something on his BlackBerry.

'The guy you're sending me. Why is he in detention?'

Mr Webber's face darkened. 'That's not important,' he said gruffly, and hurried off down the corridor.

Whatever. If this Hero kid wanted to help, then he could help. Otherwise, I didn't care what he did, as long as he left me alone.

I made my way out behind the gym to the garden, and unlocked the gate.

I'd started the kitchen garden program last term. There was some disused land behind the footy oval that had once been a bike shed, but was now just bare earth surrounded by a chain-link fence. Mr Webber had rolled his eyes when I'd asked if I could turn it into a school garden. He said in a sneering way that I could if I raised the money to build it myself, as if he thought I wouldn't be able to. That made me all the more determined. I convinced the woodwork teacher to let his students build some raised garden beds as an assignment. Then I organised sponsorship from the ginormous fancy gardening centre in Cambridge Hills – they donated the soil, a water tank and a hundred dollars' worth of seeds, as a pity gesture to all us poor downtrodden Valentine souls. My plan was for the school canteen and the home economics classes to use as much of our produce as possible, and to harvest lots of seeds so that the garden could be self-sufficient.

The only problem was, I was *terrible* at gardening.

I couldn't make mould grow on a three-week-old tomato sandwich. I was getting A-pluses in Biology, but a single seed was yet to sprout.* I didn't *get* it. I was usually good at everything I tried my hand at. I was pretty close to giving up entirely, but what kind of environmental crusader was I, if I couldn't grow so much as a sprig of parsley?

I pulled on my gardening apron and gloves. Time to try again. I watered all the seedling trays with the special seaweed fertiliser I'd bought. Maybe today I'd try planting some new vegetables. Beetroot, perhaps. Or celery.

---

* There is a plant that grows in the Galapagos Islands in the cracks of volcanic rock. There's no soil or anything. The seed blows in from wherever, gets stuck in a crack, gets a tiny bit of moisture from the tropical air, and that causes it to germinate. As it starts to grow, its lower leaves die and drop off rapidly. Then the leaves break down and create their own soil, so the plant can grow bigger. And here I was, with organic soil and nutrient-rich fertiliser, and I couldn't get a freaking cucumber seed to sprout.

Even though it wasn't a success yet, I quite enjoyed my time in the garden. It was peaceful and still, and working with my hands was a pleasant break from all the brain-work I did for school. There was something relaxing about pouring potting mix into punnets, and pushing seeds deep into the earth. Plus, it was better than going straight home after school. Home hadn't exactly been a super-fun place lately.

There was a scuffing noise behind me, and I turned to see a guy slouch into the garden, his head down and shoulders hunched.

No, wait. It wasn't *a* guy. It was *the* guy. Shopping Trolley Guy. He of the comic book and smiling eyes.

Shopping Trolley Guy?

They'd sent me Shopping Trolley Guy as an assistant?

I knew he'd looked familiar. He wasn't in my year – maybe the year below me? I didn't know him at all – I'd never seen him participate in extracurricular activities or anything.

'Wh-what are you doing here?' I asked.

He scowled, but didn't look at me. 'None of your business,' he said.

What was his problem? He'd been so nice on the weekend. He'd been funny and interesting and we'd had that *moment* when he held my gaze for too long, as though I was the one he'd been searching for. Now, he was almost unrecognisable. He looked like he'd been sucking on something sour. Everything about his posture and expression told me he didn't want to be there.

'What are you looking at?' he demanded.

'Oh,' I said. 'Sorry. Um.'

He didn't recognise me. Not wholly surprising, given that when we'd met, I'd been dressed in a giant foam lobster costume, with red face-paint. He had no idea who I was. He just thought I was one of *them*. A Missolini.

'You're Hero, right?' I said. 'Mr Webber sent you to me?'

A one-shouldered shrug, which I chose to take as a yes.

'Hero is an interesting name.'

A pause and another sullen look. 'Hiro,' he muttered. 'With an *i*.'

'Is it Japanese?'

Another twitchy shrug. I realised that he was one of the stonery losers who had disrupted my speech at assembly. That was probably why he'd been sent to detention. Maybe he'd been the one who set that Year Seven girl's bag on fire.

I tried a bright smile. 'Well, I think it's a lovely name. What does it mean?'

Hiro cocked his head and narrowed his eyes at me sarcastically. 'It means *bite me*.'

Nice. I waited for as long as I could stand it, then asked, 'Don't you want to know my name?'

He raised his upper lip in a sort of snarl. 'I know who you are,' he said. '*Everyone* knows who you are.'

Did he? Did he know I was the lobster girl? Maybe he'd figured it out, and was so disgusted to learn I was a Missolini that now he hated me. Well, fine. It wasn't like I was short of boys following me around like drooling puppies. If Shopping Trolley Guy Hiro wanted to sulk in my garden for an hour after school every day, then he could be my guest.

'Great,' I said. 'Well, you're welcome to help me if you want. Or if you'd rather mooch around oozing disaffected attitude, you should feel free to do that too.'

Hiro pointedly put on his ridiculously oversized headphones and slunk away to sit on a bench.

I went back to planting seeds. Whatever. I didn't like him anyway. I knew those stonery kids, they were all the same. They made a lot of speeches about rejecting the System and fighting the Man, but actually all they wanted to do was lie around getting wasted and playing videogames.

Mum was banging about in the kitchen when I got home, which meant that Dad was around somewhere. She only got aggressively domestic when he decided to grace us with his presence. I'd thought that their splitting up would make things better, but it had just shifted the mood of the house from angry and hurt to passive-aggressive and resentful.

'Where is he?' I asked.

Mum yanked a saucepan from the dishwasher and shoved it in a cupboard. 'Upstairs,' she said shortly. 'Sorting out his clothes.'

I wished they'd get it over with. That Dad would properly move out, instead of staying at a hotel and coming home to use the washing machine. He usually wandered around the house, picking up two or three things – a book, a paperweight, a T-shirt – and took them with him when he left. Why couldn't he get a bunch of big cardboard boxes and do it all at once? After all, it had been three months since Mum kicked him out.

I left Mum to her dishwasher rage, and trudged up the stairs.

'Can you remind your father that he needs to call his mother tomorrow for her birthday?' Mum called after me.

'Talk to him yourself,' I replied.

My parents were so immature.

I found Dad sitting on the floor of the bedroom that he and Mum used to share. He was holding a lone black sock and crying. There is nothing – I repeat, *nothing* – worse than seeing your parents cry. Parents aren't supposed to. They're supposed to be strong and look after you when you're upset. Not the other way around. I was tempted to leave him to it, but clearly someone in this family had to be an adult.

'Dad? Are you okay?'

He looked up, surprised to see me, and used the sock to wipe his eyes. Then he adopted a nonchalant expression like he hadn't been caught crying over an unpaired sock by his teenage daughter.

'Hey, kiddo,' he said croakily.

'Hey,' I said. 'I can see the packing is going well.'

Dad looked down at the sock. 'I can't find the other one. It's supposed to be a *pair*. And now this one is all on its own. It's useless.'

It didn't take a gargantuan intellect to figure out that we weren't actually talking about the sock.

'I'm sorry, Dad.'

Another tear squeezed out and rolled down Dad's cheek. He looked awful, as if he hadn't shaved for a few days. Or showered.

'I miss your mother,' he rasped. 'I don't want this.'

'Well, then you probably shouldn't have slept with the Whippet.'

The Whippet was the twenty-six-year-old dental nurse who had destroyed my parents' marriage. No, that's not fair. My dad destroyed the marriage. The Whippet had just happened to be there, on the dental chair in Dad's surgery,

23

wearing only high heels and one of those little surgical masks, when Mum had popped by to drop off some paperwork for Dad. The Whippet had an actual human name, but I was determined not to learn it. I called her the Whippet because, even though she ticked all the conventional boxes of attractiveness in being tall and skinny and blonde, she looked spindly and pathetic, with bulging dark eyes like a hungry whippet. I *so* didn't get it.

Dad looked uncomfortable. I probably shouldn't have mentioned the Whippet. I wondered if she and Dad were still seeing each other. Ew. It's gross enough thinking about your own parents having sex. It's a million times worse imagining a parent having sex with *someone else*.

'Do you want to do something later?' asked Dad, looking hopeful. 'I could take you out for pizza.'

'No, thanks,' I said, and his face fell. 'I have heaps of homework.'

I had no idea how I was supposed to act around Dad anymore. I'd tried being angry at him, but he was so sad and pathetic it was hard to stay mad. And I figured Mum was mad enough for both of us. Not that I wasn't on her side. Dad totally shouldn't have slept with the Whippet – Mum was absolutely right to kick him out. So I didn't want to hang out with him. But he was still my dad, and I felt rotten every time I rejected him.

3

I got an email from Mr Gerakis on Tuesday, asking if I could pop by and see him. Mr Gerakis was in charge of Home Economics at Valentine High, and he fancied himself a kind of Greek Heston Blumenthal. He was always encouraging the students to experiment with texture and flavour – which was a pretty big ask considering most of the students couldn't successfully boil an egg. There'd been at least three cases of acute food poisoning, and one incident where the Home Ec lab nearly burnt down after a student got a little over-enthusiastic with a brûlée torch.

'Astrid!' It was Tyson Okeke chasing me down the corridor. Tyson was Valentine High's star full-forward, and one of the friendliest guys I'd ever met – a definite red ten.

Back in Year Eight, Dev had invented this complicated system of who was allowed to date whom. Everyone was assigned a colour, depending on what type of person they were. Red was sporty. Purple was creative. Green was scientific or academic. Paige, Dev and I were gold – general all-rounders. Black was the goth-emo types. Brown were the anti-establishment stonery dissidents. Within each colour, you were assigned a number, which had to do with your status, popularity, talent and success. We, naturally, were tens. Dev's rule was that you could date anyone who was the same colour as you, *or* anyone who was the same number as you. It was totally ridiculous, but there was a certain demented logic to it.

'Hey,' I said, craning my neck to look up at Tyson.

He smiled his usual ear-splitting grin. 'So, um. Slightly embarrassing question. I've got tickets to the Junior Brownlow this weekend. Is Paige still dating her aikido instructor?'

'I'm afraid so.'

Tyson shrugged ruefully. 'Always worth checking. So . . .' His grin took on a slightly cheeky twist. 'What are *you* doing this Saturday night?'

I laughed. 'Wow, Tyson. You really know how to make a girl feel special.'

'Sorry.'

'I'm used to it. And I'm busy this weekend. But have fun!'

Tyson threw me a mock salute and jogged off down the corridor.

I slipped into Home Ec lab after school, just before heading to the garden. The room reeked of something sweet, salty and altogether unpleasant.

'What *is* that smell?' I asked Mr Gerakis, who was cleaning purple goop off his desk.

'Beetroot and caper foam,' said Mr Gerakis, pushing his glasses up his nose with a pink-stained finger. 'It didn't work so well.'

'I'm sorry to hear that,' I said, thankful once more that I'd never taken Home Ec. 'You wanted to see me?'

'What?' Mr Gerakis rubbed his temples for a moment. 'Oh, right, yes. I gave your proposal to the canteen, and they've turned it down.'

I stared at him. 'I'm sorry?'

I'd written up a proposal for the canteen, letting them know that once the garden was producing, they could use as much of the harvest as they liked, and that if there was anything in particular they'd like me to grow, I'd give it a shot. I wasn't going to charge them any money or anything – it seemed like a win-win. They got free vegies, our students got to eat fresh local produce, and we'd considerably reduce the school's carbon footprint. I figured we'd be at full production before the Christmas holidays.

Mr Gerakis blinked. 'They said no.' He shrugged. 'The canteen isn't independent – it's owned and staffed by a company that services most of the schools in the state. It keeps costs down.'

'Costs and *nutrition*,' I said. 'All they serve is sausage rolls, deep-fried food and rubbery ham sandwiches.'

'Well, they've signed a new exclusive contract with the bulk supplier,' said Mr Gerakis. 'They're not allowed to use any externally sourced food or food-related product.'

'What does that even mean? What's a *food-related product*? And we're not talking about externally sourced produce – we're growing it right here at school!'

'They mean produce sourced from outside the company,' explained Mr Gerakis with a sigh. 'Also, their insurance people say it's a health risk.'

'Health risk!' I felt my voice rising in indignation. 'Have they seen the deep-fried chicken and corn in a roll that they serve?'

Mr Gerakis shrugged. I felt a wave of despair, but shoved it away. 'What about here, then?' I asked, looking around the Home Ec room. 'What if you used the produce from the garden in Home Ec class?'

Mr Gerakis shook his head gloomily. 'The canteen supplies me with all the Home Ec ingredients.'

'So you can't use *anything*? Not even for garnish?'

'Believe me, Astrid, I've been trying for years to get my own supplier. Can you imagine how difficult it is for me to *create* anything using such basic ingredients? But this new contract is written in stone.'

'I'll write to the new mayor,' I said. 'Maybe things will be different now she's in charge.'

Mr Gerakis gave me a flat look that told me what I already knew. I'd written countless emails to our council over the years, asking for them to improve our recycling scheme, to run seminars at our local library (or even buy some *books* for our local library), to start up a community gardening program, to protect the nearby wetlands from developers. I'd never received a single reply. Not even a form *we appreciate your feedback* email. Nothing. It was like every email I sent got sucked into a black hole.

I could write. I could petition. I could stamp my feet until I was blue in the face. But I knew that it wouldn't do any good. Valentine City Council was a closed book, a locked vault. There was no way in, new mayor or not.

I went back to the garden, feeling numb. The whole *point*

of the project was to encourage students to grow, cook and eat their own food. But I couldn't do that when the school's idea of a healthy meal was frozen fish sticks or soggy pies.

An icy rage spread through me. I *hated* our council. If Paige were here, she'd tell me that hate wasn't a constructive emotion, and that I was disrupting my *ki*. But I *hated* them. I hated the way they never *did* anything, but still managed to destroy my plans. It was like they *wanted* the whole planet to die.

I kicked over a watering can, but only succeeded in stubbing my toe. I swore, hopping around on one foot.

I heard the crunching of gravel behind me. It was Hiro, hood up and ridiculous headphones on, staring at me as I clutched my foot. I felt my cheeks redden, which made me even more angry.

'What are you looking at?' I snapped.

Hiro put up his hands in mock surrender, and slunk off to his bench. I could hear the tinny thumping of music from his headphones, which only served to irritate me more. Stupid sullen Hiro and his stupid attractive face. I hated him too.

I stomped over to the seed-raising punnets so I wouldn't have to hear his stupid music or look at his stupid head in its stupid hoodie.

Bare earth stared back at me.

Not a single sprout. I'd been trying for over a month, and nothing.

I retrieved the watering can and filled it, determined not to even look at Hiro. Rage seethed inside me. Water soaked into the mockingly empty punnets.

Maybe I was kidding myself. Maybe this whole kitchen

garden plan was a waste of time. Who cared if the canteen wouldn't take my produce – I didn't *have* any produce. The International Space Station had a microgravity growth chamber where they could get seeds to germinate. In space. I couldn't even make a sprout. I wasn't even growing *weeds*.

'You're watering them too much,' said Hiro from behind me. He'd come over to the potting shed and was watching over my shoulder.

I glared at him. 'And I suppose you're an expert.'

He shrugged. 'You're drowning the seeds,' he said. 'They'll rot. Soil needs to be damp for germination, not wet.'

Hiro moved closer and bent to look at my carefully labelled punnets. My rage melted into confusion. Sulky Hiro was talking to me. In real, proper, multisyllabic words. Talking about something useful. Maybe he'd been in a bad mood yesterday. Maybe Shopping Trolley Guy was his true persona, and he just had to get warmed up to me.

Surely if I could get Hiro to talk to me, I could get a snow pea seed to sprout.

Maybe everything would be okay after all.

'You won't have any luck with snow peas anyway,' he said. 'It's too warm this time of year. Try tomatoes or cucumbers. And you're sowing the seeds too deep. They should only be a couple of centimetres below the soil.'

I stared at him. His face had come alive as he poked around in my seedling tray. The sullen stare had vanished, and had been replaced by a keen alertness. I felt an excited flutter of recognition as I saw the cute guy I'd met on the weekend. He looked up and met my eyes. A shivery thrill ran through me, and for a moment I was certain that he'd finally recognised me. Then, like blinds being drawn, his face shut again, and once more he was angry and disconnected. The transformation was so sudden, I felt like I'd been given an electric shock.

'Whatever,' he mumbled. 'Do what you want.'

I opened my mouth to reply, but stammered incoherently. I wanted to get him back. 'H-h-how do you know so much about gardening?' I managed to choke out.

He just looked away and scuffed his sneakered foot on the ground, then made a show of pulling up his headphones and turning his music up loud. But he didn't go back to his bench. He sorted through my seed packets, separating them into four piles. I watched him, fascinated.

'Summer. Autumn,' he said, pointing at the stacks in turn. 'Winter. Spring.'

I blinked. 'I didn't know you were supposed to plant them all at different times.'*

Hiro slid his headphones off with a weary sigh. 'Is it shocking?' he asked sarcastically. 'To discover that there are things you don't know?'

He was *mean*. 'There's lots of stuff I don't know,' I told him. 'Anyone who thinks they know everything is deluded.'

Hiro raised an eyebrow, but I thought I saw the teensiest flicker of respect in those dark eyes. Or maybe it was

---

* Although I totally should have. I know that one of the biggest problems with our food industry is the way supermarkets import out-of-season fruit and vegies. We think it's possible to grow oranges all year round, but it isn't. Not in the same place, anyway. In winter, most of our fruit is imported from China, and then dosed with toxic fungicides in supermarket warehouses.

just wishful thinking. But he did leave his headphones slung around his neck, and showed me how to soak the seeds before we planted them, and how much the seaweed fertiliser needed to be diluted. With only a minimal amount of eye-rolling.

'Hey,' I said. 'You're really good at this. Thank you.'

In an instant, Hiro's face clouded over. 'Don't patronise me,' he muttered, and stumped away to his spot near the water tank.

'Astrid!'

Dev and Paige were on the other side of the chain-link fence that separated the kitchen garden from the rest of the world. I saw Hiro stiffen and pull up his headphones. I walked over to the fence.

'Nice outfit,' said Paige.

I looked down at my gardening apron and flowery gloves. 'I know, right?' I said, striking a pose.*

'We're heading to Patchwork Rhubarb to study for that algebra test tomorrow. Come with us.'

'I can't,' I said. 'I've got more work to do here, and I promised Mum I'd be home for an early dinner.'

Paige and Dev made exaggerated sad faces.

'Are you sure?' said Paige. 'Not even for half an hour? I'm going to need a break from listening to Dev go on about his music teacher.'

'I friended him on Facebook,' said Dev breathlessly. 'And he *doesn't have any relationship status*. That means he's single!'

Paige shot me an imploring look.

---

* Rule one of being a Missolini: take all snide comments as compliments. It throws everyone off balance.

I shook my head. 'Sorry.'

Paige sighed. 'How's it going, anyway?' she asked. 'The Great Gardening Project?'

'Better,' I said. 'I'm learning a lot.'

Paige glanced at my raised garden beds. 'I don't see any actual plants.'

'Er,' I said. 'No. Still working on that.'

'What did Mr Gerakis want?' asked Dev.

Anger washed through me again. I told them about the canteen, and the school's contract with the bulk food supply company.

'How awful,' shuddered Dev. 'I'm so glad we never eat there.'

'Can you imagine the kinds of preservatives they use?' said Paige. Although Paige wasn't particularly enthusiastic about my kitchen garden idea, she was *very* much in favour of organic food. She said that preservatives were toxins that polluted the body, clouding the *ki*. She made her mum drive her to Cambridge Hills every weekend to buy kale, avocado, chia seeds and dried goji berries for her lunch salads, and had been very supportive of my campaign to get her dad's cleaning business to use only green cleaning products.

'Um, Astrid?' Dev was frowning. 'Why is there a drug dealer in your garden?'

He'd noticed Hiro. A sudden thought occurred to me. What if Hiro was good at gardening because he grew pot? He could be a drug dealer. A hydroponics expert. It wasn't a comforting thought.

I tried to put on a bright smile. 'Mr Webber sent him here. Detention.'

Dev made a face. '*Him?* He's the guy who stole the box of finished exams from the office and put them up on the roof.'

Really? That was Hiro? It had been a huge deal. The fire department were called to get the box of papers down so they could be sent off for marking.

Paige nodded. 'Isn't he also the guy who got caught calling in a bomb threat so he wouldn't have to do a maths test?'

'Maybe we should stay and protect you,' said Dev, eyeing off Hiro, who was apparently engrossed in his phone. 'He might be dangerous.'

I laughed. 'The only danger he poses is to himself. He might eye-roll too hard and cause permanent damage.'

Paige peered through the fence at Hiro. 'I think he'd be quite cute,' she said. 'If he stopped looking so slouchy and miserable.'

I felt a little zing of . . . something. What was it? Pride? Jealousy? That was ridiculous. Paige could have him if she could convince him to look at her without sneering. I certainly wasn't interested. Even if he was cute. Anyway, he was obviously immune to the Missolini glow.

'Too young,' said Dev with a dismissive sniff. 'Did I mention that Sanasar studied music at a Belgian conservatory? He's definitely a purple ten.'

Paige groaned. 'Come on,' she said. 'I want to get this algebra done so I can watch *Runaway Amish*.'

I could feel the scorn coming off Hiro in waves. And I could feel myself growing prickly. It was okay for *me* to judge Paige for her reality-TV obsession, but it was *not* alright for stupid Shopping Trolley Guy to do it. She was *my* friend, and if she wanted to watch *My Alien Lover Wants a Divorce* or *Dance Senator**, then she could. After all, it wasn't as if *she* was wasting her life. As well as being Queen Missolini and universally adored, Paige was also a straight-A student and an aikido champion. *And* she meditated for an hour every single morning to focus her *ki*, so she definitely wasn't neglecting to nurture her soul. How exactly was Hiro bettering himself? Skulking around, setting Year Sevens' bags on fire and working as a supermarket stacker? Whatever.

I farewelled Dev and Paige, and returned to the seedling beds. Hiro had fled to the far corner of the garden, but he crept back after they were out of sight. He fiddled with a bag of potting mix.

'Is that true?' he said. 'About you not being able to give any of the food you grow to the canteen or Home Ec classes?'

I frowned. 'Of course it's true. Why wouldn't it be true?'

Hiro didn't say anything for a moment, just trailed his fingers along the side of one of the raised beds. He had long, thin fingers. I wondered if he played piano, in the days before he became too cool to make an effort with anything.

'So is that it?' he said at last. 'You're giving up?'

My anger, which had been lying like a lump in the pit of my stomach, suddenly boiled over into white-hot rage. 'Absolutely not,' I said. 'If the school thinks that they can pump our students full of additive numbers and imported,

---

* It is possible that one time Paige forced me to watch an episode of *Dance Senator*, and it was actually kind of awesome. Who would have thought our publicly elected officials had such a diverse range of talents? It's just a shame none of those talents are ever employed to do anything useful like, oh, I don't know, saving the Southern Corroboree Frog from extinction, or cutting our greenhouse gas emissions by eighty per cent.

processed rubbish, then they can think again. We'll sell our produce – there's no rule against having bake sales for fundraising, so we can sell fruit at recess and lunch for some totally token amount. And . . . and we'll hold a little farmer's market, once a month, so parents can pick up some fresh vegies to take home. I am *going* to make this garden work.'

Hiro had taken a step back away from me, as if he were slightly frightened by my outburst.

'And anyway, maybe things will be different with the new mayor. Maybe she'll listen.'

Hiro snorted.

'Do you think I'm crazy?' I asked, calming down a little.

Hiro shrugged. 'I don't know why you bother,' he said, and pulled up his hood, stumping out of the garden and out of my sight.

4

At seven on Saturday morning, I double-checked the email I'd composed the night before to the new mayor about our kitchen garden program. It was still looking good, so I hit send. After a quick shower and a bowl of muesli*, I pulled on my lobster costume.

'Really?' said Mum, looking up from the kitchen table where she was reading the newspaper. 'You're going back?'

'The Margaret River Hairy Marron isn't going to save itself,' I said. 'Someone's got to step up.'

Mum looked dubious. 'And you think the lobster costume helps?'

'At least people notice me,' I said. 'And if they come up looking for a free sample, then maybe they'll stay and listen to what I have to say, and sign my petition. Also, I hired it from the costume place for a fortnight.'

---

* I make my own muesli because the shop-bought stuff is so full of sugar. Did you know that many of the so-called healthy commercial breakfast cereals contain more sugar than ice-cream or soft drink?

'Well,' said Mum, taking a sip of tea. 'It's an impressive effort, if nothing else. I hope the Hairy Marron is grateful.'

I shrugged. 'It's the right thing to do.'

What I could barely admit to myself was that I wanted to see Hiro again. I wasn't sure if I'd totally misread him on our first meeting. Maybe he was always sullen and slouchy. Or maybe there was more to him. I had to know. He was intriguing, so different to all the handsome, high-achieving boys I'd hung out with before. He was darker, and seemed kind of dangerous in an exciting way.

'Do you want a lift?' asked Mum.

I raised my eyebrows at her. I'd made a pledge in January that I wouldn't get in a car for a whole year. I'd catch public transport, walk and cycle everywhere, to demonstrate how overly reliant we are on cars.*

'Sorry I asked,' said Mum, holding up her hands with a smile.

It was good to see her smile. It had been a while.

'Hey, Lobstergirl.'

Hiro put down his comic and grinned at me. His face was warm and open, his smile wide and his eyes crinkled. He looked so genuinely chuffed to see me that I totally forgot about his awful grouchy attitude at school, and his terrible

---

* There's a guy in the US called John Francis who is a planetwalker – he hasn't got into a motorised vehicle for twenty-two years. He's walked all over America raising awareness about sustainability and respecting the planet, and now he's a UN Ambassador. He didn't speak for seventeen years – and got three degrees including a PhD, all while never saying a word. Obviously this could never be an option for me. I really like talking.

reputation as a troublemaker. I hadn't expected to be so pleased to see him, or feel so happy that he was pleased to see me.

'Um,' I said. 'Hi.'

'I was hoping I'd see you here again,' he said. 'How's your week been?'

He didn't recognise me. We'd hung out in the garden every afternoon that week, and he'd been so disaffected that he hadn't noticed that I, Astrid Katy Smythe, the Missiest of the Missolinis, was also Lobstergirl. How could he not even recognise my voice?

I knew I should tell him. I should tell him and then he'd laugh and realise how judgemental he'd been at school, and we could hang out in the garden and talk and it'd be awesome.

Or, he'd never speak to me again.

'Are you okay?' he asked.

I blinked. 'Fine,' I said. 'I'm fine. My week was busy, you know. School.'

Hiro made a face. 'Six hundred and eighty-four days,' he said.

'I'm sorry?'

'Of school. Six hundred and eighty-four more days I have to go to school. Unless I can get suspended, or contract some sort of disease.' He looked hopeful.

'You must really hate school,' I said.

'Don't you?'

I shrugged and felt awkward. I *loved* school. School was where I was in charge. I couldn't get anyone to take a flyer or sign a petition in this stupid shopping centre, but at school

39

I could talk about the danger of desalination schemes at assembly when everyone *had* to listen. 'Um. School's okay, I guess.'

Hiro screwed up his nose. 'It's just a way of keeping us docile.' He waved his *X-Men* comic at me. 'It's all in here. I mean, think about it. We're locked up every day. We work for no pay, but we *legally have to go*. We wear uniforms and listen to adults filling our heads with propaganda about how they think the world should be. And all our movements are controlled by the ringing of bells.' He dropped the comic onto the table and thumped his fist on it for emphasis. 'We're living in a dystopia, I'm telling you.'

A bit dramatic, perhaps, but I suppose he had a point. 'I'd never thought of it like that,' I said.

'You would if you went to my school,' he said darkly. 'It's like a cross between *1984* and *The Hunger Games*.'

I busied myself with rinsing out a glass, desperately trying to think of a way to either a) come clean, or b) change the subject.

Hiro cocked his head to the side. 'Wait,' he said. '*Do* we go to the same school? I don't think I've seen you there. I'm sure I would have noticed a giant lobster in Humanities, or lining up at the canteen.' He made a snapping motion with his hands.

This would have been the perfect opportunity to come clean. Explain who I was. Laugh about it. Maybe make a joke about the seaweed fertiliser and being a lobster. But Hiro's mention of the school canteen had sent up a flash of rage, which threw me off-target. So instead I did something completely and utterly insane.

'Er,' I said. 'No. I go to St Catherine's.'

What was I saying? Why was I lying to him? Where could this possibly go?

Hiro looked slightly ill. 'Really? My dad's a science teacher there.'

Uh-oh. What if Hiro asked his dad about me?

'I hate it,' I said quickly. 'It's awful. Everyone's so stuck-up. I just try to keep a low profile.'*

Hiro appeared to be satisfied by my disdain for a school I didn't go to, and he smiled. 'I didn't ask you your name, the other day.'

I didn't even hesitate. 'Katy,' I said, amazed at how easily the lie rolled off my tongue. 'It's Katy.'

He smiled that lazy, cocky smile. 'Nice to meet you, Katy. I'm Hiro.'

'Oh,' I said. 'Cool name.'

'It's Japanese,' he said. 'It means *generous*. My mum's Japanese. Dad's Italian.'

Well, that explained why he was so freaking *cute*. When he wasn't sulking, anyway.

'Do you speak Japanese or Italian?' I asked. 'When you're at home?'

Hiro scratched his nose. 'I only know a few Japanese words,' he said. 'But my Italian's pretty good. My nonna's English is terrible, and she used to look after me and my sister after school, when we were little.'

I was drinking in this information like a dying person in the desert. All of the questions he wouldn't answer at school, and now he was *volunteering* information about himself! He had a sister! And a nonna!

---

* I knew nothing about St Catherine's, except that the uniforms were fancy, the fees were exorbitant, and they had an Olympic-sized swimming pool that they heated all year round. I'd written to the principal several times informing her that a solar-heating system would not only save her thousands of dollars every year, but also save thousands of tonnes of carbon emissions. Of course, there'd been no response.

'You must be close,' I said. 'If you spent so much time with her.'

'I guess,' he said. 'She's your standard nonna. Does all the usual Italian cliché nonna things. Gardening. Cooking. Cheek-pinching.'

Gardening. That was how he knew so much about gardening. I imagined little Hiro toddling down a windy garden path with a rosy-cheeked Italian nonna with her hair in a bun. They'd pick tomatoes and basil and zucchini, and he'd learn the Italian words for everything.

'What are you smiling about?'

Hiro was staring at me, a soft smile on his face mirroring my own. I felt my cheeks get hot, and once again was grateful for the lobster costume. I was having *feelings*. Unfamiliar, squirmy feelings. Feelings about Hiro.

'Nothing,' I said. 'So, you like comics.'*

Hiro nodded. 'I do.'

'Do you read manga?'

Hiro frowned. 'Why do you ask? Because I'm half Japanese?'

'Because everyone I know reads manga.'

'Fair point. No, I don't read manga. The big eyes creep me out. I'm a traditional Western comics kind of guy. With a name like mine, you grow up thinking about superheroes a lot.'

'So what kind of a superhero am I?'

He raised an eyebrow. 'You're a superhero?'

I gestured at myself. 'I'm wearing a disguise, aren't I?'**

---

* Yeah, I know. Worst flirting ever. I was totally off my game.

** Much better. I was warming up to it.

'So you are,' said Hiro with a smile. 'And from what I can tell, you are trying to save the world.'

'Precisely. So what's my superhero name?'

'Lobstergirl, of course.'

I sighed. 'You know I'm supposed to be the Margaret River Hairy Marron.'

'Yes, but Margaret River Hairy Marrongirl doesn't sound as good as Lobstergirl.'

I scowled at him. 'Fine, if I'm Lobstergirl, you have to be Shopping Trolley Guy.'

'I've been called worse,' said Hiro with a shrug. 'Now, what are your superpowers?'

'Well, impenetrable armour for one.' I rapped on the foam suit.

'Maybe,' he said, the soft smile still on his face. 'I think it's something better, though. Like, once you grab hold of something with one of your lobster claws, you never let it go, no matter what.'

I felt a bit taken aback. That was . . . surprisingly accurate. Hiro had *seen* me, in a way that I wasn't sure anyone else ever had. Even though I was wearing a giant foam lobster outfit.

'Er,' I said, feeling flustered. 'So what's your superpower?'

Hiro sighed. 'I don't know,' he admitted. 'I've spent sixteen years trying to figure it out.'

'What's the one thing you wish you could do?'

'Fly, maybe. That seems so generic. Do you have one? A superpower you always wished you had?'

'Easy,' I said. I had actually given this plenty of thought. 'The one that Mary Poppins has, where she clicks her fingers and everything gets tidied up.'

Hiro raised an eyebrow again. 'Seriously? That seems a little ... boring. You don't want to fly? Have X-ray vision? Telepathy?'

'Think about it,' I said. 'You never have to wash dishes again. Clean your room. Mow the lawn.'

'You have surprised me, Lobstergirl,' said Hiro. 'I thought you'd have a more worthy superpower. Something more planet-saving.'

'Ah!' I wagged a finger. 'That's the genius of the cleaning finger-click. Why should it only apply to domestic mess? Surely I could also use it to clean up oil spills or accidents at nuclear power plants.'

'Huh. Now I'm imagining you clicking your lobster claws at hundreds of oil-soaked penguins.'

'And don't those penguins look grateful? Best superpower ever.'

Hiro smiled again and nodded. 'Okay,' he said. 'Fair enough. It's a cool superpower.'

'Except, to be honest, I prefer my superheroes without superpowers.'

'Really?'

'Definitely.' I said. 'Like Hawkeye and Black Widow. And Batman. And DangerMouse.'

'DangerMouse is a multilingual, secret agent rodent. I think that's a superpower.'

'Okay, fine, not DangerMouse. But the others.'

Hiro cocked his head. 'Am I mistaken, or does the black heart of a nerd beat underneath that crustaceous exterior?'

I rolled my eyes. 'This is the twenty-first century,' I said. 'Everyone's a nerd. And liking Batman and the Avengers—'

'And DangerMouse.'

'—and DangerMouse, doesn't exactly make me a mouth-breathing geek. Everyone likes that stuff. I haven't read any comics, so I can't claim to inhabit the upper echelons of nerdery like you do.'

Hiro looked unconvinced, but he was still smiling. I liked his smile. I liked it a lot. I liked that I could make him smile. There was a warm, fizzing energy between us, as if we were feeding off each other. I could tell he was feeling it too. He made eye contact a lot – long, gazing eye contact that made me feel all shivery inside. He hadn't met my eyes *once* in the garden. Now he couldn't seem to look away.

'Anyway,' I continued. 'My point is, Superman is boring because he has superpowers. He's *obliged* to do good, and doing good is easy for him. But if you actually have to *train* to be a superhero, if it takes courage and willpower and obsession, then *that's* an interesting character.'

'And you think we can all be superheroes.'

'Sure. I mean, not spandex-wearing crime-fighting ones. Unless that kind of thing floats your boat. But we should all be working hard to make the world a better place.'

'Sounds a little cheesy.'

I shrugged. 'Doesn't make it wrong.'

Hiro raised an eyebrow in a slightly patronising, cynical way that made me itch with irritation.

'What,' I said. 'Don't you agree?'

Hiro tipped his head to one side. 'Not really,' he said. 'I don't see the point. I mean, look at you. How many signatures did you get today?'

I looked down at my clipboard. 'Three,' I said with a sigh.

'And two of them thought they were signing up to some cheap seafood newsletter.'

'See?' Hiro said. 'What can you do with three signatures? People don't care, so I don't see why I should waste my time.'

'I don't see it as wasting my time. And even if those three people change their minds, then I've made a difference.'

Hiro shook his head. 'I wish that was true. But those three people are going to go home and eat their awful rubbery supermarket tomatoes and watch TV and forget all about the Margaret River Hairy Marron. People don't change. Trust me.' His face grew dark, and he turned back to his comic.

I felt like the sun had gone behind a cloud. Hiro had shut me out, just like he did at school. I suddenly felt enormous and ridiculous in my big red lobster suit.

'Er,' I said, and glanced at my watch. 'I should go.' I was supposed to meet Dev and Paige for lunch, and it'd take me forever to scrub off this stupid red face-paint.

'Really?' He looked up, his face suddenly disappointed. 'We were just getting started.'

He gave me a twinkly, decidedly flirty smile. Flirty! Hiro! How could this possibly be the same guy as the one from my kitchen garden who grunted in response to any question?

'Can I have your number?'

He wanted my number. Hiro Silvestri, Shopping Trolley Guy and Sulky Gardening Companion, wanted my number.

My number.

I couldn't give it to him, of course. Even though he was cute and interesting and funny and cared about things. Even though he gave me *feelings*. Because sooner or later he'd recognise my voice, and realise who I really was, and then he'd hate me. And even if he didn't, it wasn't like we could *date* or anything. I didn't need Dev's dating model to tell me that Hiro and I were not suited. We came from completely different worlds, and not in a romantic way like Romeo and Juliet.*

No, I'd just politely tell him I couldn't give him my number, and then I'd leave, and he'd never see me again. I was sick of spending my Saturdays dressed up as a lobster anyway.

'Sure,' I said.

What.

It was like an out-of-body experience. I watched myself grab a pen and paper from the break-room table and scribble my number on it.

'Text is better,' I heard myself tell Hiro. 'My parents are pretty strict.'

This was in no way true, but it might help with the voice-recognition issue. It seemed like my giant lobster head was enough to keep Hiro from connecting Astrid to Katy, but I suspected that without any crustaceous distractions, he might join the dots.

This wasn't good. I was getting myself into deep, deep trouble. But I couldn't stop. I liked him. I liked Hiro, and even though I knew the whole thing was doomed before it had even started, I wanted more.

---

* And anyway, look at how that turned out.

5

I finally gave in and agreed to have dinner with Dad. He offered to pick me up, but I explained again about my no-car vow for the year, and he agreed to meet me at a nearby pizza place that I could walk to.*

Dad looked different. Older. He had dark rings under his eyes and his already-thinning hair had all but given up and left the building. He gave me a hug and he felt thinner, more frail. It was as though in three months he'd turned into an old man. I ordered tap water and Dad tried to order an imported beer, but I made him change to a local organic red wine. Then we ordered pizzas – Dad had the meat lovers, I had a vegetarian with bacon. I've tried to go full-vego, but I can't, because, well . . . because bacon. Also, it's almost impossible to avoid genetically engineered soy products if you're a vegetarian. So I stick to small amounts of organic meat. And bacon.

---

* One of the biggest drawbacks of my no-car vow was having to eat at local restaurants. Like everything else in Valentine, our local eateries are either fast and multinational, or old, ugly and utterly joyless.

48

Dad asked about school and I told him about the kitchen garden project, leaving out the part where I was totally failing to grow anything, and the part where I was babysitting a guy who I kind of had a crush on, but who didn't know about my secret identity as a lobster-suited superhero, and who was also awful to me sometimes.

No need to overcomplicate things.

I tried to think of a similarly polite personal question to ask Dad. But I couldn't ask him about his new diode cavity-detecting laser, or whether he'd done any really exciting root canals recently, because I didn't want to give him the opportunity to talk about the Whippet.

'Did you call Grandma for her birthday?'

Dad nodded.

Our pizza arrived and the waitress shot me a sympathetic look. Was our awkward conversation so obvious?

'So how is your mother?' asked Dad at last. It was obviously the question he'd been wanting to ask since I arrived.

I bit off a giant piece of pizza so I could think about how to answer while I chewed. It was super hot, and the molten cheese fused to the roof of my mouth. How was my mother? She was . . . . actually kind of okay, now that Dad had stopped coming over to use the washing machine. She was different too, but not old and tired like Dad. It was as if she'd been playing the role of Mrs Smythe for the past sixteen years, and now she was finally able to take off her costume and be *her*. But I couldn't tell Dad any of that.

'Pretty good,' I said at last. 'Keeping busy.'

Dad looked disappointed. I guess he wanted her to be sad and pining like he was. 'Do you think she misses me?'

I squirmed in my chair and took another bite. 'I dunno,' I said. There's nothing like an awkward conversation about your parents' marriage breakdown to turn a normally articulate teen into a monosyllabic pool of resentment.

'I understand she's upset,' said Dad. 'I did a bad thing. But . . . I was hoping that she would have worked through that by now.'

Worked through that? I wanted to tell Dad that Mum *had* worked through it, and she'd come out the other side realising that her life was better without him in it. I wanted to tell him that cheating on Mum with the Whippet was not *a bad thing*, it was *the worst* thing. That he was lucky *I* was still talking to him.

'Don't you think I deserve another chance?' Dad's face was drooping like a sad cartoon character's. I was afraid he was going to cry, right there in the restaurant. That would be so embarrassing.

'It's not up to me to decide that,' I said. 'And it's not up to you either. It's Mum's decision, and we both have to respect that.'

'But you think she should give me another chance.'

I looked down at my fingernails. They were still rimmed with red from where I'd washed off the lobster face-paint. 'You can't ask me that. It's not fair.'

Dad sighed and nodded. 'You're right,' he said. 'I'm sorry. It's just that . . . we all go through difficult times in our lives. I know I reacted in a way that was inappropriate . . .'

I wondered if it would be rude to check my phone. Not that I was expecting Hiro to text. Not straight away, anyway. And I didn't even know if I wanted him to. I mean, I wanted him to like me. He was cute and interesting and funny. But he was also an enormous pain in the arse – I'd seen what he was like when he *wasn't* trying to be charming, and it was not pretty. We'd never be able to work out as a couple. Especially not since the only way I could go on a date with him was if I wore the lobster suit so he wouldn't recognise me. I imagined sitting next to him in a cinema, wearing the suit. He'd try to put his arm around me, but all he'd get would be red foam. He'd hold the chair out for me at a fancy restaurant, and all the other diners would have a sudden craving for seafood. We'd walk along a beach, him holding my giant foam claw. I chuckled.

'Astrid?'

I realised I'd stopped listening to Dad a while ago. And he was staring at me, baffled and a bit hurt. He'd been pouring his heart out and I'd zoned out and started imagining lobster dating scenarios.

'Sorry,' I said to Dad. 'I'm a bit tired. Got up early this morning.'

Dad smiled weakly. 'That's okay, kiddo,' he said. 'How do you feel about dessert?'

I heard my phone chime in my bag, and my heart leapt into my throat. It was Hiro. I knew it was. I pulled my phone out of my bag.

Hiro: Why didn't the lobster share its toys?

I stared at it. He'd texted me.

Why did I feel so nervous? It wasn't as if I'd never been texted by a boy before. I'd gotten plenty of boy texts. Occasionally inappropriate ones. It was no big deal.

'Are you okay?' Dad asked.

Who was I kidding? It was *totally* a big deal. Hiro wasn't like any guy I'd met before. He was smart and he cared about the world. He was kind of dangerous. He was *super* cute. But most of all . . . he *got* me. He didn't want to hang out with me because I'd increase his social standing. He wasn't intimidated by me. And it seemed he was more interested in my brain than my . . . other parts. I mean, he'd never actually seen my face. Not without red face-paint, anyway. I could be a hideous beast underneath that lobster costume.

'Astrid?'

I looked up at Dad. 'Fine,' I said. 'I'm fine. But, um, I should go home. I've got . . . homework.'

'Oh,' said Dad, looking disappointed. 'Okay, sure. Um, do you want me to walk you home? I know you won't come in the car, but it's dark outside, and I don't like the idea of you walking by yourself.'

'I'll be fine,' I told him. 'It's just around the corner.'

I could tell he wanted to walk me home so I'd invite him in and he could talk to Mum. Well, that wasn't going to happen. It wasn't fair to Mum, and also, I wanted to be alone with my phone.

'How was it?' asked Mum as I walked in the door. She was curled on the couch reading a book, a bottle and glass of red wine on the coffee table. I couldn't remember the last time I'd seen her look so relaxed. Usually at this time of night she was cleaning up after dinner or ironing Dad's work shirts.

'As expected,' I said. 'He's still all mopey.'

Mum sighed. 'Sorry,' she said. 'You shouldn't have to put up with all this nonsense.'

'It's okay,' I said. 'I can see why he's upset. But I also totally think you're doing the right thing.'

Mum's gaze grew soppy. 'How did I end up with such an amazing daughter?'

I grinned. 'Just lucky, I guess.'

I disappeared to my room and spent a good five minutes staring at Hiro's text.

Hiro: Why didn't the lobster share its toys?

What was I supposed to reply to that? I wanted to come up with something witty. Something smart and sassy. At last I gave up.

Me: Why?

Pathetic. It was lucky that flirting wasn't a subject at school, I would have broken my straight-A streak. What was wrong with me? I'd never had any trouble flirting before. I was an *expert* flirter!

My phone chimed again, and I nearly had a heart attack.

Hiro: Because she was shellfish.

I laughed out loud, and suddenly, I wasn't scared anymore. This was Hiro. Hiro understood me. I didn't need to pretend to be someone or something that I wasn't.

Me: :-)
Hiro: I'm glad you texted back. If you hadn't I'd be in a PINCH.
Me: I see what you did there.
Hiro: Hopefully if we keep talking you'll come out of your shell.

Me: Ha ha.

Hiro: Am I cracking you up?

Me: Not really.

Hiro: I'm running out of jokes.

Me: Thank goodness.

Hiro: Something something Santa Claws?

Me: . . .

Hiro: Seriously, though. Hi Lobstergirl.

Me: Hi yourself, Shopping Trolley Guy.

Hiro: How is your Saturday night going?

Me: Okay. Had dinner with my dad. Now I'm catching up on some homework.

Hiro: Exciting.

Me: IKR?

Hiro: So I did some research. And there is ALREADY a lobster superhero. Lobster Johnson.

Me: Really? Does he have a giant claw?

Hiro: Nah. Actually he's not a lobster at all. But he burns his trademark lobster claw onto the foreheads of his victims.

Me: Victims? I thought you said he was a superhero!

Hiro: Well, he was a vigilante. Killed mobsters and Nazis.

Me: Hmm. I'm not sure I approve of vigilantes.

Hiro: I thought you said they were the best superheroes?

Me: Not having superpowers isn't the same thing as being a vigilante!

Hiro: Batman is a vigilante.

Me: Batman is different. He's noble in his motivations. And he doesn't burn a lobster claw onto anyone's forehead.

Hiro: That you know of.

Me: I'm prepared to put money on it.

Hiro: You're a funny one, you know.

I felt an incredible glow spread through me. Hiro really wasn't like anyone I'd ever met before. My previous text adventures with guys had been either soppy* or sleazy.** But Hiro talked about superheroes and saving the world and he told silly jokes about lobsters. He listened. He saw me. My phone pinged again.

Hiro: Katy? Are you still there?

The glow evaporated. He didn't see me at all. He saw Katy. And the moment he realised that Katy and Astrid were the same person, everything would go horribly, horribly wrong.

On Monday after school I wandered across the footy field to the kitchen garden. I wasn't sure if Hiro would show up – his general attitude suggested he wasn't exactly committed to the rules of detention.

I lifted the plastic covers from our mini greenhouses, and set about watering the seeds with a mix of water and seaweed solution. Hiro had explained that the seaweed encouraged root growth, so was good for sprouting seeds. I covered the tray of basil and parsley seeds, making sure not to overwater. Then I moved on to the next tray and let out an involuntary squeal of excitement.

A sprout.

One of our lettuce seeds had sprouted. A tiny green tendril peeked cautiously up through the dirt.

---

* *I think about you all the time. Your eyes are like two sparkling sapphires in a pool of milk* EW EW EW.

** . . . Yeah, I'm not reproducing any of those.

I was doing it! I was gardening!

Hiro wandered in, and I grabbed his hand and dragged him over to the sprout.

'Look!' I said. 'Isn't it beautiful?'

Hiro shook his hand free and wiped it on his jeans. What was he, five? Did he think he'd get girl germs? Whatever, I wasn't going to let it dull the gloriousness of this day. My own hand was tingling from where I'd touched him.

'We did it!' I said. 'The kitchen garden project is really happening!'

Hiro snorted, but I could tell he was at least mildly amused. 'Well done,' he said. 'You've achieved something that humans have been doing for ten thousand years.'

'I couldn't have done it without you,' I said. 'Seriously, you're amazing. You've taught me everything I know. Thank you so much.'

'Thank Mr Webber,' said Hiro, scowling. 'I'm not choosing to be here.'

I rolled my eyes. Why did he have to be so irritating? I knew he wasn't always like that. I'd seen the real Hiro. Why did he have to put up a wall every time he saw me without my lobster suit on?

I spotted another speck of green emerging from the soil, and all my irritation evaporated.

'Hiro!' I squealed. 'I found another one! Another sprout!'

I nearly hugged him. That was what Katy would do. Not Astrid.

But I wanted to.

After Hiro had sulked over by the fence long enough to establish his scowly street cred, he came back to the garden, and we worked side by side, setting up a raised garden bed for our future seedlings to be transplanted into. I desperately wanted to start a conversation with him. See if I could coax out the funny, interesting Hiro I'd met in the shopping centre break room. And see if he'd recognise me for who I really was, not the bitchy Missolini monster that he saw.

'Can I ask you something?' I said at last.

'No.'

'What did you do?'

Hiro looked at me blankly.

'To get a whole month's worth of detentions. Was it you who set that girl's bag on fire?'

Hiro shook his head. 'No,' he said. 'Well, sort of. Kyle did the actual lighting of the fire, but I was involved. However, that's not what the detention is for.'

'What, then?'

A ghost of a smile flickered over Hiro's face. He hesitated, like his inner cool was competing with his urge to brag. 'Do you remember Dogshaming? When people were obsessed with posting photos of their dogs wearing signs admitting to all the dumb stuff they do?'

I vaguely remembered Paige showing me something along those lines.

Hiro pulled out his phone and showed me a photo. It was of Mr Webber, asleep on one of the benches near the football oval. Every time he had yard duty, he'd always sneak off and have a quick nap. Someone had hung a sign around his neck.

I ATE A BOX OF CRAYONS. NOW I POO RAINBOWS.

The letters were in multicoloured, wobbly crayon. I let out a snort. It was immature, but it was funny.

'I figured out his computer password and made it his email signature. And his Facebook profile picture.'

'Hence the detentions,' I said.

'It was totally worth it.'

I turned back to the garden bed, feeling a surge of victory. We'd done it. We'd had a conversation. The first step had been taken. But Hiro didn't join me. Instead, he wandered away, tapping on his phone.

A few seconds later, my own phone pinged, and I froze. Hiro was texting me. Or, more accurately, he was texting *Katy*. I sneaked a look at him, but he had his headphones on and hadn't heard my phone chime.

Phew.

I snuck my phone out of my pocket.

Hiro: I'm stuck in the most boring detention ever. What are you doing?

I felt stung. I thought we'd been having fun! We grew a sprout! Two sprouts! Didn't that mean anything to him? And we'd laughed together over the rainbow poo, hadn't we? I slipped my phone back into my pocket without replying.

'You can go if you want,' I said to Hiro. 'I won't tell Mr Webber.'

He didn't even hesitate. 'Cheers,' he said, and headed out of the garden without a backward glance.

I looked down at my little lettuce sprout. It was so fragile. How would it possibly survive the wind and sun, not to mention hungry snails? And even if it did survive, even if it grew and stretched and spread into a whole lettuce, what then? It'd get plucked and eaten. All that work, all that energy and growth. All to be a salad. Was it worth it?

I sighed and put away my gardening tools for the day.

Mum was out when I got home. I checked my email, and made myself some toast. I didn't have any urgent homework. I didn't feel like texting Hiro – not after the way he'd blown me off earlier. I felt at a bit of a loose end. I picked up my phone and called Dev.

'Hey,' he said. 'I never get to see you anymore. Are you still alive?'

'You saw me in Chemistry. All of two hours ago.'

'You know what I mean,' said Dev. 'You're always busy at recess and lunch, and after school. We haven't gone to Patchwork Rhubarb for weeks.'

'Yeah,' I said. 'Just busy in the garden and stuff.'

'Grown anything yet?'

'A lettuce seed sprouted.'

'Congratulations! Will there be a baby shower? A big announcement on Facebook? Do you have any names picked out?'

'Very funny. Anyway, who knows whether or not I'll be able to *do* anything with the lettuce.'

'No word about the canteen?'

I sighed. 'Nope.'

'Well,' said Dev. 'You tried, and that's what matters.'

I felt irrationally irritated. 'It *isn't* what matters,' I said hotly. 'Trying means nothing if you fail to make a difference.

If you declare your undying love to this music teacher, and he rejects you, are you going to feel better because you *tried*?'

Dev fell silent on the other end of the line. 'Yes,' he said at last. 'Because at least then I'll know I did everything I could.'

I snorted. 'You'd be just as heartbroken either way,' I said. 'And if you *try*, you'll end up humiliated *and* heartbroken.'

'So what do you suggest?' asked Dev, his voice rising a little. 'Never do anything, in case you fail? Never even take a risk?'

'Of course I'm not suggesting that.'

'Then what? What's the solution?'

'You don't fail.' My own voice sounded cold and brittle.

I heard Dev sigh. 'Well, sometimes you don't get to decide that. Sometimes you fail, and you pick yourself up, learn from your mistakes and try again. And next time it'll be better.'

He didn't understand. He didn't *get* it. I couldn't just try again later. If the garden failed, then Mr Webber would win. Nothing would change, and we'd just go round and round again, forever, until the polar icecaps melted and we all died.

'Look,' said Dev, 'I have to go. I'll see you at school.'

He hung up without waiting for me to say goodbye. I sat staring at my phone. I knew I wasn't exactly being a stellar friend. I shouldn't have been so dismissive of his new crush. But didn't he get that what I was trying to do was *important*?

My phone pinged again.

Hiro: Are you still out there?

I hesitated. Was I? Hiro and I had shared a moment that afternoon – a connection, and he'd thrown it away. He'd judged me the second he first saw me, and nothing was going to change that. As far as he was concerned, I was a Missolini. I was bitchy and shallow and spoilt. He was never going to change his mind.

And yet . . .

I wanted to talk to him. He'd understand how I felt. Dev didn't. Paige wouldn't either. My parents were too wrapped up in their own dramas to care about little things like saving the planet. Only Hiro. He was the only one who'd really *heard* me. I turned to my phone.

Me: Yep. Sorry about before, I was busy.
Hiro: Doing what?

I bit my lip.

Me: School stuff.
Hiro: :-(
Me: How has your afternoon been?
Hiro: Oh, you know. Boring detention. Then the usual dramas at home.

I was hurt again by *boring detention*, but was too overcome with curiosity to care too much about it.

Me: What kind of drama? Did you get in trouble about the detention?
Hiro: Nah, nothing like that. I don't think they even noticed I'd been in detention. My house is crazy at the moment. A week ago, my perfect sister told our parents that she's moving out of her college dorm into an apartment with her girlfriend.
Me: They don't like her girlfriend?

Hiro: They didn't know she was gay.

Me: Oh! Really?

Hiro: Yeah. Dad's fine with it, but Mum is . . . being weird. She likes order. This doesn't fit her idea of the perfect family.

Me: What about you? Were you surprised?

Hiro: Oh, I've known forever. Michi told me when I was five, and she was eleven. Her girlfriend is awesome. Plus the new apartment is in the city and Michi says I can crash there sometimes.

Me: Well, that's cool. I'm sure your parents will get used to the idea. It must be a bit of a shock.

Hiro: Yeah. They're supposed to be mature adults though. They could be more supportive. I get why Michi didn't tell them for so long.

Me: At least she has you!

Hiro: What about you? Any gay siblings? Mad aunts locked in attics? How's your family?

I hesitated. I hadn't actually told anyone about Mum and Dad splitting up. Not even Dev or Paige. Every time they'd suggested coming over to hang out, I'd made up some excuse, like we were having the carpets steam cleaned, or a distant relative was staying. I wasn't quite sure why I hadn't told them. It seemed too private. And also . . . a big part of who I was at school hinged on me being, well, perfect. I had this perfect life where I was pretty and popular and smart. I didn't want to admit that *some* parts of my life were far from perfect.

But Hiro didn't think I was perfect. Hiro didn't know me, or my reputation.

Me: Not great. My parents are breaking up.

Hiro: Wow. That sucks. I'm sorry.

Me: It does suck. Dad cheated on Mum so she kicked him out. I'm not convinced it was the first time, or even that he's stopped doing it. I still love Dad, but I think maybe Mum is better off without him.

Me: That was a bit of an emotional unload, sorry. I haven't really talked to anyone about this.

Hiro: That's okay. I'm glad you trust me.

Me: :-)

Hiro: I like talking to you, Katy. You make being different feel less lonely.

Me: Are you lonely?

Hiro: If there's anything I've learned from comic books, it's that people who are different are always lonely.

My thumb hovered over the phone, ready to reply. But I didn't know what to say. Lonely? I'd never been lonely. I'd always had friends. More than I needed, and then plenty of others who *wanted* to be my friend. And even though my parents didn't seem to like each other very much anymore, I knew that they both loved me. But was I *different*? And what did that even mean?

I thought about how Dev sounded on the phone, and realised I'd barely seen him and Paige over the last week, except in class. My brain had been so full of the kitchen garden, and Hiro. Dev's latest romantic adventure and Paige's obsession with reality TV seemed . . . inconsequential. Maybe *I* was becoming different.

Hiro: I've been thinking about what my superpower might be.

Me: Yes?

Hiro: I can't find it. I'd love to ride dragons, or be able to turn into a wolf, or control some kind of elemental force, like darkness or fire or water. But none of those feel right. I don't know, maybe I don't have one. Or worse, maybe I've got a lame one, like HEART.

Me: Um, isn't it obvious?

Hiro: What?

Me: Your superpower. It's obvious.

Hiro: It is the opposite of obvious.

Me: You make things grow.

As soon as I'd hit send, my hands turned clammy and I wished I could take it back. How could I have been so stupid? My blood ran cold, and I waited for a reply.

And waited.

And waited.

I'd blown my cover. Hiro had to realise who I was now. It was all over. He'd be furious. Wouldn't he?

Ping.

Hiro: What makes you say that?

Um. You know that girl at school who you kind of hate?

Me: You said you did a lot of gardening. With your Nonna. When you were little.

I needed more.

Me: Oh, and because you're Shopping Trolley Guy. You start off with one shopping trolley, and you *grow* them until you have a whole stack, that you can use to corral baddies. Or form bridges to rescue poor orphans dangling off cliffs.

Hiro: My superpower is growing tomatoes and trapping villains with shopping trolleys.

Me: Yes.

Hiro: . . . okay. I don't know if that's enough to get me into superhero school, but if you say so, Lobstergirl, then it is so.

Me: Good. Anyway, I should probably go to bed. It's late.

Hiro: I'm already in bed.

I felt an excited shiver run over my skin. Hiro was in bed. What was he wearing? Pyjamas? Boxer shorts? Nothing? I wondered what his room looked like. What kind of doona cover did he have? Did he sleep on one pillow, or two? What posters did he have on his walls?

This was bad. Very bad. I'd thought that my *feelings* were going away, but they weren't. They were getting stronger. I brushed my teeth as quickly as I could and changed into pyjamas, slipping into bed with my phone clutched in my hand.

Me: Are you still awake?

Hiro: Just.

I pressed my phone against my cheek for a moment.*

Me: Goodnight, Shopping Trolley Guy.

Hiro: Sweet dreams, Lobstergirl.

---

* I know, I know. I was probably giving myself some sort of horrific face cancer.

6

After all my efforts in the garden, I finally had something to show. Lettuce, basil, tomatoes and capsicum had all sprouted and were valiantly pushing up into the light a little further each day. And Hiro was thawing a bit, too. He was still sullen, but he'd talk to me about gardening. It made my insides feel like they were on spin cycle. Seeing Hiro, being physically close to him, was electric. Our texting sessions were getting longer and more intimate. Sometimes it was as if he was right there in my bedroom with me. Sometimes I felt I'd go mad because he wasn't. So standing next to him in front of a garden bed, close enough that I could reach out and touch him, was a kind of exquisite torture.

Sometimes I'd forget that it was Katy that he liked, and that he only barely tolerated Astrid.

Something had changed between me – Katy-me, not Astrid-me – and Hiro. It wasn't as though we'd *done* anything, or even *said* anything. And he still didn't know that I was Lobstergirl. But something had changed. Texting in bed – even though we weren't texting anything, you know, *sexy* – still felt intimate. It wasn't something casual friends did. Texting in bed brought a closeness. A privacy. A promise of more to come.

He slouched in twenty minutes after the end of school as per usual on Thursday. I'd spotted him loitering by the canteen with his friends Kyle and Barney. I couldn't believe Hiro was friends with such stonery losers. Kyle and Barney always looked half asleep, and seemed to move at a different frame rate to everybody else. They said incomprehensible things to each other and guffawed loudly, but never spoke to anyone else or participated in class. I didn't see the *point* of being alive, if the only thing you were ever going to do was slouch around and eat salt and vinegar chips. What on earth did Hiro see in them? Hiro, who was smart and sensitive and cared about the world? Hiro who texted me such sweet things deep into the night?

I tried to tell myself that if the rumours were true, Hiro was also the one who had broken into his homeroom before school one morning and filled it with about five hundred plastic cups, each one half filled with water. This was horrific for three reasons – firstly they had to be removed one by one so as not to spill the water and ruin the carpet, which meant the teacher had to skip homeroom and English. Secondly, plastic cups. Thirdly, water. What a waste! And for what? But maybe Hiro hadn't been the one behind it all. Maybe it had been Kyle or Barney's idea. Maybe. But if I was honest with myself, I knew it was too clever for Kyle or Barney.

'Hey.' He nodded at me and went to check on the seedling trays.

In some ways, it was a victory. He'd never greeted me before. He'd sounded almost friendly. But I wanted more. I was hungry for it. I nearly pulled out my phone and texted him. I nearly told him everything.

'Tomato seedlings looking good,' he said.

I went over to look, but I could barely focus on the little fuzzy green tendrils. Hiro was close enough to touch. Close enough that I could smell laundry detergent and deodorant and something else, a boy-smell that made my heart pound. I wanted to touch him. I *ached* to touch him.

'I got a reply from the mayor,' I said, in a desperate effort to keep things civil.

'Really?' said Hiro, looking dubious. 'An actual reply? Not a form reply, or something written by an underling?'

'An actual reply.'

It had been pretty exciting, really. Mayor Tanaka had written to me personally, thanking me for the information about the kitchen garden program, and commending me for my efforts. Then she'd told me how committed she was to transforming Valentine into a truly beautiful suburb – a suburb where people actually *wanted* to live. The way she'd described it all . . . it was exhilarating. Finally, things were going to change. I'd replied immediately with my ten-point plan to make Valentine the most sustainable suburb in the country, and was checking my email every five minutes to see if she'd written back.

Hiro was looking sceptical. 'Did she actually say she was going to do anything? About the food supply deal with the canteen?'

'It was definitely implied,' I said.

'*Implied.*'

'Trust me,' I said. 'She's on our side.'

Hiro raised his eyebrows. 'If that's what you want to believe.'

I was getting irritated with him again, but confusingly that made me want to kiss him even more. 'Why are you so anti-mayor?' I asked. 'Do you know her or something?'

'I'm sorry?' Hiro drew back. 'You think that because she has a Japanese name, we must know each other? Do you think we're all related?'

'No,' I said. 'Of course not. I—' I shook my head, confused, and took a deep breath. 'Never mind. What do we do with these tomato seedlings?'

Hiro shot me a long, scowly stare, but turned back to the tray of seedlings. 'Once they grow their second set of leaves, we pick out the best-looking ones and put them in their own pots.'

'Okay.'

'But today we'll sprinkle them with a little diluted Seasol.'

He walked away, and I felt myself being drawn after him. There was nothing else for it. I pretended to stumble, and fell against him. My cheek brushed his hoodie and I put out my hands to steady myself on his arms. He felt warm and solid and strong and *real*. More real than anything I'd ever touched before. I closed my eyes, trying to drink it all in so I could remember it and replay it over and over in my head.

'Whoa,' said Hiro, pushing me upright again. 'Have you been drinking?'

I mumbled an apology. What was wrong with me? I was supposed to be Hiro's *supervisor*. Faking accidents just so

I could grope him was sexual harassment. I was a terrible person, and I needed to get a grip on myself.

'So I read this interesting article last night,' I said, trying to focus my mind on something else. 'There's this organisation in the UK running a program where they give refugees and asylum seekers garden allotments and help them to grow their own vegetables.'

Hiro shrugged. 'So?'

'So it's such a great idea. Helping people find a new home by encouraging a connection with the land. Enabling them to be self-sufficient.'

'Um, I think you're mistaking me for someone who cares.'

My desire evaporated, and I felt myself physically recoil. Why was he so nice to Katy, and so mean to Astrid? This double-identity thing was no fun. I'd spent so long wishing Batman or Spiderman would take off their masks so their romantic interests could know the truth. Yet every day I dreaded my unmasking more and more. I knew it was inevitable, but I also knew that it definitely wasn't going to be like it was in the movies.

'Are you okay?' asked Hiro. 'Sure you're not drunk?'

I *felt* drunk. This was crazy. This wasn't me. I'd decided not to do this anymore. I'd already returned the lobster costume. I had to let it go.

My phone pinged on Saturday afternoon as I was working on an essay for English.

Hiro: Have you given up on the lobster campaign?

Maybe just *one* more text. Just to clarify my position. Something cool and noncommittal.

Me: Yeah. It wasn't very effective.

Hiro: You converted one poor ignorant soul.

Me: You didn't sign my petition.

Hiro: I guess you'll have to come back to the shopping centre so I can.

Me: Nice try.

Hiro: It was so boring today without you. I stacked at least two hundred trolleys, but didn't see a single supervillain or dangling orphan. Just morons stuffing their faces with junk food.

Me: Too bad. Maybe next time.

Hiro: Maybe. Anyway, I missed you. You're the only thing that makes Saturday worthwhile.

Me: I'm sure you don't work at the supermarket out of the goodness of your heart.

Hiro: Yeah, but that's only money. Money doesn't make you FEEL anything.

Me: And I do?

Hiro: . . . I realise that you can't see me right now, but I am looking embarrassed and attempting a manly cough. Now I'm going to try changing the subject.

Okay, so the not-texting thing clearly wasn't working. Fireworks were exploding inside me. I couldn't stop thinking about his smell, and the feeling of his arms under my hands.

Hiro: So how goes your plan to save the world?

I thought about the email from the Mayor. But I couldn't tell Hiro about that – he'd guess the truth.

Me: The Hairy Marron is still endangered. There still aren't any wind turbines along the dried-out creek bed. Our recycling program is a joke. But I'm still fighting the good fight.

Hiro: So . . . what exactly do you want to achieve?

Me: I want to make people care. I'm sick of being the only one who cares.

Hiro: Good luck with that. People suck.

Me: *sigh* I'm beginning to think you might be right.

Hiro: You will come to understand that I am ALWAYS right.

Me: Uh-huh. Sure.

Hiro: So . . . when do I get to see you, then?

Me: You want to see me?

Hiro: Yes. Ideally sans claws.

Me: Why?

Hiro: Because you're funny and interesting and I'd like to know what you look like when you're not a lobster.

Me: What if I'm ugly?

Hiro: I don't care. You're not ugly on the inside, and that's all that matters to me.

Me: That is very sweet. But we'll see if it holds up when you realise that my face is an oozing mass of slimy tentacles.

Hiro: Sounds hot.

Me: You have no idea.

Hiro: So?

Me: So what?

Hiro: Will you come out with me? Tentacles and all?

Me: Like . . . a date?

Hiro: Gah. You know I don't like using that kind of Missolini cultural bullshit. Could we say . . . a Meeting of Like Minds?

Me: If it's my mind you're interested in, then why so eager for me to leave the lobster suit at home?

Hiro: You're cruel.

Me: I know.

Me: . . .

Me: I'm waiting.

Hiro: You're going to make me say it?

Me: Yes.

Hiro: Fine. Would you like to join me for a Meeting of Like Minds with Possible Romantic Consequences?

I squealed out loud.

'Astrid?' called Mum from downstairs. 'Are you okay?'

'Fine, Mum.' I took a few deep breaths.

Me: There, that wasn't so hard, was it? ;-)

Hiro: I hate you.

Me: Now, now. That's no way to talk to a lady you're about to take on a date.

Hiro: Is that a 'yes'?

Me: Yes.

Hiro: :-)

I felt a wave of nausea. It would be a disaster. As soon as Hiro saw me without my Lobstergirl outfit, he'd recognise me. And hate me. Or realise that he hated me all along.

But I needed to do it. I realised I owed Dev an apology. In matters of the heart, you had to do everything you could, even if you knew you'd fail.

My hands shook as I sieved compost for the seedlings on Monday, excited and terrified to see Hiro. We were going on a *date*, in five days. Five days till he knew the truth.

'Do you have a plan of where everything's going to go?'

At least Hiro was speaking to me. That was an improvement on last week.

I nodded. 'I thought alphabetically. Then it's easy for anyone to find what they're looking for.'

Hiro blinked. 'Alphabetically. Like, asparagus, basil, carrots, daikon?'

'Is that crazy?'

'Yes.'

'Are you going to explain why? Or are you going to look superior and smug?'

Hiro raised an eyebrow drily. 'I think I can manage both.'

Was it just me, or was that *almost* flirting?

'Do you know anything about companion planting?'

I shook my head. 'Nope.'

'Right. Well, some plants are good friends with other plants. Marigolds go well with tomatoes and roses. Nasturtiums will distract bugs from squash and broccoli. Oregano will keep pests away from cucumbers. Chives make carrots taste sweeter, and basil makes tomatoes taste better.'

This was amazing. How awesome was nature? 'Go on,' I said.

'Some plants aren't friends with other plants. Dill doesn't like tomatoes or carrots. Garlic and onion should be kept away from beans. Strawberries shouldn't be planted where tomatoes, potatoes, eggplant or capsicum have been previously.'

'So alphabetical order probably isn't the way to go, then.'

Hiro shook his head. 'Probably not.'

We spent the next hour planning out the garden beds on a piece of paper. Hiro told me about crop rotation, and we split up our seeds into four different groups – fruits, leaves, roots and legumes. We'd plant one bed with each, and every year rotate the beds, so that the soil could be replenished with different minerals. Well, not me, obviously, because I wouldn't be around for that much longer. But I'd train up some Missolini wannabes and make sure they knew all about the crop rotation method.

'So, um.'

I glanced up from our garden plan at Hiro, who was wearing a pained expression.

'I'd like some advice,' he said.

'Wow. That looked like it hurt coming out,' I said.

'Shut up. Forget it.'

'I'm sorry.' I smiled. 'I'm shocked that you want advice from me. I thought *you* were the advisor in this relationship.'

As soon as the word *relationship* left my mouth, I felt myself blush. Hiro visibly winced at the word, and looked like he might bolt.

'Please,' I said. 'I'd love to help you out.'

Hiro scowled, and stared at his shoes. 'I'mgoingonadate.'

'I beg your pardon?'

'A date. I'm taking a girl on a date. I'd like some advice.'

Yikes.

Hiro was asking me advice on what to do with his date. His date, who was me.

'W-what kind of advice?' I asked, trying to keep my voice level.

'I don't know. I . . . like this girl a lot. And I've never really . . . You know.'

'Gone on a date?'

Hiro shrugged.

75

'You've *never* gone on a date?'

'You don't need to make it sound like I've been living in a cave,' he said, narrowing his eyes. 'Dating is lame.'

'Does that mean you've never . . . with a girl . . .'

Hiro gave me a withering look. 'Don't be an idiot,' he said. 'I've hooked up with plenty of girls. I've just never done the whole white picket fence, fifties diner *date* nonsense. I didn't even know people still *did* that.'

I tried not to picture the kind of 'hooking up' Hiro had done. 'But now you're going on one. A date.'

'Yes.'

I couldn't help myself. 'You must really like this girl.'

'Don't push your luck,' Hiro said. 'This isn't going to be a bonding experience where you and I talk about our feelings. Tell me the kind of thing that girls like to do on dates.'

I shrugged. 'It depends on how serious you want it to be. If you want the full date experience, then it's dinner and a movie. If you want to play it cool, meet for coffee, and then if that works you can extend the date to something else.'

'Like what?'

'A walk by the river, although obviously not in Valentine*, or a trip into the city. If you're feeling brave you could invite her back to your place to watch a movie.'

'Right.' Hiro twisted his fingers together. He looked genuinely terrified, which somehow delighted me. This date wasn't just a casual hook-up for him. He must really like me!

---

* Our local creek is more like a concrete drain, choked with plastic bags and drink bottles. Given that your chances of coming into contact with a dead animal, syringe or new strain of E-coli are pretty high, it's not exactly the kind of place I'd recommend for a romantic interlude.

Or at least, he must really like Katy.

'And should I . . . bring her anything? Flowers or something?'

This was ridiculous. I was designing my own perfect date. How many girls got this opportunity?

'Bring her one flower. That you picked yourself.* Then it's romantic, but not overboard. Not a rose, either, that's too much of a cliché. Something that makes you think of her when you see it. Something pretty, but interesting.'

Hiro nodded. 'Pretty, but interesting. That's the perfect way to describe her.'

How the hell did he know? He'd never seen me outside my lobster costume. This was a good opportunity to come clean. Tell him the truth. Give him time to come to terms with the whole thing before our date.

'Thanks,' said Hiro, looking as if the word tasted disgusting coming out of his mouth. 'I appreciate your help.'

Tell him.

'You're welcome,' I said. 'And good luck. I hope it goes well.'

I really, really did.

---

* This also avoids supporting the cut-flower industry, which I'm not an enormous fan of. You want to give someone a naturey gift? Buy a pot plant, or better still, donate money in their name to the Wilderness Society.

7

What did one wear on a date with a smart, environmentally conscious guy who had only ever seen one dressed as a lobster?

Nothing too dressy – we were only meeting for a coffee, after Hiro had finished his shift at the shopping centre. And nothing too preppy – I didn't want to scare him off once he discovered I was a Missolini. I settled on jeans with a green, floaty blouse and a yellow cardigan. I spent a good forty minutes getting my hair to look effortlessly tumbled around my shoulders, and added lip gloss, mascara and a simple gold necklace with a hammered oak leaf pendant.

I surveyed the results in the mirror. Pretty, casual and softly romantic.

Perfect.

The truth was, I was terrified. One half of me was sure that Hiro would hate me once he found out who I was. He hated the Missolinis. Moreover, I'd lied to him. I'd been lying to him for weeks. How could he not hate me? But the other half of me didn't care. The other half knew that if there was the tiniest sliver of a chance that he'd understand,

I had to take it. And even if he didn't, it'd be worth it to be close to him for a moment.

This was pathetic. I was going out of my mind over a *boy*. I wasn't that kind of girl! I'd never written a guy's name over and over again in my diary. I'd never tried out his surname with my first name, imagining how it'd be if we got married.* I wasn't the kind of girl who swooned and sighed and obsessed over every little detail.

And yet here I was, reading over our text messages for the millionth time. Three hundred and twelve texts. That was how many he'd sent me. And I'd sent him three hundred and nine.

It'd be fine. He'd understand why I did it. He understood *me*. And I was still the same person. Maybe he'd be *pleased*. I was hot property at school, lots of guys wanted to date me. Hiro's social status would go through the roof when people found out we were together. I'd be the best thing that ever happened to him.

💋

I saw him long before he saw me, waiting on the street corner outside Patchwork Rhubarb. He was wearing dark skinny jeans and a grey T-shirt under a black jacket. He held a single, blush-pink flower. Not a rose. Something softer and wilder. I paused before I crossed the road and took a few deep breaths. If this didn't go well, it could be the last time Hiro

---

* Who was I kidding? As if I'd ever change my name when I got married. And anyway, I wasn't getting married until Dev could.

ever spoke to me. But that wasn't going to happen. I would explain, and he'd understand.

He looked nervous, jiggling up and down on his feet and twisting the stem of the flower between his fingers. I was sure he couldn't be even remotely as nervous as me. I clenched my fists and stepped off the kerb, crossing the road and coming up behind him.

'Hey.'

Hiro turned around. His brow wrinkled when he saw me.

'What are *you* doing here?' he asked.

I tried to ignore the sudden freezing feeling in my gut. 'I'm here for our date.'

He looked blank. 'Um,' he said. 'I think there's been a misunderstanding.'

'No,' I said. 'It's me. Katy. My middle name is Katy.'

He stared at me.

'Surprise!' I said weakly, thinking I might throw up.

I was waiting for realisation to dawn on his face. I hoped it would be closely followed by relief, or pleasure, or good-humoured astonishment.

It wasn't. Hiro's brows drew together in outrage. He shook his head slowly.

'Why . . .' He shut his eyes for a moment. 'Why would you *do* something like that?'

'I meant to tell you sooner,' I said. 'I wanted to make sure you'd understand—'

'Is this all a big joke to you?' He took a step back like my mere presence was physically repulsive to him. 'You think this is funny?'

'No!' I said. 'I don't. I wanted to—'

'I thought you were different,' he said, ignoring me. 'I thought you understood.'

'I do!' I said. 'I do understand.'

'You're just the same as the rest of them,' Hiro said, his mouth twisting. 'You're *worse*. I bet you've been giggling over this with your little comrades.'

'What? No. I haven't told them about you.'

Hiro snorted. 'Great. I'm such a loser that you're embarrassed even to be messing with me.'

My heart was beating fast, and I felt colour rising to my cheeks. 'Hang on a minute,' I said. 'What happened to you promising that you wouldn't judge me for the way I looked? What happened to you knowing me so well on the inside that the outside didn't matter?'

'I was wrong. I don't know you on the inside at all. And I don't want to.'

'That's not fair.'

'Says the spoilt Missolini princess. Always getting exactly what she wants. Well, you've got what you wanted. You fooled me. Well done.'

'You don't know what I want.'

'I know everything I need to. You're controlling, manipulative and shallow.'

My mouth fell open. 'How dare you!' I said. 'You think you're so awesome, sitting outside the system that you say is so broken. But here you are, judging me because I'm popular. You've stuck me in a labelled box, and you refuse to even consider that I might be a real person as well. I meant every single word I said to you. I didn't tell my friends about you because I didn't think they'd understand. But I thought that *you* would understand. *You* were supposed to be different. *You* were supposed to see the real me, regardless if I was a lobster or a Missolini. But you didn't. You can't.'

I could feel tears running down my face. Hiro's face was shut up and cold. I took a step forward to touch his arm, and even though he was so angry and I was getting more and more upset, touching his skin sent a bolt of electricity through me.

'Don't touch me,' he said, his voice low. 'Don't text me again. And don't talk to me. You and I – we're finished.'

He dropped the pink flower and walked away, turning sharply around the corner.

'Hiro!' I called after him. 'Wait.'

But he was already gone.

I didn't understand what was happening. *Nobody* rejected me. Ever. I was Astrid Katy Smythe, Missolini. There was not a single boy at our school who didn't want to date me.*

Except Hiro.

Hiro didn't want to date me. He didn't even want to *speak* to me.

I felt as though someone had punched me in the stomach, leaving me sick and hollow and trembling. This wasn't fair. It wasn't supposed to happen like this. I bent down and picked up the pink flower, its petals already bruised and wilting. I wanted to cry and break things and curl up in a ball and sleep for a million years.

He hated me.

---

* Obviously after they'd first been rejected by Paige. And not including the ones who wanted to date Dev, although to be honest there was the occasional crossover.

I'd been lying to myself earlier, when I'd told myself that I didn't care. I cared. I cared a lot. I'd dated plenty of guys before. I'd had a few makeout sessions at parties, and been awkwardly groped at the movies. But I'd never felt like this. I'd never felt so alive, full of raging storms and spinning, turbulent winds. I'd never really *felt* my heart before, felt it beating and aching and breaking. I knew I should *do* something. I should go home and eat my feelings, or throw myself into a new campaign. Or go and confess everything to Paige and Dev and let them cheer me up with organic popcorn and new episodes of *Psychic Cheerleaders* and *Fraternity Exorcism*. But I couldn't move. I couldn't see the *point* of moving, if Hiro hated me. There was no point in anything. Maybe I'd stand here forever. Maybe I'd put down roots and become a tree. I bet trees never got their hearts broken. That giving tree in the picture book never got upset, even though the little boy was awful to it and cut it down until it was just a stump. Maybe it'd be better to be a tree.

I'd never felt so completely, utterly alone.

Hiro hated me.

And could I blame him?

I'd lied to him. I recognised him the moment he stepped into the kitchen garden, and I hadn't said anything. Would it have made a difference if I'd confessed straight away? Would he have turned against me so utterly?

Maybe. Maybe not. I should have told him the truth.

It was all my fault.

'Did somebody die and nobody told me?' asked Paige, as I slumped down next to her and Dev at Patchwork Rhubarb the next morning. 'You two look terrible.'

I glanced up from the laminex table at Dev. Paige was right. Dev's eyes were red-rimmed, as if he'd been crying. As for me, I hadn't been crying, but my mood could sour milk, and that must have registered on my face.

Paige pushed a cup of coffee across the table to me, and I took a grateful sip. It was unseasonably warm outside, even though it was still early. I hoped my little seedlings at school would survive. I had a key to let myself into the garden over the weekend so I could pop in and give everything a good drenching.

Normally I didn't approve of air conditioning*, but the pleasant coolness of Patchwork Rhubarb was a relief. It was the only café in Valentine that didn't belong to some kind of evil multinational chain, as well as being the only one that sold single-origin coffee. For this, we put up with the ridiculous chintzy decor (think lots of florals and teddy bears) and the hordes of gumnut-earringed ladies who used it as a venue for their scrapbooking club meetings.

'I did something terrible,' said Dev in a quiet, hollow voice.

Paige clucked her tongue. 'You told him, didn't you? Your music guy? You told him you loved him.'

Dev sniffed.

'And he said he didn't love you. Is it because he's straight?'

'He—' Dev gulped. 'He didn't say anything. He didn't exactly get the opportunity to say anything.'

---

* One kilo of air conditioning emissions has the same greenhouse impact as running a car for six months.

Paige narrowed her eyes. 'What did you do?'

Dev looked down at his hands, neatly folded on the table.

'Dev. What did you do?'

'I wanted to surprise him. Show him how much I love him. I wanted to make a grand romantic gesture.'

Paige hit herself in the forehead with the palm of her hand. 'Go on.'

Dev swallowed. 'I broke into his apartment and filled it with candles.'

'You *broke into his house*?'

The scrapbooking ladies peered over at us disapprovingly. Paige frowned and lowered her voice. 'How did you even know where he lived?'

'I . . . might have followed him home a couple of times.'

Paige closed her eyes. 'So you stalked him until you found out where he lives. Then you broke into his place and . . . filled it with candles. So what did he say when he saw them?'

Dev's mouth twisted. 'Well . . . Um. He didn't exactly get to see them. Not properly.'

Paige gestured for him to continue.

Dev took a deep breath. 'The candles set off a smoke detector. And his apartment is new, so it has an automatic sprinkler system. Which also alerts the fire department.'

Paige stared at him, then started to laugh. 'So the love of your life came home to find his apartment soaking wet and full of extinguished candles and firemen?'

'It's not funny.'

'I think you'll find it is a little bit funny.'

Dev let his head fall onto the table with a *thunk*. 'I ran as soon as the fire alarms went off, and watched from behind a fern in the lobby.'

'So he doesn't know it's you. Then everything's fine, you're off the hook.'

'But he still doesn't know how I feel.'

Paige shook her head. 'When are you going to stop modelling your life on romantic comedies? We've talked about this. Grand romantic gestures *do not work*. They are *creepy* and *stalkery*. People do not want to come home and find their house full of candles or flowers. They don't want to be proposed to in front of hundreds of strangers. They don't want a flash mob or a skywriter or a viral YouTube video. People respond to genuine emotions, not overblown flashiness. Trust me, I've seen every single episode of *Extreme Proposals*.'*

Dev lifted his head and scowled. 'I suppose I should have just sent him a text message then. Would that satisfy you?'

'I'm not saying there can't be *any* romance,' Paige replied, rolling her eyes. 'But would it kill people to aim for a *medium-sized romantic gesture*? Mr Darcy bursting in and unloading on Lizzie. John Cusack declaring his feelings in the rain in every movie he's ever made. Bridget Jones running through the snow in her undies. That awesome *feelings* noise that Emma Thompson makes in *Sense and Sensibility*.'

I blinked. A *medium-sized romantic gesture*. Maybe that's what I should be doing. Instead of just waiting and hoping for Hiro to speak to me again.

---

* Paige had also seen every episode of *The Prisoner Wants a Wife*, *Last Fiancée Standing* and *Savannah Shotgun Weddings*, so she was definitely an expert on the subject.

Paige looked over at me. 'So what's your deal, then? Did you set someone's house on fire too?'

'I didn't *set it on fire*,' said Dev indignantly.

I shook my head and smiled. 'I'm fine,' I said.

Or at least I would be.

8

One of the many perks of being a Missolini is that as a year level captain, I could access the school intranet from my laptop at home. I had my hands on Hiro's home address within minutes. And the weather forecast predicted showers for the afternoon, so it looked like I was all set for my Medium-sized Romantic Gesture.

I waited until four, but there was no sign of rain. I checked the weather radar, and realised I'd either have to wait for another rainy day, or downgrade my Medium-sized Romantic Gesture to a Smallish Romantic Gesture. I checked the weather forecast for the following week. It was predicted to be the driest, warmest November on record. I was going to have to bite the bullet.

Hiro's house was a twenty-minute walk from mine. I scoured every front yard and median strip I passed for an extra piece of romantic gesture. Hiro had brought me a flower on our failed date. I wanted to take him something too. Something to show him I was sorry. Eventually, after garden after garden of concrete blocks and straggly weeds,

I found what I was looking for – a withered, sick-looking olive tree. I ducked into the front yard, hoping that nobody would see me, and snapped off a twig.

This was going to work.

I wouldn't fail this time.

Hiro's house was somehow cleaner and newer than the others, with modern white render and a perfectly manicured front lawn. It wasn't what I'd expected. I thought it would have been more . . . scruffy. Like Hiro. I took a deep breath and marched up the path.

A pretty girl a few years older than me answered the door. If my life was a romantic comedy, I'd assume she was Hiro's new girlfriend, and be consumed with jealousy. But I wasn't that stupid. She had the same dark hair and eyes as Hiro, as well as the smattering of freckles across her nose.

'Hi,' I said. 'I'm Astrid. You must be Hiro's sister Michi.'

The girl blinked. 'I am,' she said. 'Hello, Astrid. What can I do for you?'

'I'm here to see Hiro.'

Michi looked confused. 'Really? Is he in trouble?'

I smiled. 'No,' I said. 'Actually, I'm here to apologise to him.' I held up the twig. 'It's an olive branch.'

Michi glanced at it. 'Are you sure?'

Suddenly, I wasn't.

'Anyway,' said Michi, 'Hiro isn't here. He'll be back soon, though. Do you want to come in and wait?'

This wasn't going how I planned. But I was committed now. 'Thank you.'

Michi led me into the house, and I tried to be subtle as I looked around, hungry for any clues about how Hiro lived. Everything was spotlessly clean and modern, all white marble and stainless steel. It was like something out of a display home, stylish but without any warmth. I couldn't imagine Hiro living here at all.

'Tea? The kettle just boiled.' Michi led me into the kitchen and pulled two white mugs from a cupboard. 'I have no idea what kind there is . . . I don't actually live here.'

I nodded. 'Hiro told me,' I said. 'Congratulations on moving to the city.'

Michi looked surprised. 'He told you? About me? About our family?'

'He told me that your parents weren't overjoyed when you came out, and that you're moving into an apartment with your girlfriend.'

'Huh.' Michi plonked a teabag into the mug, and pushed it across the bench to me, looking me over with a more calculating eye. 'So Hiro actually can talk in actual full sentences? Not monosyllabic grunts?'

I glanced around the spotless, shining kitchen.

'It's weird, isn't it?' said Michi, as if she could read my thoughts. 'Teen rebel Hiro and his lesbian sister coming out of such a sterilised environment.'

'It does seem a little strange,' I admitted.

'So you and Hiro are . . . friends?' Michi looked as if she thought this was unlikely.

'Yes,' I said firmly. 'Although I did something stupid and he's angry at me.'

Michi cocked her head. 'Does this have something to do with Katy?'

I nearly spilled hot tea on myself. 'You know about Katy?'

'She's all Hiro's been talking about lately. Katy says this, and Katy says that. It's been a super big deal – I'm sure he's dated girls before, but this is the first time he's mentioned it to me. So I figure he must really like her. He was supposed to go on a date with her yesterday, but I think something went wrong, because he hasn't mentioned it since and he's been in a foul mood. Fouler than usual.'

I swallowed.

'So do you know her?'

I winced. 'In a manner of speaking.'

Michi narrowed her eyes. 'Okay,' she said. 'Spill. Tell me everything.'

I did. It was easy. There was something about her open face that made me want to tell her things. She listened, nodding occasionally, and sometimes letting a slight frown furrow her brow.

'Well,' she said, when I'd finished. 'This isn't good.'

'What do I do?' I asked. 'How do I fix it?'

Michi shrugged. 'If there's anything I've learnt, it's that honesty is always the best policy. Apologise and tell him how you feel.'

'Do you think it'll work? Will he forgive me?'

'I honestly don't know.'

I sighed. 'I wish we could go back to being Lobstergirl and Shopping Trolley Guy.'

Michi raised her eyebrows. 'Kids today. I never understand a word you're saying.'

The front door banged, and my heart banged too. I shakily put my tea down on the bench.

Michi winked at me. 'Good luck.'

Hiro came into the kitchen and stopped dead when he saw me. His face clouded over. I wanted to run to him and touch his hair, his face, his hands. I wanted to slide my hands inside the pockets of his hoodie. I wanted to lay my head against his chest and listen to his heart beating. But I straightened my spine and waited.

'What the hell are you doing here?'

It was just good to *see* him. To drink him in. Even though he looked like he wanted to kill me. Hiro glanced at Michi, who shrugged and smiled.

'Is Mum here?' Hiro asked her.

Michi shook her head. 'At work.'

Hiro seemed momentarily relieved, before dialling up the anger again and turning to me.

'I thought I told you yesterday I never wanted you to talk to me again.'

'You were wrong,' I said. 'You forgot about my superpower. I never let go.'

'Well,' said Michi, clearing her throat awkwardly. 'I've got some very important . . . things . . . to be getting on with. In a place that is not this place.' She headed out of the kitchen, jabbing Hiro in the ribs as she passed him, and hissing, 'Don't be too much of a dick, okay?'

And then it was just the two of us. We stood there in silence for what felt like hours.

I took a deep breath and pushed my olive branch across the benchtop. 'Please let me explain,' I said. 'I deserve that.'

'You don't deserve anything.'

'Just *listen*,' I said.

Hiro rolled his eyes, crossed his arms and turned to stare

out the kitchen window. I took that as a good sign. At least he wasn't leaving.

'You were so nice to me that day at the shopping centre,' I explained. 'And you talked to me like nobody else did. You *thought* about things and you listened and you cared about stuff. You weren't sucking up to me like everyone else does. And I honestly thought you'd recognised me at school, that first day in the garden, and that was why you were being so sulky. But then I realised that's how you *are*, and you had no idea. And then I saw you again and we talked about superheroes and I didn't want that to stop. Because I like you. A lot. And I'm sick of having a secret identity. And I know I'm a Missolini and that you hate us, but I'm sure if you give me a chance you'll see that I'm still Lobstergirl. Just without the protective shell.'

'You lied to me.'

'I'm sorry,' I said. 'I should have been honest with you from the beginning. But I liked you, and I thought that if I told you who I was, then you'd write me off as a shallow Missolini.'

'You should have trusted me.'

I couldn't quite let that one go. 'In all fairness, you *did* write me off as a shallow Missolini as soon as you found out.'

Hiro scowled, but I could see that he knew I was right.

'Please,' I said. 'Don't judge me on who you think I am. Judge me on who you *know* I am.'

Hiro looked down at the twig. 'You know this isn't olive, right?'

'It isn't? But I found a picture online and everything. I walked around for *hours* looking for one.'

93

'Sorry,' said Hiro. 'It's a wattle.'

'Will you take it as a token of my regret anyway?'

Hiro didn't say anything.

'Come on,' I said. 'Have you never kept secrets before? Held back because you didn't want to ruin the possibility of a good thing?'

I couldn't read his expression at all. I ploughed on, feeling desperate.

'We . . . had something,' I said. 'I don't really know what it was, but it was good. And I wanted to see where it went. I still do. And . . . I think you do too.'

Another long, excruciating moment.

At last, he nodded. 'Okay.'

'Okay . . . okay what?'

'Okay I accept your apology.'

It was lucky Hiro was so cute, because he could be insufferable. 'Thank you,' I said.

Hiro rubbed a wattle leaf between his thumb and forefinger, and I tried not to melt into a puddle of nerves and anticipation.

'So what happens now?'

'This.'

Hiro leaned over the bench, slid his hand into my hair and kissed me. It was warm and sweet and soft and totally unlike any of my previous fumbling, gropey kissing experiences. I was feeling *everything*, all at once. I felt nervous and happy and excited and relieved and terrified. I felt parts of me that I'd never truly been aware of come to life with aching sweetness. But more than anything, I felt *right*. As though this was exactly where I was supposed to be, in this moment, in all of space and time. The hairs on my arms stood up, and I leaned forward, trying to get closer to him. The benchtop dug into my stomach, and I started sliding off my stool.

'This is kind of awkward,' said Hiro, breaking away.

Awkward? Awkward was one of the few feelings that I *wasn't* experiencing. Until now.

'Oh,' I said, taking a step back and feeling like an idiot. Had I been doing it wrong?

Hiro placed his palm on the kitchen bench. 'There's something coming between us,' he said, and then he vaulted up and over the benchtop, so we were both on the same side. I was overwhelmed by the sheer *physicality* of him – strength and grace and closeness. I could smell his boy-smell, and it made me dizzy. He stepped even closer, and I slid off the stool to press up against him.

Someone cleared their throat behind me, and Hiro and I jumped apart, guiltily.

A man who I assumed was Hiro's dad was standing in the doorway. He had dark eyes and shiny cheeks, and wore jeans and a blue-and-white checked shirt. He was handsome, in a dignified, silver-haired way. I remembered that he was a teacher at St Catherine's.

Neither Hiro nor his dad said anything. I took a step forward and held out my hand. 'Hi, Mr Silvestri. My name's Astrid. I go to school with Hiro.'

Mr Silvestri looked bewildered. 'Nice to meet you, Astrid,' he said, shaking my hand. 'Call me Carlo.'

I smiled, hoping Hiro would say or do something to prove that he was a living, breathing human being.

'Your mother just called,' said Mr Silvestri to Hiro. 'She's on her way. Is your sister home?'

Hiro jerked his head towards the back of the house.

Mr Silvestri's lips tightened. The air in the room had grown even more laden with awkwardness. I could tell Hiro's dad was utterly baffled to see me, and I could understand why. I was neat, polite, conventionally pretty – everything a parent would want in a girlfriend for their son. But I was *definitely* not the kind of alternative, black-nail-polish girl he would expect Hiro to bring home. In fact, I was confident Hiro had never brought a girl home before. Or even *mentioned* a girl to his parents.

Another few excruciating seconds passed, and I realised that Hiro wasn't planning on saying anything. It was up to me to be the grown-up, as usual.

'You know, it's getting late,' I said. 'My mum will be expecting me home for dinner. Mr Silvestri – Carlo – it was lovely to meet you. Hiro, I'll see you at school?'

I wanted him to speak. To tell me to wait. To invite me into his room, or at least offer to walk me home. Instead he nodded vaguely, without making eye contact. I let myself out.

I walked home with mixed feelings. Hiro had obviously forgiven me . . . the kissing proved that. But he had been deeply uncomfortable about me meeting his dad, and I couldn't figure out why. Was he embarrassed to be seen with me? That didn't make sense. I was . . . *me*. I was a catch. My lips still buzzed.

9

'Hey.'

I should have been excited to see Hiro. It was less than twenty-four hours since we'd last been together. I'd lain awake for hours, thinking about him, about lying on his bed, and his hands, and his lips. And now everything was out in the open. We'd work together in the garden, just like before, but there would be honesty and openness. And kissing.

Except I couldn't feel anything except my white-hot supernova of rage.

Hiro took a step forward, as if he was going to hug or kiss me, but stopped when he saw my face. 'What's going on?'

I shook my head.

Hiro faltered, and his face grew cautious.

'No,' I said. 'It's not you. Not about you. I just spoke to Mr Webber.'

It had been awful. Talking to Mr Webber was never a highlight of my day, but this time, instead of looking at me with his usual irritated frown, his dry, flaky face had been plastered with a smug grin.

'I'm sorry, Astrid, but we've decided not to continue the kitchen garden project next year.'

I tried to tell him why he was wrong, but he spoke over me, almost as if I wasn't there. He told me that the school had recently been offered some funding to develop a new building, and that the site they'd picked just *happened* to be in the same place as the kitchen garden. Construction was due to start at the end of February.

I'd spluttered. I'd argued. I'd cajoled. But Mr Webber wouldn't budge.

'He wouldn't even tell me what kind of new building they were planning,' I told Hiro through clenched teeth. 'Just looked even more smug than before and said it was "currently being scoped", whatever that means.'

Hiro nodded. 'Typical,' he said. 'Webber is a fascist.'

Nice, polite Missolini Astrid protested – Mr Webber was just doing his job. But the rage-monster roared in agreement with Hiro.

'What are we going to do?' I asked.

Hiro put up his hands. 'We?' he said. 'There is no *we* in this. I mean, there's a *we* in the sense that there is you, and there is me, and we seem to like each other and yesterday some very nice things happened. But here,' he gestured around the garden, 'here there is no *we*.'

I felt like he'd slapped me in the face. 'What do you mean? I thought you liked working on the garden?'

Hiro looked uncomfortable. 'You know how I feel about this kind of thing. I mean, the garden is cool, and we've done some good work here. But this is the way the system goes. You try to challenge it, and it crushes you.'

'So you think I should give up.'

Hiro sighed. 'In my experience, these things never work out. You're upsetting yourself unnecessarily.'

I looked around at our garden. in every bed, plants were springing to life. Every day there was a new patch of little green sprouts, and every day the sprouts got taller and stronger. And Mr Webber wanted to get rid of it all. Just when it was starting to work.

'I can't give up,' I said. 'I can't. It's not in me.'

Hiro shrugged. 'Your call, Lobstergirl.'

Even though my hands were still shaking with rage, I tried to calm down. I ran through some of the breathing exercises that Paige had shown me. I tried to centre my *ki*.

'Can we work for a bit?' I said. 'The garden's still here, and we have lots to do.'

But the rage-monster was controlling me, and I couldn't do anything right. I kept crushing the tiny seedlings with my rage-monster hands. I spilled a bag of chicken manure and broke a terracotta pot.

'Okay, I think we need to get out of here,' said Hiro at last, stripping off his gardening gloves. 'Your head isn't in it today. You're like The Hulk.'

'But we're supposed to transplant the new zucchini seedlings today.'

Hiro chuckled. 'The zucchini will wait. Come on.'

He gently pulled my gloves off too, and a warm, fuzzy feeling flickered inside me, soothing the rage-monster for a moment.

'Wh-where are we going?'

'I'm taking you to Nonna's house.'

'Your nonna? The one with the garden?'

Hiro nodded. 'Nonna can fix anything,' he said. 'She'll cure your Hulkness.'

'Really? Now?'

'Now. It's only a few blocks away.'

'But you're in detention.'

Hiro gave me a flat look. 'Are you planning on turning me in?'

He grabbed my hand, and pulled me away from the garden.

I couldn't believe I'd never seen it before. All along the narrow suburban street were identical brown brick houses with identical yellowing lawns.

And then, an oasis.

Even the sight of it soothed the rage-monster.

It was still the same boring brown brick house, but I could barely see it. There was no lawn, just an enormous lemon tree, heavy with fruit, surrounded by a confusion of basil, swiss chard and about a million other green, interesting-looking plants that I didn't recognise. Green tomatoes hung like heavy jewels, some of them just beginning to blush pink. There were three apple trees carefully pruned against one fence – Hiro told me it was called espalier. They were covered in new greenery and swelling fruit. The opposite fence was lined with tall, upright plants with pods bursting from the stems.

'Broad beans,' said Hiro, following my gaze.

'Is your grandmother a witch?' I asked.

Hiro laughed. 'It's not totally out of the question,' he said. 'Come on.'

'Shouldn't we call first? How do you know she's not busy?'

'Nonna is never too busy for a visit from her only grandson.'

He led me up the path towards the front door. Bees and butterflies flitted around the garden. Everything was so green it practically *glowed*. It was probably producing about eighty per cent of Valentine's oxygen.

The door opened before we reached it. Hiro's grandmother was tall and thin, with wiry grey hair swept into a messy bun. She wore a simple black dress, and intelligent eyes glinted behind black-framed glasses. Her eyes flicked over me and her mouth curled in a smile as she reached out and pinched Hiro's cheeks before hauling him in for a hug.

'Hi, Nonna,' he said, his voice a little muffled, before extracting himself. 'This is Astrid. Astrid, this is my grandmother, Maria.'

'Hi,' I said, feeling suddenly shy. Shy? I hadn't felt shy for *years*.

'Nice to meet you,' said Maria, in heavily accented English. 'You too.'

She looked me over with a shrewd eye, and for a moment I felt like she could actually hear my thoughts. I wanted her to like me. I wanted her to approve of me as a good girlfriend for Hiro. Finally she turned back to him and said something rapidly in Italian. He replied, and I drank it in. I couldn't understand a word, but there was something very, very appealing about Hiro speaking fluent Italian.

'We have to stay for dinner,' said Hiro, turning to me. 'We have no choice in the matter.'

'As long as it's not an inconvenience,' I said, 'I'd love to stay.'

Hiro snorted. 'I don't think you understand how this works. Staying for dinner isn't some generous offer that she's made. It's an order. Non-negotiable.'

He said a few more words in Italian, and Maria nodded and smiled. Hiro took my hand.

'She's going into the kitchen,' he said. 'I'll take you out the back and show you around.'

Hiro led me through the house, which was full of so many knick-knacks and ornaments that I felt a bit overwhelmed. I noticed a preponderance of cows – china cows, brass cows, paintings of cows, cushions embroidered with cows. Hiro grinned.

'This place drives my mother crazy,' he said. 'She hates clutter.'

'Why all the cows?'

'Nonna's family back in Italy owned a dairy farm,' he said. 'But she fell in love with a mechanic who wanted to move to Australia.'

'Is he still . . .?'

'Alive?' Hiro shook his head. 'He died when I was a baby. I don't remember him at all.'

He pushed open the back door and led me outside.

Maria's back garden was even more amazing than the front. More fruit trees, as well as a whole grove of olive trees and a huge trellis of grapevines. Pumpkin vines sprawled between rows of staked vegetables. At the very back of the garden was a potting shed covered in passionfruit, a chicken run where five or six fat birds scratched around, an enormous compost heap, and what looked like a beehive. I tried to take it all in, my mouth hanging open.

'Cool, huh?' said Hiro. 'She's pretty self-sufficient.'

'It's the most incredible thing I've ever seen,' I said, and I meant it.

I breathed deeply, closing my eyes. I could smell basil and mint and *green*. I pointed at a plant with droopy red bunches. 'What's this one?'

'Amaranth,' Hiro replied. 'It's a kind of cereal grain.'

'This one?' I pointed at a bush with little round leaves and fat green buds.

'Capers.'

'How about this one?'

'Bay tree.'

Hiro walked me around the garden, pointing out broccoli, cabbage, beetroot and garlic, as well as neat rows of young eggplant, zucchini and capsicum. There were also lots more tomatoes. The smaller varieties were all bearing fruit in a riot of yellow, green, red and even purple.

'Isn't it too early for tomatoes?' I asked, thinking of our tiny sprouts in the kitchen garden.

Hiro nodded. 'Nonna has a special touch.'

'So she *is* a witch.'

'It's all organic, too,' said Hiro. 'Nonna doesn't believe in pesticides.'

I shook my head. 'It's amazing,' I said. 'I wish people knew how amazing it feels to produce fresh, delicious vegetables, without pumping them full of chemicals.'

Hiro winced. 'Please don't say that.'

'Say what?'

'*Pumping them full of chemicals*. You're saying that chemicals are bad. But *everything* is chemicals. Every single thing in the universe is made from chemicals. So don't blame the carcinogenic toxicity of a few chemicals on *all* chemicals.'

I stared at him.

'What?'

I grinned. 'I love it when you shed your sarcastic, disaffected exterior to reveal your squishy inner dork.'

He stuck his tongue out at me.

'What's this?' I asked, looking at a rubbish bin that had green leaves poking out the top.

'Potatoes,' said Hiro. 'It's much more efficient to grow them vertically. I'll show you how back at school.'

A warm glow spread throughout my body. This thing with Hiro and me, it was not going to be just a small thing.

'Nonna lives for this garden,' Hiro explained. 'Dad wanted her to come and live with us after my grandfather died, but she wouldn't leave her garden. She produces all her own fruit and vegies and eggs. And all her own honey, of course.'

So it *was* a beehive. Amazing. Hiro was amazing, too. His slouch was gone, and he was more alert, open and happy than I'd ever seen him. I realised that this was the real Hiro – that the sulky, angry guy who stomped around at school was just a mask. In his nonna's garden, surrounded by green growing things, Hiro came alive, like a blooming flower. I squeezed his hand.

He shot me a sly smile. 'How's your Hulk monster?'

I smiled back. 'All gone.'

Maria opened the back door and presented Hiro with an empty wicker basket, rattling off a list of instructions in rapid Italian. Then she went back inside, and Hiro and I pulled up carrots, beetroot and radishes, then cut fat leaves of silverbeet and lettuce. Hiro showed me how to tell which tomatoes were ripe, and explained the difference between the five different varieties of basil. He showed me Maria's garden shed, where plaited ropes of onion and garlic hung, filling the shed with a spicy, earthy scent. We also inspected the chicken run and the roosting boxes, and discovered four brown speckled eggs and one greeny-blue one, which Hiro said came from a kind of chicken called an Aracauna. We took our overflowing basket back into Maria's kitchen, which was warm and full of jars and pots and appealing smells. She bossed us around, and Hiro showed me how to make pasta, mixing flour with the eggs and then hand-cranking the resulting dough through a small machine that flattened and sliced it into fat fettucini strips.

Hiro clowned around with his grandmother and me, getting flour all over himself and making me giggle. He was like a completely different person. His guard was totally down, and if I'd liked him before, I *adored* him now.

We carried full plates into the dining room. I couldn't believe it had all come together so quickly and easily. There was pickled zucchini and eggplant next to a bowl of plump purple olives. Maria had cooked the pasta we'd made and mixed it with a simple tomato, garlic and basil sauce. There were four kinds of dip, and a loaf of crusty bread. The vegetables we'd picked had been simply cooked and combined with olive oil and vinegar. There was *so much* food, and it was all amazing. And we'd picked most of it from the garden only an hour or so previously.

'Wow,' I said.

'In our family,' said Hiro, 'eating is serious business.'

'*Grazie*,' I said to Maria as we sat down. It was the only thing I knew how to say in Italian, other than *ciao*.

Maria beamed. '*Prego*,' she replied, and then said a bunch of words to Hiro that I didn't understand.

'She likes you,' said Hiro. 'Says you're very pretty.'

I felt myself blush. Maria said something else.

'*Nonna!*' Hiro scowled at her.

'What did she say?'

'Nothing.' Hiro shot Maria a dark look. 'Nothing at all.'

Maria chuckled.

'Okay,' said Hiro. 'Enough of the chit-chat. Let's eat.'

I didn't need a second invitation. I dug in, loading up my plate with a bit of everything. Maria watched approvingly. Hiro flashed me a grin and I felt such a wash of warm contentment to be sitting here with Hiro and his grandmother, in front of such a glorious feast. I realised I hadn't eaten a proper meal at home with Mum for *ages* – I'd fallen into the habit of eating in my room while I finished my homework. I'd forgotten how wonderful sharing a meal was, how intimate and beautiful. And I realised that the garden I was making at school wasn't just about the environment. It wasn't just about minimising food miles and providing fresh organic options to our students. It was about this. It was about passing a dish of beans over the table. It was about meeting someone's eyes over a glass of perfectly clear water. It was about tearing a piece of bread in half to share it with the person sitting next to you. Gardens made food, and food made families.

It was a perfect moment, and I wanted to remember it always.

And.

The.

Food.

I'd never eaten beans so crunchy, tomatoes so sweetly acidic, herbs so full of flavour. It was as if in my whole life I'd never really heard music before, just the tinny rattle of someone else's earbuds on the train. And now a symphony orchestra was playing live inside my mouth.

I ate everything. Even eggplant, which I didn't think I liked. I had spent my entire life hating anchovies, but in Maria's white bean salad they were the most astonishing little salty parcels of deliciousness I'd ever eaten. And when I thought I'd never be able to eat again, Maria brought out an enormous lemon cake, dripping with honey from her hive.

'I don't know if I can fit anything else in!' I protested.

Hiro snorted, and cut me a piece of cake.

'What did you think?' he asked.

'Apart from the fact that I can barely move?' I said. 'It's the best meal I've ever had.'

Hiro said something in Italian to Maria, who looked smugly satisfied.

'Thank you,' I told her. 'Really, you have no idea how much this has meant to me.'

'You're welcome,' she said.

After a suitable period of digestion had passed, we said goodbye to Maria and wandered back out. The sun was setting, drenching everything in golden light, and I paused for a moment, breathing in a last lungful of the fresh green air, listening to the chirping of crickets, and running my hand over the bark of the lemon tree.

'Are you okay?' asked Hiro. 'You're unusually quiet.'

'I was trying to remember the last time I ate dinner with Mum. A proper dinner, not just pizza in front of the TV. Even before Dad left . . . we used to have family dinners all the time, but in the last few years everyone got so busy.'

Hiro nodded. 'We never have family dinners at home anymore either,' he said. 'Mum doesn't usually get home from work until eight or nine.'

'I wish everyone could experience this, you know?' I said. 'Everyone in Valentine. I wish they could see how wonderful it is, how beautiful. How good everything tastes. How sitting down to a home-grown, home-cooked meal with family can make you feel *so good*. I wonder if we all did it more often, perhaps there wouldn't be so many fights and tears and dental nurses.' I shook my head. 'Do you think I'm crazy?'

Hiro put his hands on my shoulders and kissed my forehead. 'No,' he said. 'I don't think you're crazy at all. I think you're amazing.'

I smiled and we started walking down the street in the direction of my home. Hiro was quiet.

'What's up?' I asked.

He smiled, distracted. 'Nothing,' he said. 'Just thinking.'

'About what?'

'About you.'

I tugged on his hand. 'You have plenty of time to think about me when you're home without me,' I said, teasingly. 'But I'm here right now, so you should pay attention to me!'

Hiro chuckled. 'Yes, *Il Duce*.'

We walked on. I counted twelve houses in a row that had ripped out their front gardens to create concreted carspaces. Valentine was the *worst*.

The thirteenth house was the same, but something made me stop.

'Are you okay?' asked Hiro, stopping too.

I nodded and bent over the low brick wall to examine the cracked concrete of the house's driveway, squinting in the fading light. There, peeking through the cracks, was a tiny green shoot.

'Looks like a geranium,' Hiro said.

The crack in the concrete was only a few millimetres wide. It had been such a dry spring everything else was utterly barren. And yet here was this one little green shoot. This one sprig of life, coming from the harshest conditions.

If this tiny little geranium could make it, without water or fertiliser or even proper soil, then so could I.

Suddenly the rage-monster was back, but this time it didn't want to smash things. This time it was clever and sharp. This time it wanted to *win*. I straightened up.

'I'll fight Mr Webber,' I said to Hiro. 'I'll get a petition. I'm not giving up.'

Hiro wrapped me in a great, crushing hug. 'Of course you're not,' he said. 'You're Lobstergirl. You never let go.'

When we reached my house, Hiro stopped and I saw his defensive hunched shoulders return.

'Do you want to come in?' I asked.

Hiro glanced warily at my front door. 'Nah,' he said. 'I'm not really the meet-the-parents type.'

I raised my eyebrows. 'You just took me to meet your *grandmother*,' I said. 'And I've met your sister and your dad.'

'Exactly,' said Hiro. 'You are the textbook example of a meet-the-parents type. My parents will be *thrilled* that I'm dating you. They'll think you'll be a good influence on me. Your family, however, will be suspicious and disapproving.'

'No they won't,' I said. 'My parents are very relaxed about that sort of thing.'

Hiro spread his hands. 'I hate to inform you of this, but I am terrible boyfriend material,' he said. 'My marks are bad, I get in trouble all the time and there is absolutely no way that I will ever take you to prom. If you want to back out now, I'll totally understand.'

He was mostly joking. I was pretty sure.

Hiro held up a finger. 'However, I'm prepared to make one small concession. One chink in my bad-boy armour. I think we should go on a proper date.'

'Isn't this a date?'

'Nah,' he said. 'This is hanging out. You think I'd take you to meet my grandmother as a date?'

I narrowed my eyes. 'How would you know what a real date is?' I asked teasingly. 'From what I hear, you've never been on one.'

For a moment I thought I'd said the wrong thing. What was I doing, reminding Hiro of how I'd deceived him? But to my relief he smiled.

'I like to think that my lack of experience in this area is a good thing,' he said. 'There'll be no tired dinner-and-a-movie clichés here. Do not expect a corsage. I won't win you a giant teddy bear at a carnival. There will be no long walk along the beach, and I won't make out with you in the back of my car. That last one is mostly because I don't have a car.'

I laughed. 'So what *can* I expect on our date?'

'Well,' said Hiro, his face deadpan. 'It'll be the most amazing night of your life, obviously. You can safely expect that.'

'More amazing than the night me and Dev and Paige had a séance and Paige was possessed by the ghost of Michael Jackson?'

'Definitely more amazing than that.'

'You don't think maybe you're building it up too much?'

'Nope. This date is going to be so amazing, that it will not only change your life . . . it'll also change the world.'

I tilted my head. 'I thought you didn't believe in changing the world.'

'I didn't,' said Hiro, with a smile that made me melt inside. 'But then I saw your face. And now I do believe.'

10

Our date was scheduled for the following weekend. Hiro said there were some things he needed to organise first. I was intrigued. I was supposed to be going to some party with Dev and Paige, but I blew them off. I'd much rather be with Hiro.

Mum was on her way out too. She looked . . . different. She was wearing a loose-fitting linen shirt and jeans. Her hair was soft and down around her shoulders, instead of pulled up into the tight ponytail that I was used to.

'Where are you off to?' I asked.

'I've signed up to an art class,' said Mum.

I blinked. My mother, an artist? She saw the confusion on my face and laughed.

'I majored in Fine Art, you know,' she said. 'At university.'

This was definitely news to me. 'Really?' I said. 'How come you didn't become an artist?'

Mum shrugged. 'You know,' she said. 'I got a real job. Met your father and got married. Then you came along. I just . . . sort of forgot about it. Life got in the way.'

I tried to picture my mother as an artsy uni student, and

wondered if her transformation into everyday, conventional Mum had been because of me. Or because of Dad. Perhaps a bit of both.

I gave her a hug. 'Good luck at the class.'

Mum beamed. 'Have fun with Dev and Paige.'

I wasn't ready to tell her about Hiro – he'd been right, my parents wouldn't be particularly overjoyed that I was dating someone so . . . academically unmotivated.

Hiro had told me to meet him in a crappy part of Valentine (I mean, crappier than all the other parts), and that he had a surprise for me. He also told me to dress in dark, comfortable clothes and sensible shoes.

Um.

I mean, Hiro had been right the other day. I knew that he was a bit . . . you know . . . *bad*. And I didn't want to be the living embodiment of the *nice girl falls for bad boy* cliché, but yeah, that was part of the attraction. His life was so different to mine. It felt as if he lived *more* than me. Experienced more. But I also liked him for his brains and his heart.*

But I was a little concerned that he was taking me on a date where we would . . . what? Shoplift? Throw eggs at teachers' houses? Knock letterboxes off their posts?** I was intrigued by the possibility of living a little dangerously, but I didn't want to live *illegally*. After all, I had my reputation to protect.

---

* And, ahem, his face and his body.

** Do people really do that? Or is it just in the movies?

It was unusual for anyone to be on the streets of Valentine after dark. I mean, why would you? I didn't see another soul as I dodged abandoned shopping trolleys and tipped-over rubbish bins. It was dark and quiet, and enough streetlights were broken that I didn't feel entirely safe.

Bloody Hiro. What kind of a date *was* this?

There weren't even any houses in this part of Valentine. Only boarded-up shops and empty industrial shells. This was not a fun place to be. Was Hiro going to make me break into somewhere? Graffiti something? Or . . . was he trying to find somewhere private so we could . . . I mean, the idea of having sex with Hiro was definitely not a repugnant idea. In fact it was . . . alluring. But it was way too soon to think about it – we'd been officially dating for less than a week. And I had thought a lot about how and when I would lose my virginity, and doing it on an abandoned factory floor surrounded by dust and mouse-poo had never been one of my fantasy scenarios.

But then I saw Hiro, and all my anxiety fizzed into excitement. He was wearing his usual dark jeans and a hoodie, leaning against a brick wall with a backpack slung over his shoulder. A slow smile spread over his face when he saw me.

'Hi.'

'Hi yourself.'

There was an awkward pause while we stared, each waiting for the other to make the first move. We made it simultaneously, both stepping in and leaning forward too fast, so we bumped foreheads.

Not an auspicious beginning, but we managed to make

up for it with a long, slow kiss that made me tingle all over.* The night was chilly, and Hiro was warm, and I wanted to wrap myself in his arms and breathe in his scent. He put his hands on my shoulders and slid them down until his fingers interlaced with mine.

'Okay, are you ready?' he asked.

No, I was not.

'Where's my corsage?' I asked.

'I told you not to expect a corsage.'

I shrugged. 'A girl can dream.'

'Come on,' he said, and took my hand. 'I have something special planned.'

'Is it going to be illegal?' I asked. 'Because I won't do anything illegal.'

Hiro laughed. 'No, it's not illegal. You'll like it, I promise.'

'You should know I don't drink or do drugs.'

'Seriously, you'll like it. Stop worrying.'

'You're not secretly a murderer, are you?' I asked, as Hiro led me down a quiet, dark street. 'Because it occurs to me that we are in the middle of nowhere, completely alone, with no witnesses.'

'I'm not a murderer.'

'I bet that's what all the murderers say.'

We stopped outside a vacant lot, and I realised we weren't that far from school. There were plenty of vacant lots in Valentine – the council had tried to sell off a bunch of land to developers a few years ago to try and pay off some of their debts, but nobody had wanted it. This particular lot was

---

* But not enough to find an abandoned factory floor appealing.

between an abandoned brick factory and a similarly empty tin warehouse. The chain-link fence had been pushed over at some point, and there was a buckled section at the bottom where it would be easy to crawl in. Other than that, there was nothing but bare, cracked earth and dumped rubbish – a TV, some broken glass and a tangle of scraggly brown weeds.

'So there's this guy in the Marvel Comics universe called the Gardener,' said Hiro. 'His real name is Ord Zyonz, and he's one of the Elders of the Universe. He's one of the oldest living creatures in the universe – so old that nobody knows where he comes from, only that he's probably been around since the Big Bang.'

'O-kay,' I said cautiously. 'What's his deal?'

'Well, the Gardener seeks out planets that have been devastated by war or other disasters. Planets that are abandoned and cold and barren, without life or beauty.'

'Sounds like Valentine,' I said.

Hiro grinned, and I knew I'd said the right thing.

'The Gardener brings life back to these wastelands. He sows seeds and grows plants and flowers and trees, making planet-sized gardens. He knows more about botany than anyone else in the universe, and can turn an Earth-sized planet into a green paradise within a year.'

I looked at the vacant lot, and imagined it thick and healthy with vegetation. 'He sounds awesome,' I said, a little dreamily.

'He is,' said Hiro, and took my hand. 'So are you.'

He leaned over and kissed me, and the dreamlike feeling intensified as my feet went numb and my insides spiralled into bliss.

'So. Are you ready?' asked Hiro, pulling away and looking at the vacant lot.

I stared at him, the dreamy feeling starting to slip away. This was *Hiro*, after all. Hiro, who had stolen all our exam papers and put them on the roof. Hiro, who had filled a classroom with plastic cups of water. Hiro, who had called in bomb threats to get out of a maths test. Hiro, who had hacked into the school intranet and put five thousand dollars on his photocopying account. Hiro, who had been *somehow involved* in setting a Year Seven's bag on fire.

'Seriously,' I said. 'What are we doing here? I don't feel comfortable breaking the law.'

Hiro chuckled. 'Have you ever broken a rule?'

I thought about it. 'I've protested about unfair rules.'

'Never stolen anything?'

'Of course not.'

'Wagged school?'

'Only with a teacher's permission.'

'Jaywalked?'

I shrugged. 'Pedestrians don't get seatbelts, airbags or helmets, you know.'

'Well, it's time to break some rules.'

'You said we weren't doing anything illegal!'

'It's not illegal,' said Hiro, then frowned. 'At least, I don't think it is.'

'Hiro!'

He laughed. 'Come on, Lobstergirl. Live a little!'

He reached into his backpack and withdrew an egg carton.

'I don't want to do anything stupid,' I said.

Hiro grinned. 'It's not what you think.' He opened the egg carton. Inside were . . . what looked like lumpy grey papier-maché eggs.

'Take one.'

I did. It felt like papier-maché too. Up close I could see it was covered in tiny black dots.

'What is it?'

'Seed bomb.'

Bomb!? Hiro saw my look of horror and chuckled, taking another egg from the carton.

'It's a mixture of paper, compost, liquid fertiliser and seeds.'

I looked at the grey egg, then up at Hiro. 'What kind of seeds?'

'Whatever I could find in Nonna's potting shed. Sunflowers, tomatoes, pansies and coriander.' Hiro grinned at me, then lobbed his egg over the barbed-wire. It thunked down onto the bare dirt, another piece of grey rubbish in among the empty drink cans and pieces of styrofoam.

'It's called guerrilla gardening,' said Hiro. 'I read about it online. You sneak around at night and plant things in weird places. It's like the opposite of terrorism. Instead of making awful things happen, you make the world more beautiful. And that's what you want to do, right? Make the world better. Well this is how I think we should do it. We'll be like superheroes – sneaking around at night bringing Valentine to life. You were right about changing things. We should be doing everything we can.'

'Why here?'

Hiro pointed into the lot. 'Look.'

I looked. In the dim orange light cast by the nearby freeway lights, and the yellow splash of streetlights, I could see . . . rubbish. 'I don't understand.'

'Look harder. Over there, by the broken TV.'

'I see a stick.'

'It's not a stick. I'm pretty sure it's an apple tree.'

I looked again. It was a small, straggly sapling, with furry grey buds protruding from brittle-looking twigs.

An apple tree. Growing among all the rubbish.

'Will it grow apples?'

Hiro shrugged. 'Hard to say. It's probably grown from seed – after someone chucked an apple core in there a few years ago. So it could be anything, really.'

'It won't grow the same apples that the seed came from?'

'Apples don't work that way. Apple varieties are all grafted – clones of one original tree. If you grow an apple from seed, it's like a lottery. You could get something useful and delicious, or you could get some kind of inedible crab-apple.'

I frowned. 'What about that American guy who planted all the apple trees?'

'Johnny Appleseed? Yeah, most people used those apple orchards to make cider, so it didn't matter that the apples didn't taste good.'

'Really? So instead of "American as apple pie", the saying should be "as American as . . . booze?"'

'Yep. Not to mention the fact that apples originate from Kazakhstan, so the phrase should be "as American as Central Asia".'

I looked at the apple tree again. I couldn't believe it had grown there, just from someone lobbing an apple core into the rubbish heap. It was a *brave* apple tree. It had survived without regular watering or fertiliser. It was a hero, and we needed to celebrate it.

'Look at this place,' said Hiro. 'It's perfect. It has a north-south orientation, so it'll get plenty of sun. The guttering on that factory is all rusted, so all the rainwater will trickle down over the dirt there, like a natural sprinkler system. It's sheltered from the wind, and there's nobody around to get suspicious when stuff starts to grow.'

He'd put a lot of thought into it. I hefted my egg. Guerrilla gardening. I'd heard of it too, in some of the environmental magazines I read. But I'd never thought of *doing* it. Maybe this was what I'd been looking for. Maybe instead of handing out stupid fact sheets and trying to convince other people to change the world, I could go and *do* it myself. Behind their backs. I could *show* everyone how much better we could be. Together, Hiro and I could make Valentine beautiful. *Then* people would start listening to us. We'd be urban superheroes.

'What do you reckon?' said Hiro. He looked nervous.

I felt a slow smile spread across my face. 'Let's do it.'

I lobbed a seed bomb over the fence, and felt a thrill of total exhilaration. I felt dangerous and free, as though finally, after years of *telling* people I wanted to change the world, I was actually *doing* something. I wanted to wriggle and dance with joy.

'So, Lobstergirl,' said Hiro, tossing another bomb over the fence. 'What's your origin story?'

I turned to look at him. 'My what?'

'Your origin story. How you got your superpowers. There

are three kinds: trauma, destiny and chance. Batman is trauma – he sees his parents get murdered. Destiny is all those Chosen One stories, you know. Like Buffy or Kung Fu Panda. And chance is like the X-Men, who were all born mutants. Or the Fantastic Four, who were exposed to radiation. There are some combinations, like Spiderman who was bitten by a radioactive spider – chance – but only started to use his powers for good once his uncle was killed – trauma. Also in the comics there are heaps of prophecies about Spiderman, so I guess he's destiny as well.'

'Right.'

'So . . . what's yours? What made you care so much about the environment? Did you see an oil-slicked penguin? Were you exposed to some radioactive pollution? Or did you have some sort of prophetic dream about melting ice-caps and homeless polar bears?'

I thought about it. 'I don't know. I suppose . . . Mum took me to see *Wall-E* when I was eight and I cried for a week afterwards. I hated the idea that the planet might end up like that, all brown and dry and empty. That was when I started my first petition.'

'What were you petitioning?'

'For Santa Claus to use more recycled and sustainable materials in his toy workshop.'

Hiro laughed.

'I figure . . . it feels wrong to be so influential at school – and I know how that sounds but it's the truth – and not be using it for something good, you know?'

Hiro nodded and handed me another seed bomb. 'You're like Superman.'

I made a face. 'Really? Isn't Superman the most boring superhero ever?'

'Not at all,' said Hiro. 'Firstly, Aquaman is the most boring superhero ever.'

'What does he do?'

Hiro shrugged. 'Talks to fish.'

I threw my seed bomb. It bounced off the top of the broken TV and rolled behind a milk crate. 'That *is* pretty boring.'

'But I think Superman gets a bad rap. I mean, yeah, he's all square-jawed and corn-fed, but here's the great thing about him. He's so strong, and so powerful, but no matter how many explosions he stops or hostages he rescues, he can't stop the greatest evil of all.'

'Which is?'

'Humanity. He can't stop the greed and the deceit and the selfishness. It's like he's constantly bailing water out of a sinking boat, but he can't plug the leak. Think how frustrating that must be.'

I took the last bomb from Hiro's egg carton. 'I know how he feels.'

'Exactly,' said Hiro. 'You understand. How helpless he must feel. How alone.'

I nodded. 'I do. I do understand.' I turned my face up to the sky. 'Sorry, Superman,' I said to the gloomy orange clouds. 'I underestimated you.'

'I think he's the most tragic of all the superheroes,' said Hiro.

'So what's his origin story? He's an alien, isn't he?'

'Yeah. I suppose there's a fourth kind of origin story –

alien or god. I suppose technically Superman is trauma, because his whole planet was destroyed when he was a baby.'

'Still,' I said. 'Much as I understand where Superman is coming from, it's not as cool as being bitten by a radioactive spider.'

I threw the last seed bomb, then wove my fingers into the fence and pressed my forehead against the chain links. Our bombs lay there, little grey lumps blending in with the hard-packed grey earth.

'I can't believe they'll ever grow,' I said, feeling a little deflated.

'Depends on whether it rains, I guess,' said Hiro.

This wasn't exactly what I'd imagined. The lush green oasis in my mind obviously wasn't going to happen overnight. But I wanted some sort of instant gratification. A hint of more to come. At the moment it looked like we'd just added to the debris. Wasn't there something more we could do to help the tiny seeds on their way? Wasn't it a superhero's job to protect the weak and vulnerable?

'I think we could do more,' I said, slowly.

Hiro looked at me, an eyebrow raised. I kicked the loose section of fence. 'I mean, surely it'd help if we improved the soil. Added fertiliser. And we've got a bunch of extra seedlings at school that we don't have room for.'

Hiro's face broke into a grin. 'I knew I could count on you, Lobstergirl.'

We met the next night, too. I told Mum I was going to Paige's house. I felt slightly hypocritical – after my big epiphany about gardening and food and family togetherness, I'd eaten a meal with a family member exactly zero times. But Mum was out a lot – either at her art class or catching up with friends. She'd never gone out much when Dad was around, so good for her, I guess. And Dad . . . I felt a guilty pang every time I wondered how he was spending his evenings. Then a sick thud when I realised he was probably spending them with the Whippet. So much for family time. But at least it made it easier for Hiro and me to sneak around.

Hiro and I packed all the spare seedlings from the kitchen garden into cardboard boxes and hid them outside the school, near the bins. Then, under cover of darkness, we collected them and returned to the vacant lot.

We crawled under the fence and filled garbage bags with most of the moveable rubbish – the broken glass, the styrofoam, the empty beer cans. Then we tilled the dirt using hand trowels we'd borrowed from school, and Hiro sprinkled fertiliser around the apple tree. We planted cucumbers and beans around the perimeter of the vacant lot, so they'd climb up the chain-link fence. We poked potting mix into the broken front of the TV and planted a geranium there. We filled an old tennis shoe and planted basil. Anything that could be a container – a styrofoam esky, a disposable coffee cup, a mouldy old suitcase – became a home for new growth.

It was amazing. My heart was beating a million miles an hour – despite what Hiro had said, I was pretty sure what we were doing *was* illegal. Somebody owned this land, and we were trespassing.

But I didn't care.

Because what we were doing felt *so right*. We were making

a tiny, ugly piece of the world beautiful. Bringing life back to Valentine. When these little plants grew and spread, this vacant lot would be a lush green oasis. People would notice. People would care.

The greyish clouds above us broke apart briefly to show thin fingers of golden light unravelling across the sky. It was morning already. My back ached and my eyes felt like they'd been propped open with matchsticks. The rumble of traffic started to sound from the freeway, but behind it, somewhere, I heard the singing of a single bird. We didn't get many birds in Valentine, and this one felt like the herald of something truly incredible. We stood back, and surveyed our efforts. The tiny seedlings looked helpless, little pops of green surrounded by drab greys and browns. How could they possibly survive?

The grey clouds grew heavier and thicker, but the occasional ray of orange still peeked through, washing our garden in a light so vivid and bright that I felt like we were on a movie set. The sky rumbled overhead, and I looked at Hiro. His cheeks were glowing with exertion and his eyes shone. He grinned at me, and slung an arm around my shoulder as we admired our new garden.

'I feel like a superhero,' I told him.

'You're a guerrilla gardener,' he said.

I made a face. 'I don't like that term. It sounds violent.'

Hiro nodded. '*Guerrilla* means *little war* in Spanish. We're declaring war on the ugliness of Valentine.'

'Mm. I still don't like it. We're not being violent. We're creating new life, not destroying it. Inviting the wilderness back into the concrete jungle.'

'*Invading* the concrete jungle with wilderness.'

I rolled my eyes. 'Why do boys have to be so violent?'

'You're the one who said you felt like a superhero. Superheroes are violent.'

'Not all of them.'

Hiro tipped his head to the side and looked at me sceptically. I thought hard.

'Okay,' I said. 'So superheroes are mostly violent. But *we* don't have to be. I want a different name for what we do.'

'Like what?'

'Beautifying?'

Hiro made a gagging sound.

'Beflowering?'

He gave me a flat look.

'Fine,' I said. 'That one was a bit much. What about bewildering?'

Hiro thought about it, then nodded slowly. 'Okay,' he said. 'I'll pay that. Bewildering.'

The sky rumbled again, and I felt a drop of rain on my face. And another. Then, fat, wet drops started to tap down onto the bare earth. I turned to Hiro and we grinned at each other, and kissed while the sun rose, and rain fell around us, and the air filled with the rich scent of wet earth.

It was just like in the movies.

On the third night, Hiro arrived pushing a shopping trolley, with two take-away coffees balanced on the baby-seat.

'Shopping Trolley Guy!' I said, grinning. 'This is just like old times.'

'Except no lobster suit.' Hiro handed me a coffee. 'It may be wax paper,' he said apologetically. 'But it's recycled, and better than styrofoam.'

I didn't care, as long as it held something hot and caffeinated. 'So why did you steal a shopping trolley?'

'I didn't *steal* it,' said Hiro, looking indignant. 'I *found* it. Abandoned and lonely down a side-street. Now we're going to give it a new lease on life.'

'How?'

'Potatoes.'

'Potatoes?'

He nodded. 'I'll get some from Nonna. We're going to grow potatoes.'

'In a shopping trolley?'

'It'll be awesome. Trust me.'

We planted the potatoes the next night. Hiro came bearing a paper bag of potatoes, and a big bag of potting mix.

'See these dints in the potato skin? They're called eyes. They're the bits that will sprout when we plant them.'

Hiro lay a large piece of scrap cardboard across the bottom of the shopping trolley so the dirt wouldn't fall out. Then we cut up the potatoes so that each piece had two or three eyes on it, then planted them in potting mix.

'Once they sprout and start to grow, we'll top up the trolley with more potting mix,' Hiro explained. 'And maybe some mulch around the sides to keep everything contained. The higher they grow, the more dirt we put in, until the trolley's full.'

127

'And they'll grow potatoes?'

Hiro nodded. 'By the end of summer, this trolley will be bursting with spuds. Like nature's own supermarket.'

As spring slipped into summer, the weather went crazy – skyrocketing temperatures punctuated with regular drenching storms. The weather bureau were predicting the hottest December on record.* Both the kitchen garden and our secret guerrilla garden responded enthusiastically – springing to life seemingly overnight, all reaching tendrils and fresh green growth.

I told Mum that I was going out for late-night jogging. I showed her an article that said that exercise just before bed could help with bloodflow to the brain, increasing mental stamina. I invited her to come with me, knowing she'd turn me down. I promised her I was being careful, and reminded her about the self-defence course I'd taken last year. I left just before she went to bed, knowing she'd be fast asleep within minutes. Then I could stay out as late as I wanted, digging in the darkness with Hiro. I'd sneak back in around two or three in the morning, and sleep until my alarm dragged me out of bed in time for school. I spent my days sitting dead-eyed and half-asleep watching the minutes tick by until the bell released us all to steamy summer afternoons, with the promise of steamier summer nights with dirt under my nails and Hiro by my side.

---

* But were any local politicians talking about climate change? Of course they weren't. They were too busy dressing up as Santa and posing for photo opportunities with babies.

'You're finally becoming a real teenager,' said Mum one Saturday morning, as I stumbled downstairs in my pyjamas. 'It's nearly lunchtime.'

I shrugged. 'I was up late reading.'

Mum chuckled. 'Are you sure you're not sneaking out to run around with boys?'

Eek. 'Very funny, Mum.'

'Astrid, is there something you're not telling us?' A frown creased the smooth perfection of Paige's brow.

I felt a stab of guilt. 'No, of course not. What would make you say that?'

'You've been super-weird lately. Blowing us off all the time. We haven't hung out other than at school in weeks.'

'I've been busy,' I said. 'School . . . you know.'

Dev shook his head. 'That's just it, we *don't* know. You barely speak anymore. It's like you're not even here.'

I forced a laugh. 'Of course I'm here.' I thumped my Chemistry textbook on the desk in front of me.

Paige and Dev exchanged a look. 'Ye-es, but we're not sure *why* you're here.'

I looked around the lab. It *was* weird that nobody else had turned up yet. 'We have Chemistry last period, right?'

'Right.'

I stared at them both. What was going on?

Dev put a hand on my arm. 'Astrid, we already had Chemistry. Don't you remember? An hour ago. We did redox equations. There was a quiz.'

I blinked. 'How did I do?'

'You got everything right, as usual. You really don't re-member? And then the bell rang, and we all went out to our lockers, and you put your books away, then got them out again and came back in here and sat down.'

I closed my books. I genuinely didn't remember any of it. Come to think of it, I couldn't remember much at all from the day. What did I have for lunch? And what had my other classes been like? All I could remember was stumbling home at three am after an epic gardening/make-out session with Hiro.

Paige was talking to me. 'You must be coming down with something,' she said. 'You need ginseng and some sinus-clearing yoga poses.'

'I think I probably just need some sleep,' I said, standing up. 'At least it's Saturday tomorrow.'

I went back into the corridor, Paige and Dev trailing behind me.

'Um, Astrid?'

'Yes?'

'Tomorrow is Wednesday.'

One night, after a day of rain and sunshine had left the garden damp and steaming, we planted the three sisters com-bination – corn, beans and pumpkin. Hiro explained that it was an old Native American companion-planting technique.

'The corn provides a support for the beans to climb up,' he said, as we made mounds of soil. 'The beans add nitrogen to the soil, and the squash covers the ground, suppressing weeds.'

'So clever,' I said. 'I love the way they all work together so well.'

Hiro grinned at me. 'Like us.'

Every night, we learnt a little more about each other. We talked about our childhoods, our dreams, our fears. Hiro told me about the long summer afternoons he'd spent at his grandmother's house, and I told him about the climate change musical that I'd forced Dev and Paige to participate in for the Grade Three talent contest. The nights seemed to race by, and I greedily drank in every moment. During the day I was a zombie, unable to function on any rational level. I lived for nightfall, when I could slip out of the house, pull the disguise of darkness over me, and find Hiro waiting in our secret growing garden.

Some nights we wouldn't garden at all, we'd just sit curled together up against the brick wall, feeling the slow unfurling of green things around us, finding new ways to learn about each other without words.

'So tell me about your favourite superhero,' I asked one night, as I leaned my head against his shoulder and closed my eyes.

'It changes all the time,' Hiro said. 'But I think at the moment it's Rogue. She's one of the X-men.'

'X-people?' I suggested.

Hiro let out a little snort, and I snuggled in closer to him. 'Tell me about her,' I said. 'Why do you like her?'

'Well, her superpower is kind of a curse. Whenever she touches someone, she involuntarily removes and absorbs their memories, their strength and sometimes their special powers or abilities.'

'So she can't ever give someone a hug.'

'No hugs. Well, not at first. At first she's vulnerable and scared and totally alone. So she gets all bitter and angry and lashes out at people around her.'

I was beginning to see why Hiro liked her.

'But then she gets through it. She learns that shutting her heart to love is much more of a curse than her actual mutation. She learns to love again, and she gets control over her powers. And now she's this awesome, kick-ass leader and role model, and she's sassy but still incredibly kind and loving.'

I sighed happily.

Hiro cleared his throat. 'This is getting a little corny,' he said. 'So I'd better tell you about my secret love for the really weird, short-lived superheroes. Or old-school ones that just seem ridiculous now.'

'Like who?'

'I have a special place in my heart for Squirrel Girl.'

'Squirrel Girl?'

Hiro nodded. 'She can control squirrels.'

I laughed. 'Are you serious?'

'Totally. They've just started a whole new series about her. She has a pet squirrel called Monkey Joe, and together they rescued Iron Man one time.'

'Who else?'

'Umm, there's also Colour Kid. He can change the colour of things, which is cool, but not very useful.'

'I wonder if he could get the tomato sauce stain out of my white jeans.'

'There's also Skateman.'

'Skateboards?'

'Roller skates.'

'Ouch.'

'And my personal favourite – Leather Boy. He looks like . . . well, like something from a bondage dungeon. Leather codpiece, hairy chest, silver studs, red ball strapped into his mouth.'

'Ew. Is he a bad guy?'

'Definitely. He—' Hiro pulled away from me so he could look me directly in the eye, and put his hand on mine, his expression serious. 'He killed Monkey Joe.'

'Monkey Joe! No!'

Hiro nodded. 'It's heartbreaking.'

I started as a car rumbled past – a taxi. Hiro and I shrank against the wall. It was so rare to see anyone around at night in Valentine. I glanced at my phone. It was three in the morning.

'I'd better go,' I said, reluctantly.

Hiro pulled me in to him for a goodbye kiss, which went on for quite some time.

'Tomorrow night then, Lobstergirl?' he murmured.

'Tomorrow night,' I said.

I wished this summer could last forever.

11

One warm night in mid-December, I met Hiro outside Valentine Station, which was less like a train station than the processing centre in some dystopian gulag. He was sitting cross-legged on the kerb reading a comic book, surrounded by shopping bags full of delicate cuttings and little plants from Maria's garden that had self-sown from the previous year – *volunteers*, Hiro called them. Our plan was to rip out the straggling weeds in the long-abandoned garden beds outside the station, and replace them with new seedlings. I loved the idea that people would be able to snag a tomato, or a handful of basil, or a stick of celery, on their way home from work. Maybe they'd realise how much better it was cooking with fresh ingredients, and get inspired to grow their own. Maybe they'd start to enjoy meals again, use them as time to talk with the rest of their families. Maybe if families ate delicious, healthy meals together, they wouldn't sleep with dental nurses.

I paused for a moment before he saw me and took him in. Him, and everything we were doing. Over the past few nights we had expanded our bewildering efforts, spreading out from the vacant lot in a wide circle, planting marigolds in potholes, herbs in cracks in the footpath. We ripped the dried brown plants out of a roundabout and replaced them with a cloud of Queen Anne's Lace and other bee-friendly flowers. We found bare corners of earth and coaxed new life into them. I imagined transforming the concrete jungle into a real, wild jungle. And slowly, the drab, industrial corner of Valentine would change, swelling with greenery and creeping tendrils. We'd find abandoned walkways and magic them into tantalising green corridors. A smashed-up bus stop would become a leafy, secret corner.

The driest spring on record had transformed in a matter of days into the warmest, wettest December in living memory. It had produced perfect growing conditions, and our seedlings were growing like crazy, thickening and spreading and unfurling almost in front of our eyes. We seemed to have no shortage of plants. Seedlings were springing up all over the place – in the abandoned lot and the school kitchen garden. We raided Maria's garden on a weekly basis, and occasionally we found little punnets outside the vacant lot, crammed with bright green sprouts. It was evidence that our efforts in Valentine were not going unnoticed, or unappreciated. Every time I saw a new donation, I felt a thrill of excitement. Things were changing.

Hiro looked up and smiled, and I was momentarily surprised that he could still have such a strong effect on me. Every time our eyes met, I felt like one of our little seedlings, unfurling and stretching delicate limbs towards the sun.

I approached him, and ducked my head to see the cover

of his comic. It was battered and dog-eared – a long way from the cliché of the meticulous comic book-reading nerd, preserving every issue in its own little plastic sleeve.

'*Green Arrow*,' I read. 'Is he the one with the magic ring?'

'That's Green Lantern.' Hiro pushed one of the shopping bags aside, and I sat down next to him, leaning in for a kiss.

'Of course,' I said. '*Green Arrow* is the film with Seth Rogan and Cameron Diaz.'

Hiro made a disgusted face and pushed me away. 'That's *Green Hornet*, and I'd appreciate it if you never mentioned it again in my presence. There's also the Green Goblin, who is a Halloween-themed super villain.'

'So what's this guy's deal?'

'His real name is Oliver Queen, and he used to be a billionaire businessman, but he lost everything. He's an archer who fights for the poor, the working class and disadvantaged people.'

'Oh,' I said. 'Like Robin Hood.'

Hiro nodded. 'Robin Hood, but with badass arrows that can explode or turn into nets or tear gas or kryptonite.'

'Cool.'

We gardened all over Valentine. We planted flowers outside the kindergarten, and strawberries outside the leisure centre. We trained passionfruit vines up the ugly brown brick wall of the library, and left pots of geraniums on the doorsteps of local businesses. Little by little, night by night, Valentine was coming alive.

And at the heart of it all, the guerrilla garden was exploding. The beans had wound their way up the chain-link fence and were blooming with bright, cheerful flowers. Tomatoes and capsicum plants had sprung up everywhere, along with fragrant basil, coriander and a whole carpet of creeping thyme. The potato shopping trolley was nearly full of dirt, with flat, healthy leaves sprouting from between the straw and steel and hopefully, growing baby potatoes under the surface. A neat circle of lettuces surrounded the old broken TV, which was bursting with marigolds. Best of all, the apple tree had sprung into life, green leaves and swelling buds all over it.

Hiro and I strolled past during the day to admire our hand-iwork, and saw a woman peering in to the lot, smiling and taking photos with her phone. Hiro squeezed my hand and we walked on, but I felt like I might overflow with excitement.

'In comic books,' Hiro murmured to me one afternoon as we watched a kid wriggle under the fence to pick some basil. 'Having a secret identity is really hard. It's a struggle for the heroes not to tell people who they really are. But this feels *awesome*.'

I nodded.

Horrible, dusty, grey old Valentine was slowly coming alive, as if it had been asleep for years and was just starting to awaken, creaking and slow at first, but getting livelier and greener every day. For the first time in my life, I heard birds twittering around the streets, and saw bees sailing from flower to flower, their pollen pants round and yellow.

And *everyone* was starting to notice.

'It's dangerous,' said Dad. 'Where does it end?'

He had come over to sign some papers for Mum, and was sitting at the kitchen table. It felt weird to have him there. A bit like déjà vu. He'd wheedled a cup of tea out of Mum, and was doing his best to pretend that nothing had changed.

'I don't know,' said Mum. 'I like it. It makes everything special, doesn't it? Reminds us that we're all living things, part of nature.'

Dad was staring at her as though she'd been abducted and replaced with some kind of crazed hippie robot.

I still wasn't used to this new improved Mum. When Dad had first left, Mum had gone all cold and businesslike, getting her new life together and disposing of the old one. She brusquely reorganised bills and bank accounts, and boxed up Dad's clothes and had them couriered to the hotel where he was staying. But now she was relaxed and happy. She came home late every Thursday from art class, covered in smears of oil paint and smelling faintly of red wine. She started letting her hair down, curling around her face. She wore soft, loose shirts instead of her usual stiff button-downs. It was . . . kind of awesome, actually. She was finally figuring out who she really was.

Dad could see Mum changing and blossoming without him, and he hated it. He couldn't accept that he had to move on too. Take some responsibility for his actions.

He was still seeing the Whippet. He didn't mention her, but I could smell her perfume on him. And there was no way he could iron his own shirts that crisply.

'You know how these greenies get, though,' said Dad. 'At first it's all flowers and loveliness, but soon it's arson and tree-spiking. Don't be fooled by the daisies and geraniums – what they're doing is illegal, and should be stopped.'

Mum rolled her eyes at me. I didn't say anything. My opinion was somewhat biased, and I didn't want to blow my cover.

'We should do something,' I said instead. 'We should be growing things out the back. We should have a vegie garden!'

Dad made a scoffing noise. 'Who has time for any of that nonsense?'

'We have a lawn,' said Mum. 'That's good for the environment, right?'

I shook my head. 'Did you know that lawns cover over 128,000 kilometres in the US? That makes it America's largest irrigated crop. Americans spend over thirty billion dollars per year looking after their lawns. And thirty per cent of the US's drinkable water is devoted to watering garden lawns. Thirty per cent! That's criminal. They could be growing something useful.'*

Dad shrugged. 'But that's America. It's not our problem.'

I resisted the urge to throw his cup of tea in his face. How could he be so complacent? Mum gave me a warning look, as though she didn't want me to start a full-fledged fight. Dad was so fragile that the littlest thing could set him off. The other day Mum had asked him to start redirecting his own mail, and he'd burst into tears.

'We'll talk about putting in some vegies,' she said soothingly.

---

* Also, apparently using a petrol lawnmower for an hour emits the same amount of pollution as driving a new car for 320km, not to mention the fact that more petrol is spilled each year refuelling lawnmowers than was spilled during the Exxon Valdez catastrophe!

Dad wasn't the only one who didn't like our bewildering. There were letters into the local paper complaining about the 'vandals' and 'eco-terrorists' who were taking over our town. A rumour sprung up that we were using the vacant lot to grow pot. One crazy old hippie tried pulling up some of our plants because he thought we shouldn't be growing anything that wasn't native. The mayor responded with a full-page announcement in the paper that filled me with excitement.

'Green Valentine,' I read out loud to Hiro, shaking the newspaper in his face. 'She says she has a ten-point plan to revitalise Valentine, bringing it into the twenty-first century and positioning it as a Suburb of the Future!'

Hiro looked mightily unconvinced. 'Sounds suspiciously dystopian.'

I shook my head. 'Don't you see? Back in September I emailed the mayor *my* ten-point plan to make Valentine more environmentally friendly.'

Hiro snorted. 'And you think that she was inspired by your plan to make her own?'

'To *adopt* my plan! Look, she's even calling it the Green Valentine Scheme!'

'I don't think you should get your hopes up.' Hiro shook his head. 'Government types always talk about these big transformational ideas. But usually it's just politico-speak for more parking fines or building high-rise apartments.'

I thumped him playfully with the newspaper. 'Whatever,' I said. 'You can choose to live in Pessimism City. But I'm excited. We've really made a difference. I think people are starting to see that Valentine can truly be beautiful.'

'What shall we call it?' I asked Hiro one night, after we'd planted a strawberry patch under the apple tree.

'The garden?' He looked around thoughtfully. 'Welcome to the Jungle.'

'No,' I said. 'That's not right. It needs to be something . . . special.'

'Eden. Gethsemane. Babylon.'

'Ugh, no.'

'Well, what do you think?'

'I'm not sure,' I said, as a sleepy, dreamy feeling crept over me. It was very late. 'The books I read as a kid were so full of gardens. There was one about a boy who was stuck in this old house because he had the measles, but every night the clock would strike thirteen, and he'd go outside to find this beautiful sunny garden. Except later he finds out that it was actually the garden in the past, a hundred years ago.'

'Sounds weird.'

'It is, in a good way. And it's like us – gardening at midnight.'

I wanted to say more, explain how in the book, Tom meets this girl called Hatty in the garden and forms a strong connection with her, even though she's from another time. It was like Hiro and me – we weren't from different times, but we may as well have been. I was the kind of girl who aced all her exams, and Hiro was the kind of guy who stole exams and put them on the roof. But here, in the garden, in the dead of night, all that fell away. And it was just us, sort of suspended in time. Just us and nobody else in the whole world.

'Well, we can't call it Astrid's Midnight Garden,' said Hiro. 'Because it sounds weird. Keep thinking.'

'Hmm.' I *was* still thinking. Gardening used to be such a vital part of survival.

'What about the Victory Garden?' I said suddenly.

'The what?'

'The Victory Garden. During the world wars, governments tried to get everyone to grow their own fruit and veg, because there were so many food shortages. And it gave all the people left behind something to do – a way to feel as if they were contributing to the war effort. They dug up the flowerbeds outside Buckingham Palace and planted cabbages and potatoes instead, and Eleanor Roosevelt dug up the White House lawn and planted beans and tomatoes. It was empowering for them. It was a way of fighting the enemy with productivity and growth instead of violence and death.'

'The Victory Garden,' said Hiro, smiling. 'I like it. Fighting the good fight with rakes and potting mix.'

We stood for a moment, looking at our Victory Garden.

'Are you impressed with my in-depth knowledge of world history?' I asked, grinning at him.

Hiro snorted. 'I can see that *you* are, and that's all that matters, right?'

'Come on,' I said. 'You have to admit it's awesome. The Victory Garden. It also sounds . . . superheroish?'

'It does, a bit,' said Hiro. 'Have I told you about all the environmental superheroes?'

'Like Captain Planet?'

Hiro chuckled. 'A little more mature than Captain Planet.'

'Tell me.'

'Well, there's Swamp Thing.'

'Sounds more like a monster than a hero.'

'He kind of is. He's made mostly of vegetable matter, and he can control the growth and movement of plants.'

'Useful. But is he a good guy?'

'Definitely. He protects his swamp from terrorism. And also, you know, the environment and humanity.'

'Like a creepy Shrek.'

'Sort of.'

'Who else?'

'Um, Animal Man can mimic any animal. He's mostly an animal rights activist, but is also a vegetarian and environmentalist. And there's Poison Ivy.'

I wagged my finger. 'Poison Ivy is *definitely* a bad guy. Girl. You know what I mean.'

'You could call her an eco-terrorist,' said Hiro. 'She creates this amazing paradise in a barren wasteland, and then some US corporation tests out weapons there and firebombs the whole place. So she goes to Gotham City and vows to make it a safe place for plants.'

'Which means killing the humans?'

Hiro shrugged. 'Her position is morally indefensible. But she does good stuff too. She rescues orphans and feeds earthquake survivors.'

'I so don't remember that bit from the George Clooney *Batman*.'

'She's often misunderstood.'

'Do you ever wish we could go on a normal date?' Hiro asked one night, as he smoothed the dirt around a passionfruit vine seedling outside the post office.

'No,' I said. 'What would be the point in that?'

'Well, I'm hardly the expert,' said Hiro. 'As you know, I've never been on a normal date. But I assume most "normal dates" are just adolescent code for make-out sessions. Hence cinemas. Comfy chairs and the illusion of privacy through darkness.'

'Well, we already have the privacy and the darkness,' I said, sidling up to him. We'd been working on the post office all night – pulling up weeds and tilling the soil before planting passionfruit and lavender. It was hard work, and we were both slightly damp with sweat. It was . . . kind of hot, actually.

'But wouldn't you like the comfy chairs?'

'This is more fun.'

We hadn't talked much about our relationship outside the Victory Garden. We didn't talk to each other at school, except for in the garden during Hiro's detentions. I hadn't told anyone I was seeing Hiro, and I assumed he hadn't told his friends about me. It was nice having a secret, although I knew sooner or later we'd have to come clean.

'I was thinking maybe we should go to Tyson Okeke's party together,' I said, resting my head against his chest.

Tyson held a massive pre-Christmas party every year that the whole year level was invited to. His parents were always down at their beach house, so there was no adult supervision and things usually got pretty messy. Last year, a bunch of people decided to go skinny dipping in Tyson's pool, and Wyatt Mitchell ended up doing something obscene involving a pool noodle and an empty beer bottle. Needless to say, Dev and Paige and I didn't engage in those kinds of shenanigans, but we did generally put in an appearance.

I felt Hiro stiffen. 'Like, together together? As a couple?'

I pulled my head away and tried to look like I didn't care. 'If you want,' I said. 'No big deal.'

'Yeah,' said Hiro. 'I'm not sure if that's such a good idea. You know how people are. Everyone will gossip about us, and stare. I'm not really into that.'

'Oh,' I said, stung. 'Okay.'

'You should go to the party, though,' said Hiro. 'Go with your friends. I'll give this one a miss.'

I nodded. He was probably right. His stoner friends were always going to despise me, and my Missolini friends were always going tell me that I could do better. It was easier to keep everything secret . . . for now.

Hiro leaned in and ran a finger along my chin.

'Your hands are covered in dirt,' I told him softly.

He responded by sliding both hands across my cheeks and winding them into my hair. 'Sorry,' he murmured.

As we neared the end of term, the days and nights grew even hotter. Teachers stopped noticing my glazed expression, because they sported matching ones of their own. Nobody was getting enough sleep, and we all stumbled through the day in our individual sticky trances, itching for the cooler evening to fall. For me, the nights were perfect. In the Victory Garden, the spicy sent of citrus blossom and warm earth filled me with tingling excitement, and Hiro and I worked long and hard in the darkness, pruning and weeding.

Despite the crippling heat, our garden thrived. We fashioned shade-cloths for the more delicate seedlings using some nylon lace tablecloths we found in a skip. Everything seemed to grow so fast we could almost see it happening. The strawberry plants flowered, and I spotted a couple of tiny hard green fruit on the little apple tree. We sat by it, admiring our handiwork. Hiro had brought tomatoes, olive oil and salt from Maria's house, and we ate them with our own fresh-picked basil leaves, red juice trickling down or chins. I'd brought along several frozen bottles of water which had mostly melted during the night. We slurped greedily at the icy water, letting it mingle with sweat and tomato juice on our skin. My clothes clung to me, and Hiro's hands on my back and waist were cool and damp. I teased a last sliver of ice from the water and placed it at the base of his throat, letting it melt into the little hollow of his collarbone. He shivered, and I kissed the cool patch of skin.

12

One Saturday, I met Dev and Paige for coffee at Patchwork Rhubarb. It was one of those hot, humid days where no amount of showering could ever make you feel really clean. My head was fuzzy from being up all night with Hiro, and moving through the streets of Valentine felt like wading through warm soup. The clouds were dark and low, and occasionally I heard a rumble of thunder. We were balanced on the edge of a storm, and I wasn't sure which was going to break first – the clouds, or my sanity.

As I passed a typical ugly Valentine house, I saw a guy from school, watering a strawberry pot on his porch. He looked up and saw me.

'Hey, Astrid,' he said, stammering a little. 'W-what are you doing here?'

'On my way to meet Dev and Paige,' I said. 'Nice strawberries.'

The guy looked proud. 'Thanks. I just thought . . . why not, you know?'

I nodded. 'Keep it up.'

I felt like a secret agent, wearing my usual Missolini face while underneath I was covered with sweat and soil and kisses.

'Maybe I'll see you at Tyson's party next weekend?' The guy was looking at me with a very familiar expression. Was he one of the ones who was also in love with Dev? I couldn't remember. What was his *name*?

'Sure,' I said.

I waved to the strawberry guy and continued on down the street. Even though I knew Hiro had been right about his reasons for not coming to Tyson's party with me, I still felt hurt. I didn't care that people might disapprove. I wanted to tell everyone about us. I wanted to announce it over the PA during form assembly every day. Spray-paint it on the basketball court. I wanted us to skip through school holding hands, wearing T-shirts that read *ASTRID 4 HIRO 4 EVER*.

I pushed open the door of Patchwork Rhubarb and breathed in a blissful (if slightly guilty) lungful of air conditioning. I spotted Paige sitting by the window, sipping an iced coffee. Apart from a middle-aged woman reading a magazine behind the counter, there was nobody else in the café. Clearly it was too hot even for the scrapbooking ladies to leave home.

'Who the hell are you?' Paige asked, squinting. 'You remind me of a friend I once had.'

I gave her a flat look. 'You saw me *yesterday*. At school?'

Paige snorted indelicately. 'I saw *something*,' she said. 'A sort of somnambulant zombie creature, shuffling around the classroom and grunting. I don't think it was you.'

It was a fair point. My memories of the school day *were* pretty sketchy.

'Are you sure you're getting enough iron?' Paige asked.

I nodded. 'I'm fine,' I said. 'Just busy with . . .' I waved a vague hand. 'You know. Environmental campaigning and stuff.'

Paige rolled her eyes fondly. 'I hope you're looking after yourself. Are you even up to date with *Ron Saskatoon*?'

'Who?'

Paige looked horrified. 'You're kidding, right?'

I shook my head.

'*Ron Saskatoon: Moose Whisperer*? It's only the most popular show on TV at the moment.'

I couldn't tell if she was serious or not.

'In last week's episode, Ron had to sleep in a tree overnight because an angry moose was waiting at the bottom. And then the moose got chased away by a bear, but the bear caught Ron's scent, and he had to distract the bear with a flare-gun, and—'

Paige kept talking, but my attention wandered away. The bell over the doorway tinkled, and Dev came in. The woman behind the counter didn't look up from her magazine.

Dev slumped into a chair. 'It is hot as *balls*,' he declared. 'I'm not built for this. How am I supposed to sneakily seduce Sanasar when I'm all sweaty and disgusting?'

Paige raised an eyebrow. 'I thought you *wanted* to get sweaty and disgusting with him.'

'Don't be indelicate,' said Dev. 'That comes *after* I sneakily seduce him, not before.'

'Still in love with your music teacher then?' I asked.

Dev sighed, which I took to be a *yes*.

I felt my own happiness buzzing around inside me, and tried to trample it down. I couldn't tell them about Hiro.

'Well,' Paige said. 'My aikido tournament was this morning. Which I won. Thank you both for asking how it went, oh and thank you also for being there to cheer me on.'

Dev and I exchanged guilty looks. 'I'm sorry,' said Dev. 'I guess I got caught up in my own drama. I can't believe I missed it. I'm a terrible friend. Let me grovel before your magnificence. You should karate-chop me in half.'

Paige regarded him fondly. 'We don't karate-chop in aikido. We centre our *ki* in order to receive *ukemi*.' She turned to me. 'What's your excuse?' she said. 'And don't be vague this time. I know something's going on.'

'Um,' I said. 'Well. It's been weird.'

'Well, that sounds intriguing,' said Dev. 'Spill.'

I swallowed. I thought about shouting Hiro's name from the rooftops, and arriving at Tyson's party with him on my arm. Then I imagined the expressions on Dev and Paige's respective faces. 'My parents,' I said. 'They split up.'

Dev and Paige both threw their arms around me and made sympathetic noises. I felt like the worst person ever. I mean, yes, my parents did split up. But Dev and Paige thought I'd been moping around listening to my parents fight, when in actual fact I'd been bewildering with Hiro, sneaking around at night being a gardening superhero.

'Astrid,' said Paige, looking awkward and apologetic. 'We already knew that. My dad cleans your dad's offices, remember? Your dad is living with his dental nurse. I'm *so sorry* I didn't say anything. But you hadn't said anything either and we thought it would be better if we waited until you were ready.'

She gave me another big hug while Dev scurried to the counter to buy me a consoling iced coffee.

'Thanks,' I said. 'And I'm sorry I didn't say anything. I needed some time, you know? To work things out.'

'Of course,' said Paige. 'I just hate the idea of you cooped up in such a toxic environment. I should teach you some new meditation exercises to help open up your centre and clear your mind.'

'Actually,' I said, deciding to lace my lie with the truth. 'I've been spending a lot of time working in the kitchen garden. It's very therapeutic.'

Kissing was also very therapeutic.

'That sounds . . .' Dev came back to the table, his head cocked. 'Well, to be honest it sounds kind of boring, but if it works for you then I'm one hundred per cent in favour of it.'

'Have you heard about the Invisible Garden Army?' asked Paige.

I felt my nose start to tingle, but tried to look nonchalant. 'The what?'

'You know, the people who are sneaking around at night planting stuff everywhere. You must have seen it. The flowers outside the kindergarten. The vegies outside the train station. Everyone's talking about it.'

Outside, another roll of thunder shook the windows of Patchwork Rhubarb.

'Really?' I said. 'Why are they called the Invisible Garden Army?'

Paige shrugged. 'That's what the local paper is calling them. Invisible because nobody ever sees them doing it, and

Army because there's *so much* of it going on. Dad says there's a whole carpet of strawberries growing outside the leisure centre.'

Dev nodded. 'My parents were talking about it last night. Mum reckons it's all an advertising campaign for that new garden centre that's opening up near the freeway.'*

The magazine lady brought over our iced coffees. 'It's not the garden centre,' she said. 'It's the local council. They're about to release this whole plan for the suburb, called Green Valentine. All the small business owners have been invited to a seminar next week where the mayor is going to explain how it will all work.'

Green Valentine. The mayor. I busied myself with my striped paper straw, but couldn't stop myself from smiling. I didn't even mind that the council was getting credit for our hard work. Green Valentine was about to go ahead, and then we really would be an army, not just a couple of kids.

As I chatted with Dev and Paige, the clouds outside grew heavy and dark, and leaves and dust whirled around out in the street.

'I'd better go home,' Paige said. 'It's about to bucket down.'

We paid for our iced coffees, and stepped out into a sticky roil of air and heat. All of Valentine seemed to be holding its breath for the storm.

---

* Ridiculous. That new gardening centre is owned by an international conglomerate that also controls most of the fracking industry – there's no way that they'd come up with something that was this a) environmentally conscious, and b) awesome.

'Where have you been?' asked Mum when I walked in the front door. She was lying on the couch, with two pedestal fans blowing air on her.*

I blinked. 'With Dev and Paige. I told you I was, remember?'

'Oh,' said Mum. 'Yes. Sorry, darling. This weather has me all foggy. Why won't it *rain* already?'

I looked out the window. 'Soon. Any minute now.'

Mum sighed. 'I thought maybe we could pick up a Christmas tree this afternoon,' she said. 'But I can't seem to get off the couch.'

I squirmed. 'Do we have to have a tree? Those cut ones aren't native. They're farmed as a monoculture and doused with pesticides. Not to mention all the plastic used to make tinsel and decorations.'**

'Really?' said Mum, raising her head and looking at me. 'You don't want a tree? You're sure?'

I nodded. 'Positive.'

Mum looked relieved. Maybe she'd been dreading her first Christmas without Dad. All our family was interstate, so it was usually just the three of us. It'd be weird without Dad this year.

'In fact,' I said, 'maybe we could skip Christmas altogether.

---

* She'd wanted to get air conditioning installed last year, but I'd told her that it was too much of a drain on energy. I'd tried to bargain with her, saying we could get air con if we also got solar panels. But Dad didn't want solar because he thought that the government should pay for energy-generation systems, and that individuals using solar weren't going to solve any problems.

** Of course a cut tree was still better than an awful PVC plastic fake one. You may as well string fairy lights around a drum of toxic waste.

It's just another stupid fake holiday created by capitalism to make us spend money on stuff we don't need.'*

Mum smiled. 'We should still do *something*,' she said. 'But you're right. Let's keep it low-key.'

Her head dropped back onto the couch and she closed her eyes. I trudged up to my room to wait for darkness.

The air grew heavier and thicker. The storm clouds rumbled and flashed overhead, but didn't burst. I tried to nap for a while, but it was too hot. Minutes ticked by like hours as sweat pooled in the small of my back. I picked up a book, but couldn't focus on the words. I put on headphones and tried to listen to music, but everything made me irritable. I texted Hiro, but he was working at the shopping centre so I didn't get a reply. I imagined the cold, fluorescent lights and the icy wash of industrial strength air conditioning. Usually the thought of that sterile, soulless building filled me with disgust, but today I would have given anything to be there.

But I couldn't even visit Hiro. The shopping centre was a good thirty-minute walk from my house, and I wasn't walking in this heat. I could break my no-car pledge and invent some excuse for Mum to drive me, but was a few hours of air conditioning really worth sacrificing my moral standards?

I stared at the ceiling and thought about Hiro and the Victory Garden, waiting for the storm to break.

It didn't. Mum and I ate cold salad and icy poles for

---

* Don't even get me started on Valentine's Day. Apart from the wastage of cards and ugly teddy bears and over-packaged boxes of chocolate, last year over seven million bunches of roses were imported into Australia for V-Day, in fuel-guzzling refrigerated transports from Kenya, Ethiopia and Columbia.

dinner, flopped on the couch in front of the TV. I drank a million litres of iced water. I checked the radar obsessively. Mum and I grew more irritable, snapping at each other. I felt itchy and sluggish and wanted to burst into tears.

Finally, at ten, I announced I was going out for my usual pre-bed run.

'In this heat?' said Mum. 'I don't think that's very safe.'

'It's not so bad now it's dark,' I said. 'I'll be careful, I promise. I'll take it slow, and I'll stay hydrated.'

Mum looked dubious, but she didn't have the energy to fight me.

I jogged over to the Victory Garden as lightning flashed overhead. The clouds were so low I felt like I could touch them. I reached the garden before Hiro. All our plants were wilting from the heat. *Surely* it would rain soon. We'd been bucketing water from a tap in the front driveway of a factory at the other end of the street, but I didn't think I could bear struggling back and forth with a heavy bucket tonight.

'I wasn't sure if you'd come,' said Hiro, arriving behind me and sliding his hands around my waist. 'With the storm and everything.'

Our embrace was brief – it was too hot for anything more serious.

'Of course I came,' I said. 'I haven't been able to think of anything else all day.'

It was too hot to move. We didn't even attempt to weed or prune or harvest the new tomatoes. We sprawled on the hot dirt, staring up at the clouds, watching the flashes of lightning and counting *one hippopotamus, two hippopotamus* until the thunder followed.

I reached out and let my fingers touch Hiro's, so they entwined.

'I've changed my mind,' said Hiro. 'About what I'd like my superpower to be. I want to be able to make it rain.'

'Like Halle Berry in *X-Men*,' I said.

Hiro chuckled. 'I love it when you reveal a new nerdy layer.'

'Oh come on,' I said. 'Everyone's seen *X-Men*.'

'I guess so.'

I drew light circles on Hiro's palm. 'Are there any other weather superheroes?'

Hiro thought for a moment. 'Thor, I guess, with his lightning and thunder hammer. And there's Sarah Rainmaker. She's a Native American superhero who can control the weather. She's a badass activist and protestor. Oh, and Weather Wizard, who's a DC super villain. He can make the weather do pretty much anything, but his name is Weather Wizard so he's automatically kind of lame.'

I chuckled, and the thunder overhead sounded like the sky was chuckling too. Hiro traced lazy lines with his finger up and down my arm.

'Your skin is so soft,' he murmured.

I shivered, and stopped caring about the heat. I sat up and reached for him, and he reached back, his arms encircling me and his head tilting towards mine. I could taste salt on his skin. We were slick with sweat. My hair was limp and damp, and I was sure I didn't smell good. But it didn't matter. All that mattered was me and Hiro, our hands and our lips, together in the Victory Garden.

With a final roll of thunder, the storm broke. Water poured

from the sky, thick and fast and hard. It was cool and wet and it filled the air with the smell of damp earth and new life.

We turned our heads up to the sky and opened our mouths, letting the water pour into us, just like the thirsty plants around our feet.

I woke up at five am to the tinny buzzing of my phone. I'd only had three hours sleep.

Hiro: Victory Garden. Twenty minutes.

I groaned, and hauled myself out of bed.

'Early morning is the best time to fertilise pumpkins,' said Hiro, handing me a coffee.

I stared at him blearily and screwed up my face, trying to process what he had said.

'What? Can't you put fertiliser on at any time?'

Hiro chuckled. 'Not that kind of fertilising. We're going to make the pumpkin flowers have sex with each other.' He pulled a paintbrush out of his pocket.

'You're joking, right?'

He shook his head. 'Nope. Pumpkins aren't great self-pollinators, and there aren't enough bees in Valentine to do it for us.'

I shook my head. 'I don't understand. I thought plants grew from seeds.'

'Humans grow from seeds,' said Hiro. 'But we still need to have sex.'

Suddenly I felt *completely* awake.

'So you're saying flowers have sex.'

'Of course.'

'There are lady flowers and man flowers.'

'Sometimes.'

'And we're going to help them.'

'Yes.'

I felt my cheeks go red. How did you help a flower have sex? Wouldn't the flowers feel weird that we were there watching them?

'Come on,' said Hiro, and led me over to the pumpkin vine, which had spilled over the edge of the rubbish bin we'd planted it in, and was rambling in among the tomatoes.

I crouched down beside him as he gently lifted one of the large orange flowers.

'This one is a male,' he said. 'See how there's nothing at the base of the flower? It just goes flower, then stem. And if you look into the flower, you'll see the stamen, which is the . . .' he coughed. 'The . . . male part.'

'Don't all flowers have . . . one of those?' I asked.

'Not exactly. Look here.' Hiro reached over and cupped his hand around another flower. 'This one is female. See inside, instead of a stamen, it has a stigma.'

I peered in. Instead of a yellow polleny stalk, the flower had something more complicated. More . . . female-looking.

'And see it also has an ovary.'

Flowers had ovaries? Surely Hiro was winding me up. But as he lifted the flower for me to see, I saw that it did. It had a hard green egg-like ball underneath the flower, between the petals and the stem.

'Wow,' I said. 'Are all flowers like that?'

'Most flowers have both male and female parts,' said Hiro. 'But all flowers have to be pollinated. That's what bees are for.'

He dipped his paintbrush into the male flower, and then gently brushed some of the sticky yellow pollen inside the female flower.

'That's it?' I said. 'That's flower sex?'

Hiro nodded. 'That's it. Some people cut off the male flowers and stick them inside the female ones, but I think that's a bit . . . you know. Invasive.'

I looked at the female flower. It looked so delicate and vibrant. Did it know what we'd just done?

'So what happens next? Does a pumpkin grow?'

'Hopefully. If the flower has been correctly fertilised, then the ovary will start to swell up in a few days. And eventually the flower part will drop off and the ovary will become a baby pumpkin.'

'Amazing.'

Hiro stood up and brushed the dirt from his knees. 'That's it,' he said. 'We just made a baby. Was it good for you?'

I laughed, feeling oddly nervous at all this talk of sex and babies. 'I had no idea it was so . . . so much like the way we . . . do it.' I felt my red cheeks grow even hotter.

'We're more like fruit trees,' said Hiro, and he reached forward to tuck a stray wisp of hair behind my ear. I suddenly felt very warm.

'How do fruit trees have sex?' I asked.

'Most fruit trees can't self-pollinate,' Hiro replied. His voice was low and husky, and he was very close. 'You need two trees that will . . . pollinate each other.'

'Oh.'

'In spring, when they explode into all those wonderful delicate blossoms. The warm spring air lifts the pollen and spreads it far and wide. Bees travel from flower to flower, dipping into one after another. Sampling their nectar and spreading the pollen.'

I swallowed, imagining warm spring air and the scent of apple-blossom. I felt giddy.

'Fruit trees can't do it alone. You have to have a pair.'

I could feel his breath on my cheek. I moved closer, feeling like I had absolutely no control over my body.

There was a sudden rattling from the other side of the fence, and we sprang apart guiltily.

It was an early-morning jogger who had kicked an empty Coke can. We froze, hoping he wouldn't notice us behind the screen of baby cucumbers that were swarming up the fence. All I could hear was my own breath, and the thud, thud, thud of the jogger's sneakers on the footpath.

He ran right past us, not even looking at the garden.

I felt a wave of adrenalin and emotion wash over me, so strong I felt my knees buckle. I was still buzzing from our almost-kiss, and tingling from the shock of nearly being discovered.

Hiro coughed awkwardly. 'Of course, there are lots of variations,' he said, as if the jogger hadn't interrupted an *incredibly* intense moment between us. 'Avocado trees are interesting. They have male flowers at one time of day, and female at another. So you need two trees, on different schedules, in order to get viable pollen.'

'Oh?' I said helplessly. 'That is . . . interesting.'

'Isn't it?' said Hiro with a grin. He dug me in the ribs, and suddenly I didn't feel nervous or weird anymore. This was Hiro. My Hiro. He understood me, and everything would be alright.

'I'd better go,' I said. 'I promised I'd have breakfast with my dad.'

'Okay,' said Hiro. 'Um.'

He was suddenly nervous, looking at me with unusually intense eyes.

'Are you okay?'

He dug in his backpack. 'I made you something,' he said, and handed me a stack of paper, folded and stapled to make a little book. 'It's stupid,' he said. 'I know it's crappy, but . . .' He broke off and kicked the dirt.

I looked down at the book. On the front cover was a picture of two figures. The guy was dressed in a tight black superhero-style suit. On his chest blazoned a bright green plant – a seedling. He was crouched on top of a shopping trolley that was flying through the air, and in his hand he held a garden trowel. The other figure was a girl, wearing a close-fitting bright red suit that emphasised her curves without being quite as objectifying as the usual female superhero getup. Instead of hands, she had two wicked-looking lobster claws, and curving antennae rose up from her blonde hair.

'*The Adventures of Lobstergirl and Shopping Trolley Guy Vol.1: The Victory Garden,*' I read. 'Hiro, you made this?'

Hiro blushed. 'It's not very good,' he said.

'It's *amazing*.'

I leafed through the comic. On one page, Lobstergirl and Shopping Trolley Guy faced up against a giant monster made of rubbish. Lobstergirl pinned the monster down with her claws, and Shopping Trolley Guy flung fertiliser from his trolley until the monster started to sprout seedlings all over him.

'It's the most incredible thing I've ever seen,' I said. 'Thank you so much.'

I kissed him, and forgot all about being discovered, and interrupting joggers, and meeting Dad for breakfast. Everything disappeared, until it was just me and Hiro, alone in our Victory Garden.

13

We arrived at the Victory Garden together the following night to find a group of strange hippy-types waiting for us. There were four of them, three guys and one girl. They looked older than us – I'd guess early twenties, but it was hard to tell under all the hemp and dreadlocks. They all blended into the same colour palette of tanned skin and earthy brown and green clothes, with lots of beads and weird symbols. Two of the guys wore sandals (probably vegan); the other guy and the girl were barefoot. The only thing that stood out from the browns and greens was the girl's bright red hair, matted into thin dreadlocks and decorated with the occasional bead or ribbon. Her eyes were outlined in thick black eyeliner, and a silver stud glinted on her lower lip. Thai fisherman's pants were slung low around her waist, exposing the kind of tanned, taut midriff that I'd only ever seen in highly photoshopped magazines. A cropped hemp singlet emphasised her cleavage, and silver chains and beads hung at her throat. She oozed raw, animalistic sexuality.

I'd always respected and envied the hippy lifestyle. They were so committed to their vision – it permeated every layer of their existence, the way they lived and dressed, the food they ate. Me? I couldn't even give up bacon. I was a try-hard when it came to environmental ethics, unwilling to give up my modern comforts no matter how damaging they were.

'So you're the one behind this,' the girl said, her voice low and husky. She was looking at Hiro.

'We are,' I said, stepping forward.

The girl's eyes skimmed over me, then returned to Hiro. The other guys stared at her. She was clearly in charge.

'It's very impressive,' she said, but I wasn't entirely sure she meant it. 'Your fame is spreading far and wide.'

'Thanks,' I said.

'I'm Storm,' she said.

I suspected *Storm* wasn't her real name, but it suited her. Sultry and powerful.

'Cool,' said Hiro.

I felt a sting of jealousy. Wasn't there a Storm in *X-Men*? Surely Hiro would be impressed by this wild, untameable super-hippy.

'Anyway, if you ever want to come and play . . .'

My jealousy evaporated. Was she *inviting* us to join them? I had visions of being part of a real environmental movement, chaining myself to bulldozers and holding up placards out-side ministerial offices.

'Of course we're a little more . . .' Storm's eyes glanced off me again, '*extreme* than you kids.'

'We're up for that,' I said, unable to control the eagerness in my voice. Hiro shot me a disapproving glare. Didn't he see what I saw? The potential for change?

'Really?' she said. 'How pleasing. We prefer the big picture, though. Your gardening project is very cute, but we're serious. Last month we destroyed an entire crop of GM canola.'

I blinked. Weren't environmentalists supposed to *protect* plants? Not destroy them? But I suppose if they were GM then that was different . . .

Storm turned her gaze back on Hiro. 'What about you?' she asked, curling her lip slightly so the stud flashed silver. 'You look like trouble. Are you up for some fun?'

Hiro shrugged, adopting his old sullen slouch. 'Depends,' he mumbled.

Storm dug in the hessian bag slung over her shoulder and fished out a biro. Stepping forward, she took Hiro's arm, pushed up his sleeve, and wrote her number on his forearm. I frowned. Why was she giving Hiro her number? I was the one who had shown enthusiasm. Maybe she didn't want to get biro on my shirt.

'Hope to see you around,' she said, and floated off, her minions shambling behind her at a respectful distance.

'Yikes,' said Hiro, watching them leave.

'That was awesome!' I said, pulling out my phone and snapping a picture of the number scrawled on Hiro's arm. 'They're really *doing* stuff! And they want us to help!'

'Help what?' said Hiro. 'Destroy people's crops? I thought we were more about *making* things, not *destroying* them.'

'But you saw how impressed she was with what we've done! Think how much more we'd be able to do if we were part of something bigger.'

Hiro shook his head. 'I . . . I like it being just us. Our thing.'

'But this is what we've been looking for,' I continued. 'A chance to really make a difference!'

'What *you've* been looking for, maybe,' said Hiro. 'I never wanted to be part of some hippy commune.'

I left it at that and turned to the garden, helping some young bean plants trail up the chain-link fence. We worked in silence for a while, and I wasn't sure whether it was companionable silence or whether Hiro was angry with me.

'Astrid,' he said finally, and his voice was serious. 'I . . . I'm not always going to want to do the things you want to do. I'm not like you.'

I blinked. That seemed blindingly obvious to me. 'I know,' I said. 'We're different people. I understand.'

'I don't know if you do.'

I looked over at him. He was holding a punnet of egg-plant seedlings in one hand and frowning. 'Like, take uni for example. I assume you're planning on going.'

What was he talking about? 'Uni?' I asked. 'Of course I'll go to uni. I think I'll do law.'

Hiro turned the punnet upside down and gently tipped the contents into his hand. 'Why?'

'Because I can. I'll get the marks, and then I can get work either in environmental law, or move into politics.'

'But do you *want* to be a lawyer? Or a politician?'

I pulled off my gardening gloves and leaned back. 'Not really. But that's not the point. I have to figure out how I can best make a difference.'

'You'll never make a difference if you end up doing something you hate.'

'Who says I'll hate it?'

Hiro teased the tiny seedlings apart and tilted his head, gazing at me. 'What would you do, if you could do anything in the world?'

I thought about it. 'Do I have to choose just one thing?'

'Pick as many as you like.'

I smiled. 'Everything,' I said. 'I want to be the first Greens prime minister. I want to head up an environmental science project team. I want to invent a new kind of clean energy. I want to protect wetlands from developers, and fragile eco-systems from resource-hungry corporations. I want to be a primary school teacher and an urban planner and a journalist and an awareness-raising rock star.'

Hiro's expression was strange. Sort of sad and proud and angry all at the same time.

'I'm aware that the last one might not happen,' I said. 'But I'm pretty sure Dev will become a massive celebrity, so I could at least help him with what to say when he's being interviewed.'

Hiro cupped one of the tiny seedlings in his palm, frowning at it.

'How about you?' I asked. 'What would you do if you could do anything?'

'Conductor,' said Hiro.

I raised my eyebrows. 'Tram or orchestra?'

'Orchestra, obviously.'

'I didn't know you were musical.'

'I'm not. I like the idea of being an orchestra conductor. Like Bugs Bunny in that cartoon.'

'Seriously, though,' I said. 'What will you do after high school?'

'Travel, I guess,' said Hiro. 'Read, think. Try and find some meaningful work that won't send me crazy.'

I suddenly realised why he'd asked me about uni. 'You're not going to uni, are you?'

Hiro shook his head.

'Are you crazy?' I asked. 'You won't even consider it?'

'Nope,' said Hiro. 'I've spent the past eleven years hating institutionalised learning. I don't want to do any more.'

I felt my forehead wrinkle into a frown. 'But you're smart. You could easily get into a good course if you applied yourself a little.'

'Ugh, you sound like my mother.'

'Well, she's right,' I said.

Hiro's face clouded over. 'Where do you want these egg-plants to go?'

I wasn't going to let him change the subject so easily. 'Hiro,' I said. 'You're amazing. You could do anything you wanted to.'

'I know that,' Hiro said. 'That's why I don't want to go to university. I can do anything. I don't need a stupid piece of paper. All it'll get me is some tiresome office job where I'll slowly die.'

My frown deepened. 'That's absurd,' I said. 'You can't shut off the whole idea of going to uni just because you don't want to be an accountant. That's like saying you won't ever visit a restaurant because you don't like anchovies.'

'I'm shutting off the whole idea of university because I don't want it, okay? It's not who I am.'

'I don't think that's true,' I said. 'I think you're afraid of failing. You're afraid to admit that you *want* to go to uni, because then you might fail. But I can help you with your grades. I could tutor you.'

'You know,' said Hiro, looking hurt. 'You can be a bit of a bitch, sometimes.'

I recoiled. 'You think I'm a bitch?'

Hiro shrugged. 'You expect everything will always go your way. You want people to be just like you.'

I didn't respond. Why couldn't Hiro see that I only wanted what was best for him?

Daytime seemed dreamlike and strange. I was exhausted from our night-time adventures. The hot, bright light was harsh and seemed to wash everything out, as if I was living in an overexposed photograph. I missed the soft embrace of night, the intimacy of being in the Victory Garden, just me and Hiro, the only two people awake in Valentine.

'Astrid?' Dev peered at me. 'Are you okay?'

'Hmm?' I looked at him. I couldn't *quite* remember sitting down in form assembly, but here I was.

'Are you okay?'

'I'm fine,' I smiled.

'Are you sure?'

His eyes flicked down to my hands and then back up to my face. I looked down. My hands were filthy – covered in dirt, the crescents of my nails crusted black.

'Oh,' I said. I'd forgotten to wash my hands when I got home after bewildering.

I must have also forgotten to shower.

'Kitchen garden,' I said to Dev. 'I-I was there this morning. Before I came here. Forgot to wash my hands.'

Paige frowned. 'You're getting weird about this whole gardening thing,' she said.

Dev nodded. 'You're putting the *cult* in *cultivate*.'

I hesitated. Should I tell them? I desperately wanted to. They were my best friends, and it had felt wrong hiding something this big from them. But I couldn't tell them about Hiro. We'd agreed not to, and I knew they wouldn't understand. But I *could* talk about the gardening without mentioning Hiro . . .

'Okay, I'm going to tell you guys something, but you have to *swear* to keep it a secret.'

'I'm sorry, have we not been best friends since we were four?' said Dev. 'Did I tell anyone about the thing that happened in Grade Two with you and the peanut butter?'

Paige cocked her head. 'What thing with the peanut butter?'

Dev spread his hands. 'See?' he said. 'I'm trustworthy.'

I took a deep breath. 'You know all the gardening stuff?' I asked. 'The Invisible Garden Army?'

'Of course.'

'It's me. I'm the one who's been doing it.'

Dev and Paige exchanged a look.

'Are you serious?' asked Paige.

'Yes,' I said. 'It's been me all along.'

'No,' said Paige. 'I meant – do you seriously think we didn't already know that?'

I blinked. 'You knew?'

Dev nodded towards my dirty hands. 'It didn't take a vast amount of deductive reasoning.'

I felt deflated. But at least now I could take some of the credit.

'Are you doing it alone?' asked Paige.

Why weren't they more excited? 'Um, yeah,' I said. I wasn't ready to come clean about Hiro yet.

'Astrid!' Dev shook his head. 'That isn't cool. You can't go wandering about Valentine at night on your own. You'll get stabbed. Or worse.'

'I'm fine,' I said. 'I'm perfectly safe.'

'No, you're not,' said Paige. 'This is not a nice suburb.'

I hesitated. 'Fine,' I said. 'I'm not doing it on my own. There's . . . someone else.'

Paige's eyes widened. 'It's a *boy*,' she said. 'That's the only reason for you to try and hide it. You're doing sneaky night-time gardening with a *boy*. And sneaky *other things*!'

'This is so *romantic*,' said Dev. 'Under cover of night, you're sneaking around in the shadows with a mysterious crusader, beautifying Valentine with your love.'

'Bewildering,' I said. 'It's called bewildering, not beautifying.'

'Even better. What's he like? Is he handsome? Do you wear masks to conceal your identities? Do you have code names?'

I laughed. 'No,' I said. 'It's not nearly that exciting, sorry. I mean, it *is* exciting. But there aren't any special outfits or anything.' I thought of the lobster costume. 'Not anymore.'

'So who is he? Does he go here?'

I felt myself colour, and remembered my deal with Hiro to keep our relationship a secret. 'Um,' I said. 'No.'

Dev and Paige exchanged a glance. Could they tell I was lying?

After struggling to keep my eyes open through double English, I slipped out of maths in third period and went to the kitchen garden. I weeded around the lettuces and tied the growing tomato plants to bamboo stakes. The work was calming, and I breathed in the scent of earth deeply. It was more enlivening than any caffeinated product I'd ever consumed. I hoped things were okay with me and Hiro, after our weird conversation the previous night. He hadn't texted me at all, but then I hadn't texted him either.

I heard the gravel crunch behind me, and my heart leapt.

But it wasn't Hiro. It was Mr Webber.

'Shouldn't you be in class, Astrid?' He was frowning.

I looked at him and considered making up a lie about a free period, but decided I couldn't be bothered. 'I've got better things to do,' I said.

The frown deepened. 'Astrid, I'm worried about you.'

I blinked. 'I'm sorry?'

'You're a good student,' said Mr Webber. 'You're very driven and motivated. Your teachers all love you.'

Didn't exactly sound like cause for concern.

'So you understand we want to make sure you . . . stay on the right path. You have a great group of friends.'

'Sir, is this about Hiro?'

Mr Webber looked disapprovingly at a slater crawling

along the edge of one of the garden beds. 'I admit that when I assigned him to do detention with you in the garden, I'd hoped you'd be a positive influence on him.'

'We've been a positive influence on each other,' I said. 'He taught me a lot about gardening.'

Mr Webber didn't seem impressed. 'I'm also aware that there are . . . other activities going on. Outside of school. Some of them aren't exactly legal.'

Did he know about the Victory Garden? About our bewildering? 'What do you mean?'

Mr Webber shrugged. 'Trespass. Graffiti. Vandalism.'

I shook my head in disbelief. 'It's not *vandalism*. Valentine has never looked better.'

'But at what *cost*, Astrid?' asked Mr Webber. 'How has this affected your schoolwork? And your social life? And where does it end? It may seem like fun now, but these environmental campaigns can get nasty. Violent.'

I shook my head. As usual, Mr Webber had no idea what he was talking about.

'You'd better get back to class,' he said, narrowing his eyes. 'Before I find you a detention slip.'

I met Hiro at Maria's the following afternoon. We were taking more cuttings from her garden to propagate all over Valentine. We'd already had some success with lavender, rosemary and geraniums, and were now trying to grow cuttings from the olive and citrus trees. Things had been tense since our almost-fight, but we both avoided bringing it up, talking instead about our future bewildering plans.

Until.

'I texted her,' I told him.

'Who?'

'Storm. She says we should meet them on Friday evening in a park near the city.'

Hiro's face drew together in all-too-familiar lines. He was shutting himself off again.

'Please,' I said. 'Come on. We have to go once, just to see what it's like. And if we don't like it, we don't have to go back.'

'Why does everything have to be *big*?' said Hiro. 'Why isn't this enough? You and me. We're making a difference. We don't need an army.'

'Don't you want more, though?'

Hiro shook his head. 'No,' he said. 'This is enough for me. *You're* enough for me.'

I drew back. 'That's not fair,' I said. 'This isn't about *us*.'

'Isn't it?'

'Come on,' I said. 'Please. Come with me. I need you there.'

'I don't want to.'

'Don't want to do what?' It was Michi, who had just stepped out the back door into Maria's garden. With her was a tall blonde girl with an asymmetrical haircut.

'Nothing,' said Hiro. 'Astrid, this is Cara. Cara, Astrid.'

'Hey,' said the blonde girl.

Michi was looking at me. 'What's going on?' she said.

Hiro glared. 'Astrid wants to go and be *radical* with a bunch of feral hippy activists.'

Michi frowned. 'Redheaded girl? Dreadlocks? Hemp? Calls herself Seagull or Breeze or something equally stupid?'

'Storm,' I said.

'That's her.' She looked at Hiro and wagged a finger. 'Stay away from those guys,' she said. 'They're trouble.'

Hiro snorted. 'What, are you going to dob on me?'

'You know what I mean,' said Michi. 'You don't want to piss Mum off. Not this week, especially.'

Maria called Michi and Cara inside, and Hiro scuffed his feet on the garden path, his face dark and unreadable.

'Fine,' he said at last. 'I'll come with you.'

I knew it should have felt like a victory, but it didn't. Something wasn't quite right, but I had no idea what it was.

14

Storm's gathering was down by the creek a few suburbs over, in a derelict children's playground. A few fires burned in rubbish bins to provide light and heat, which seemed overkill on an already muggy December night, and not exactly environmentally friendly. I started to feel uneasy, but swallowed it down. I had to be open to new ideas.

There were about twenty people gathered in the park, all dressed in hemp or Thai fisherman's pants. I could smell incense burning.* A guy was banging on an African spirit drum, while a waify blonde sang high, whispery nothings. Another woman wearing an orange skirt fringed with bells stomped around making the bells jingle.

'I can't believe you made me do this,' Hiro muttered.

I was starting to wish I hadn't. I jumped as a huge jet of fire burst out of one guy. Fire twirlers? Weren't these people

---

* I'd forgotten about hippies and incense. Paige used to burn it, until I'd explained to her that it releases carbon monoxide, carbon dioxide and sulphur dioxide into the atmosphere. Also, it makes me sneeze.

supposed to be environmentalists?* Through the stomach-turning stench of kerosene and incense, I could smell something else that I was pretty sure was pot.**

'I think we might have made a mistake,' I said to Hiro, but it was too late to turn back.

Like some kind of supernatural entity, Storm emerged from smoke and flame, wearing something that managed to be shapeless and revealing at the same time. Her red dreadlocks burned bright in the light of the flickering fire.

'You came,' she said in her low, throaty voice.

'Here we are,' I said, and my voice sounded chirpy and false.

Storm ignored me, but gazed at Hiro, licking her lips. What was going on?

She gestured to a tall man standing next to her. He wore an Indian-style tunic, and I couldn't tell where his matted hair ended and his tangled beard began.

'This is Revolution.'***

'*Namaste*,' said Revolution, gazing at us with heavy-lidded eyes.

'Hi,' I replied. 'Um, when does the meeting start?'

Storm smiled lazily. 'It's already started.' She swept a hand to indicate the dancing, braiding and smoking.

---

* You know what fire twirlers use as fuel? Kerosene. And you know what produces more greenhouse gases than petrol, aviation fuel and propane? Kerosene. The only thing worse for the atmosphere was the wood they were burning in those rubbish bins.

** Super bad for the environment. Illegal cannabis farms use millions of litres of water, not to mention the energy that goes into powering all the fans, light globes and dehumidifiers they need.

*** Revolution? Really?

Right.

'I don't suppose there's an agenda?' I asked. 'Actionable items from previous minutes?'

Storm gave me a flat look. 'We're anarcho-primitivists,' she said. 'We don't subscribe to the capitalist bullshit that's poisoning the planet.'

'Anarcho-what?' I asked. 'What even is that?'

'Anarcho-primitivists.' Storm smiled in a patronising way. 'We acknowledge that the human race is over – we're tumbling into ecological catastrophe. The only way for us to survive is by reverting to our natural hunter-gatherer state.'

I blinked. That was obviously completely impractical. There were way too many humans on the earth to sustain a hunter-gatherer lifestyle. Without structure and government and sanitation, the whole human race would die of dysentery and other infectious diseases. Not to mention the fact that without civilisation, we wouldn't be able to maintain our (ideally renewable) power plants or process waste products to stop them polluting our air and water and soil. But Storm looked utterly serious.

I glanced at Hiro, but he didn't seem to be doubled over in laughter the way I would have expected.

'There is no other option for humanity,' said Storm. 'We need to purge our bodies of all these chemicals.'

I looked at Hiro again. Why wasn't he taking her to task? Where was the speech about how everything is chemicals? But he didn't blink an eyelid.

'I know things are bad,' I said. 'But climate scientists have predicted that if the whole world commits to cut carbon emissions by—'

'Climate scientists are all fascists,' said Revolution. 'They're deep in the pockets of the oil industry.'

Well, *that* made absolutely no sense. 'I'm sure a quick google will find that—'

'We don't *google*,' said Storm, her voice dripping with disgust. 'Technology is the scourge of humanity.'

Was she serious?

'Technology is going to *save* humanity,' I argued. 'Technology is finding new ways to harness renewable energies. It's bringing species back from the brink of extinction. Technology is the *only* way we can reverse some of the damage we've done to the planet.'

Storm and Revolution exchanged a knowing look. 'They've already got to you,' she said with insincere sadness. 'And so young.'

I felt myself bristle. 'You can't claim that *all* scientists and *all* technology are evil. Science made that disgusting kerosene those fire twirlers are using. It made the vinyl that your vegan sandals are made from. And it made the hair dye that you use, although I'm sure you tell people it's natural. Scientists are finding new ways to harness green energy, and they're even developing nanotechnology that can clean up pollution, improve manufacturing efficiency and make alternative energy sources more effective.'

'Nanotechnology?' said Storm with a graceful shudder. 'It won't seem so wonderful when the self-replicating nanobots escape from science labs, enslave humanity and consume the earth.'

She did *not* just say that. 'Okay,' I said. 'Now you're just being silly.'

Storm scoffed. 'You say that now,' she said. 'But wait until we're being farmed for energy by an army of sentient computers.'

I couldn't help myself, I actually laughed aloud. 'You know that the whole premise of *The Matrix* is ridiculous, right? It totally contradicts the laws of thermodynamics. The energy that humans generate is *significantly* less than the amount of food you have to put in them to keep them alive. The evil machines would have been better off just burning whatever they were feeding the humans. Or, you know, using nuclear power, which would be thousands of times more efficient.'

Storm closed her eyes as if she were feeling genuinely nauseated. 'I should have known you'd be *pro-nuclear*.'

I wanted to hit someone. 'I'm not *pro-nuclear*,' I said, trying not to raise my voice. 'I'm just saying that if I was an evil machine, that's the power source I'd use. As I'm not an evil machine intent on destroying humanity, I'd obviously prefer wind or solar.'

Hiro took a step forward and spread his hands in a peaceful gesture. 'Maybe we should agree to disagree,' he said. 'After all, we have the same goals, don't we?'

I was pretty convinced we didn't. I was so disappointed. I'd thought that Storm and her friends would be kindred souls. That we'd join forces and make the world a better place. But they didn't want to *fix* anything. They were too busy being angry and negative.

'Our goal is to save the planet,' said Storm. 'And we do it by fighting the planet's enemies.'

'So who are these enemies?' I asked.

'Anyone who destroys nature for personal gain and profit.'

That seemed like a broad definition of *enemy* to me.

My phone pinged, and I dug it out of my back pocket. Storm recoiled as if I'd produced a gun. I gave her a withering look.

'I know you have a phone of your own,' I said. 'I texted you.'

Storm narrowed her eyes at me, and I moved a few steps away from the group to look at my phone.

Paige: Where are you? Dev made a medium-sized romantic gesture to his music teacher, and as expected it all went horribly wrong. He could really use some ice-cream and love.

My thumb hovered over the screen. I didn't have time to deal with whatever crisis Dev was having this week. I mean, when was he *not* having his heart broken? But still, he was my friend.

'We should go,' I murmured to Hiro. 'You were right, I'm sorry.'

Hiro shrugged. 'We're here now,' he said. 'May as well stay and see what they have to say.'

What?

Hiro and Storm were staring at each other, clearly sharing some kind of . . . moment.

'You can go,' said Hiro, without looking at me.

There was *no way* I was leaving Hiro alone with Storm. I turned back to my phone.

Me: Sorry. Promised Mum I'd have a quiet night in.

The reply came immediately.

I felt a sick twisting in my gut. I'd been caught out lying to Paige. She was one of my best friends. But she wouldn't understand what was going on. Clark Kent had to lie all the time. It didn't make him a bad person.

While I'd been busy with my phone, Hiro had somehow moved closer to Storm, and he was staring at her with what looked suspiciously like admiration.

'So what are we going to do?' he asked.

We?

'That's up for discussion.' Storm flicked a glance at me. 'Maybe we'll torch it,' she said with a cold smile.

'Torch what?'

'The Green Valentine Display Centre,' said Revolution. 'The mayor unveiled it yesterday. It outlines her whole totalitarian vision.'

I blinked. I couldn't believe I'd missed the unveiling of the Green Valentine scheme!

'But . . . isn't the mayor's scheme what we want?' I asked. 'The ten-point plan?'

Storm chuckled. 'You obviously haven't seen it. It's pure evil.'

More hyperbole, I was sure. What would these hippies know anyway, with their pot-smoking and their carcinogenic incense?

'And you're planning to *torch it*?' I said. 'You think that setting a building on fire is going to save the planet? *Really*? Are you *insane*? Do you have any idea what kind of toxic gasses that will release into the atmosphere? Burning stuff to get what you want . . . isn't that kind of like a *coal plant*?'

'That's a very simplistic take on it.'

'You know they'll just rebuild it, right? The mayor isn't going to say *oh, some anarcho-primativists burnt down my display centre – well, now I see the light, I'm going to devote my life to rescuing the Southern Corroboree Frog and preserving native wetlands.* This has never happened, ever, in the history of ever. The council will rebuild it, so not only will you have polluted the air with greenhouse gases, you will have *doubled* the building's production carbon footprint. Nice work.'

Storm looked smug. 'I don't expect you to understand,' she said, with a patronising head-tilt.

'What if someone's there? What if they get hurt?'

'There are casualties in any war.'

I shook my head. Storm wasn't the wild, elemental force of nature I'd first seen her as. She was a noxious weed, spreading poison and choking out everything that was green and good. Storm was the wrong name for her. She was Poison Ivy. I wanted to leave more than anything, but I couldn't let Hiro stay without me, under the influence of these awful people.

'How can you say that?' I asked. 'How can you just casually dismiss violence like that?'

'I've been arrested eight times,' she said, as if it was something to be proud of.

'You think that being arrested gives you, what, credentials?'

Poison Ivy shrugged. 'I've earned my stripes.'

'You're supposed to be a hippy!' I said. 'What about peace? What about love? Where does that come into it?'

'You really don't get it, do you?' said Poison Ivy. 'This is a *war*. We are *soldiers* battling for the earth. We have to win the war, before we can start to heal the earth's wounds.'

I snorted, but Hiro was nodding.

'No,' I said. 'This is stupid.'

'And I suppose you have all the answers?'

'No,' I said. 'I don't have all the answers, but I know enough to be sure that nothing is going to be solved with violence and destruction. That's the whole point of what Hiro and I have been doing. We're *making* things, not destroying them. We're showing people that they can be better, not making them angry and defensive by turning them into the enemy.' I turned to Hiro. 'Tell her,' I demanded.

I glanced at Hiro, who looked . . . unsure. He flashed me a quick smile, but his eyes were dragged back to Poison Ivy.

'Your . . . *efforts* are commendable,' said Poison Ivy in a tone that suggested they very much weren't. 'But you're doing more damage than good. Planting all of these European plants – it's just more pollution. You may as well be filling that vacant lot with used syringes or toxic sludge.'

'What, so you think that we should pull up all our vegies and replace them with natives?'

'That'd be a start,' said Poison Ivy. 'Everything you're planting comes from Europe. It doesn't belong here.'*

'If we got rid of everything here that wasn't native, *we'd* all have to go, too. *We're* not native.'

---

* Except for, you know, the corn, and the tomatoes, and the potatoes, which come from the Americas, and the variety of Asian greens that we've been growing, not to mention the native finger lime and lillypilly trees we'd planted on a dusty median strip near school.

Poison Ivy looked at me coolly. 'And you think that would be such a terrible thing?'

'Now you're being ridiculous. What are you suggesting, that we exterminate all the non-native humans?'

'The world would be better off without *any* humans.' Poison Ivy's look of smug superiority made my teeth hurt. I wanted to scratch that smile off her stupid face.

'That's insane,' I said. 'And it's pointless. Humans are here to stay. And anyway, it's massively conceited to think that humans aren't a part of nature.'

'You think *I'm* conceited?' Poison Ivy laughed a low, throaty laugh. 'Says the little girl who thinks her lame gardening project is going to change the world.'

'There's a difference between conceited and optimistic.'

'Well,' said Poison Ivy, speaking only to Hiro and totally ignoring me. 'If you're interested, feel free to join us.'

Hiro nodded. I could see how hard he was trying not to look eager, and it made me want to scream. Why couldn't he see how ridiculous these people were? How impractical? They were all talk and no action, or at least no action that would actually make a difference.

I had a sudden flashback to me, just a few months ago, standing in the shopping centre handing out fact sheets. Had I been making a difference then? My fact sheets had been full of guilt-inducing statistics about how humanity was spoiling the party for so many other species. I'd berated and badgered people, telling them off for buying four-ply printed, bleached and scented toilet paper. Had my message been as negative and alienating as Poison Ivy's?

As my expression faltered, Poison Ivy's lip curled into a sly smile. 'That's the end of the official business,' she said to the crowd. 'But of course you should all feel free to stay for the spiritual component.'

One of the dreadlocked hippies brought out his djembe and I cringed inwardly. He started to thump on it, and the wispy blonde girl raised her breathy, tuneless voice in something I could only assume was supposed to be song.

'Come on,' I muttered to Hiro. '*Surely* you don't want to stay any longer.'

Hiro nodded, but as we were turning to go, Poison Ivy dragged Revolution out into the centre of the circle. She shot Hiro an arch look, and then lightly drew her nails over Revolution's bare chest. Revolution reached around under her mass of red dreadlocks and tugged at the ribbon tie on her top. The whole thing fell away, exposing her bare breasts. I looked away, embarrassed. Hiro, of course, stared openly. I couldn't help looking back.

Poison Ivy raised her hands up above her head and began a slow, swaying dance. Her Thai fisherman's pants sat low on her hips, and she thrust them provocatively towards Revolution. She didn't seem at all concerned about the fact she was half naked. Her eyes were closed and her face was turned up to the sky. Her breasts were . . . well, I didn't have much experience in the breast area, but they looked like the kind of breasts that people paid significant amounts of money to obtain via surgery. Perfectly formed and just the right size.

Hiro was mesmerised. I tugged on his arm.

'You're drooling,' I said, through gritted teeth.

'Hmm?' He didn't look away.

Poison Ivy and Revolution were dancing, a close, grinding

dance that seemed to be only a few thin layers of clothing away from actually having sex. It was gross, and made all the grosser by how obvious it was that Poison Ivy was doing it so people would watch. I thought about how low and husky Hiro's voice had become when he told me about the flower sex. This was what he wanted. He was a teenage boy, of course that was what he wanted. And what had I done? I'd gotten nervous and stammery, and had been grateful when we'd been interrupted.

I watched Poison Ivy writhe and gyrate, oozing sexuality. I couldn't compete with that. I didn't want to. If that's the kind of thing Hiro wanted in a girlfriend, then he was going to have to look elsewhere.

And he was. He was looking elsewhere with his mouth hanging open, like a hungry dog being offered a bone.

I tried to maintain a dignified silence on the train home, but I couldn't help myself.

'Those people were *the actual worst*,' I burst out.

Hiro shrugged. 'I don't know,' he said. 'Maybe you were right. Maybe they *are* the ones making a difference.'

'No!' I shifted uncomfortably in my seat. 'I wasn't right. I was wrong. Those people are wrong. About everything.'

'Not about everything,' said Hiro darkly. 'Not about the council.'

'What makes you so sure that the Green Valentine Scheme is so evil?'

Hiro looked out the window. 'You heard them tonight. Nothing good is coming out of that scheme. It'll be diabolical.'

'They think *we're* diabolical for planting non-native vegetables.'

'Trust me, Astrid. There will be nothing good in the Green Valentine Scheme. Nothing at all. I don't want you to get your hopes up, because they will be crushed.'

'Destroyed . . . like the display centre?'

Hiro rolled his eyes. 'You're being immature. Try and see things from a different point of view. You said it yourself: if we were part of something bigger, we could really make a difference.'

'By blowing up a council building? That's what you call making a difference?'

'I'm sure they're not actually going to blow it up,' said Hiro, his voice mild. 'But I bet they're planning something spectacular. Maybe they'll destroy that billboard for Green Valentine on the freeway.'

'Do you hear yourself?' I said. 'This isn't what we do. We don't destroy things. We *create* things.'

'Well, maybe it's time to change things up a bit. Make some space. Make some noise.'

'You read too many comic books,' I said. 'Violence isn't the only way to solve problems.'

'I'm not saying we should go out and *kill* anyone,' Hiro retorted. 'Just make them notice.'

'Can't we make them notice by doing *nice* things?'

'It's not enough. There aren't any superheroes who get stuff done by being *nice*.'

I didn't like this fight. I tried to lighten the mood. 'What about Super Grover?'

Hiro rolled his eyes. 'Super Grover is for little kids. And I'm sick of eating at the kids' table.'

'So you think Poison Ivy has the answers?'

Hiro tipped his head to one side. 'Are you *jealous*?'

'What?' My mouth fell open. 'Jealous? Of that feral, fleabitten hippy? I don't think so.'

I totally was.

'You said you wanted to be a hero, right?'

'Yes, but—'

'So *do* something! Be a hero! Don't sit around and wait until you're an adult, because it'll be too late by then. It'll be all tax returns and babies and subcontracting out your kitchen redesign. We have to act *now*.'

'I *am* acting!' I said. 'What do you think I've been doing for the past four years?'

Hiro snorted. 'Handing out fact sheets at the supermarket? A school vegetable garden? They're hardly world-changing heroics.'

I pulled away from him, stung. 'I'm only sixteen. This is the best I can do.'

'Is it?'

My mouth hung open. I had spent *my whole life* trying to make the world a better place. Hiro had been working on the Victory Garden for what, three months? And suddenly he was this amazing eco-warrior? What right did he have to tell me I wasn't doing enough?

'Great,' I said. 'So whenever I've talked about big change, you've been all *who cares* and *what's the point*. But the second some hippy gets her boobs out, you're suddenly on the bandwagon?'

'It's not about that, and you know it,' said Hiro. 'Look, I know their methods are extreme . . . but sometimes you have to break something in order to put it back together.'

What was Hiro *talking* about? Couldn't he see how wrong he was?

'What about the Victory Garden? And all our other bewildering? We've changed Valentine. Everyone is noticing it. Don't you think that *means* something?'

Hiro shook his head. 'It's not enough,' he said.

I hesitated. There was a part of me that agreed with him. It *wasn't* enough. It was all very well seeing people plant strawberries on their front porch, but was that going to change the world? Was the Victory Garden going to reverse global warming and ecological disaster?

I didn't know what the answer was. But I knew what it *wasn't*.

'So what, you think the planet's going to be saved by Poison Ivy and her goons?' I jerked my head back in the direction of the hippies.

'Her name was Storm. And you're being immature.'

I couldn't believe what I was hearing. 'Violence isn't the answer,' I said. 'Violence isn't going to change anyone's mind. We're not going to save the world by scaring people.'

I stopped again, remembering how many scare-mongering fact sheets I'd handed out, and how many doom-and-gloom proclamations I'd made at school assembly. Had *I* been trying to save the world by scaring people?

Hiro rolled his eyes. 'So we should all hold hands and dance in a circle and sing songs?'

I didn't know this Hiro. My smiley, gentle Hiro had vanished. This Hiro was as hard and smooth as glass. But like glass, I could see right through him. I knew that this was all a front. I knew my Hiro was there somewhere inside. But he didn't try to kiss me as we went our separate ways.

We said a terse goodbye at the train station, and I stomped home in a white-hot rage.

Fine, then. If that was the way he wanted it, then that's how it would be.

It wasn't until I was lying in bed with the lights out that I finally admitted to myself why I was so angry. It wasn't just that Hiro had acted like a typical drooling teenage boy when confronted with a pair of (admittedly very nice) breasts. It was everything else. Listening to Poison Ivy's negative, ugly rhetoric had cut too close to the bone. Because although I hated her and her stupid red dreadlocks and her inappropriate number of piercings, I recognised myself in her. Her sense of superiority over all others. Her unshakeable belief that her solution was the only one. She didn't listen. She only gave orders.

Was I like that? Was I just a cleaner, less feral version of Poison Ivy?

15

Saturday was scorchingly hot. I spent the morning lying on my bed staring at the ceiling, waiting for Hiro to call. I felt itchy and feverish. Why wasn't he calling? I wanted to pull out my phone and call or text him. I wanted a reaction. I wanted him to want me, to fight for me, to tell me that everything that had happened last night had been in my imagination.

Except it wasn't.

So I didn't call. Didn't text. I just lay there, like a zombie.

At midday, I got up and made myself a sandwich. There was one thing I could do to prove that I was right. I was going to the Green Valentine Display Centre, so I could inspect the mayor's ten-point plan myself. I *knew* it would be good. I knew it. She would have read my recommendations, and she'd have to be a crazy person not to see the financial and environmental benefits that I'd outlined.

The display centre was near the Town Hall, in a demountable painted green and white. There didn't seem to be anyone about, so I climbed the steps and pushed the door open, and was greeted by a blast of air conditioning. The room was blindingly white, with each of the ten points illustrated by a scale model and explanatory board. I made my way over to #1, my heart pounding in my chest.

1. Domestic greenspace: all front gardens to be laid with Lush Underfoot™, a luxurious specialty turf engineered to be vibrantly coloured and silky-soft underfoot. Other plants approved for domestic greenspaces include Weeping Elegance™, Variegated Vogue™ and Urbane Spray™. Due to health and safety concerns, the following gardening practices will be banned: composting, backyard chickens, bees, water recycling, use of animal manures as fertiliser.

I stared at the board. Genetically engineered lawns? Trademarked plants? Maybe I was mistaken. Maybe this was an early phase. Maybe the mayor thought that lawns were better than the existing concrete front yards that most Valentine houses had? I moved on.

2. Public greenspace: all median strips, verges, round-abouts and other public areas will be transformed into streamlined greenspace. They will reflect the stylish uniformity of our private gardens by using the same suite of designer greenery.

3. Domestic homes: uniform render and paint (white) on all homes. Grants will be made available to achieve this uniformity, in addition to domestic greenspace grants.

I thought I might throw up. This wasn't what I'd outlined. Had the mayor used *anything* from my ten-point plan?

4. Valentine High: a proposal is being delivered to the State Government to transform Valentine High into Valentine Business College. This would create a streamlined secondary educational experience designed to prepare students for careers in executive business positions. As well as a focus on standardised testing, the college will also deliver classes on networking, business vocabulary-building and leadership. State-of-the-art facilities will be included – including an e-business training hub, putting green and heated swimming pool.

The little scale model of Valentine High was pristine, all edges and angles. My heart sank as I looked at where the kitchen garden currently was. Mr Webber had known about this. That's why he'd looked so smug when he'd said the garden project would be cancelled. It was going to become an indoor heated swimming pool. I peered at the model in the desperate hope that, at the very least, there might be solar panels, but there was nothing. I felt myself drawn on, each white board delivering more and more bad news.

5. Valentine Heights: a multilevel deluxe shopping precinct featuring international brands and flagship stores, as well as cinemas, thirty restaurants and a 2000-space car park.

6. Valentine Acres: the unoccupied land in the northern wetlands will be repurposed into a premiere housing development, featuring luxury homes with spectacular views of a constructed lake, parklands, and the new Valentine Country Club (see below).

7. Valentine Country Club: an elegant, world-class private facility boasting an architect-designed 18-hole golf course,

indulgent day-spa, restaurant, gaming lounge and extensive conference facilities.

8. Rates: new price-point system for council rates – only pay for what you use!

9. Public buildings: Maternal Child Health Centre, Public Library, Youth Space Community Centre, Valentine Public Leisure Centre and Valentine Senior Citizens Centre to be streamlined, with services outsourced to Highfield Business Development Practice.

10. Safe Streets Scheme: a crackdown on vandalism and environmental terrorism. Installation of 1200 security cameras in commercial and residential areas.

I dragged myself home and went to bed, lying on my back and staring at the ceiling. I couldn't believe it. Poison Ivy had been right. The Green Valentine Scheme *was* diabolical. It wasn't a scheme, it was a *scam*, designed to remove every ounce of community from Valentine and replace it with a soulless, corporate toy village. There wasn't a single solar panel or water tank in sight. It was all big business and concrete. Valentine had been ugly before, but at least it had been *real* and ugly. And people had been starting to change!

My phone vibrated, and I nearly leapt off my bed, fumbling and dropping it on the floor before scrabbling for it, desperate to see the screen. Was it Hiro?

It was Tyson Okeke.

Tyson's Annual Christmas Bash 8 tonight. BYOB & thirst for shenanigans.

I threw my phone aside. As if I was going to Tyson's party.

I glanced at the calendar hanging on my wall. Only a few days left of school. What was I going to do with my summer holidays? I'd had visions of more sluggish hot days and glorious secret nights with Hiro. But all my dreams were gone. Dried up and wrinkled like old leaves. Maybe it was for the best.

I wondered what Hiro would be doing tonight. Would he be with Poison Ivy? There was a bitter, metallic taste in my mouth. What if he was with her right now? What if he hadn't called or texted because he was with *her*?

I paced my bedroom floor, feeling trapped and claustrophobic. I couldn't stay here. I couldn't just stew in the soupy heat and let my imagination run away with me.

Maybe I *would* go to Tyson's party. It would take my mind off Hiro. And Dev and Paige would be there. If anyone could cheer me up and distract me, it was them.

The party was in full swing by the time I arrived, just after nine. Music thumped in the lounge room, and there were people everywhere, the girls in skimpy dresses and bikinis, the boys in boardshorts, T-shirt optional. Everyone was drinking and laughing. Through the kitchen window, I could see fairy lights twinkling along the verandah, and the cool, inviting glow of the pool, lit by underwater halogens.*

'Astrid!'

---

* I know, I know. A heated pool. With lighting. Full of awful chlorines and chemicals. Worst environmental sinkhole you could find in suburbia. But it was really hot, and whinging about the pool to everyone wasn't going to make a difference.

A guy was walking out of the kitchen, holding a plastic cup overflowing with beer. I blinked, and it took a moment to remember where I had recently seen him. It had been outside . . . outside a house.

'Hi,' I said. 'How are your strawberries?'

His mouth twisted. 'The first one was amazing,' he said. 'But the birds got the rest.'

'You need some netting,' I said.

What was his *name*? I knew he'd been in my Chemistry class in Year Nine. He was on the soccer team. But what was his *name*?

'Um,' I said. 'I better go . . .' I hiked my thumb towards the backyard.

'Yeah, sure,' said Strawberry Guy.*

I found Dev and Paige sitting by the pool with their feet dangling in the water.

'Hey,' I said, plonking myself down beside them in relief. 'I was starting to think you guys weren't here. Do you know the name of the guy in there with the light brown hair? He was in Chem with us in Year Nine, and he plays soccer?'

Dev glanced at Paige, who looked down at the pool. 'Nope,' she said eventually.

I sighed. 'I'll ask Tyson,' I said. 'He knows everyone.'

We sat there for a moment, while I waited for them to ask how I was. I was going to tell them everything. About Hiro, and Poison Ivy and everything. I needed someone to

---

* Strawberry Guy? Was he going to be a superhero too? Was I going to fall in love with him and embark on a sweet yet doomed summer romance? No. I had to find out his real name. Paige would remember.

talk to. I needed my friends. I swished my feet through the water and rehearsed how I'd say it in my head.

'Aren't you going to apologise?' asked Paige at last.

I stared at her blankly. Apologise for what?

'For lying to me? For pretending you were at home when you were obviously off with your secret gardening boyfriend?'

I'd totally forgotten about her text message last night.

'I'm sorry,' I said. 'It's complicated.'

Neither Paige nor Dev said anything. I noticed that Dev's eyes were red-rimmed and he looked exhausted. Paige looked like she was waiting for me to say something. I didn't know what she wanted.

'So,' she said eventually, a frown creasing her forehead. 'You're not going to ask what happened? Ask Dev how he is?'

'Of course,' I said, as I heard my phone ping in my bag. 'I'm so sorry. Tell me everything.'

'Well . . .' said Dev, his voice small.

I glanced at my phone. It was him.

Hiro: I'm here. Meet me in the garage.

Hiro was here. At Tyson's place. He was *here*, and he wanted to see me. Maybe he'd changed his mind about going public with our relationship. I felt like I'd been given an electric shock – a massive jolt of fear and excitement and an aching need to touch him again.

'Hold that thought,' I said to Dev. 'I'll be back in a minute, okay? I promise.'

Tyson's parents' garage was the usual enormous concrete

box with a fuel-guzzling four-wheel drive parked in it.* It stank of petrol and cleaning fluid. Romantic, no. But it did offer us privacy.

My arms were prickling with nerves as I slipped in the side door and saw Hiro waiting over by the far wall. Was he still angry? Were we going to fight again? Was he going to dump me and tell me he was in love with Poison Ivy?

But then I saw his face, and I read everything there. He looked anxious and pleased to see me and vulnerable all at once. I smiled hesitantly, and he seemed to sink in relief, like he'd been tight with worry. He looked at me with his beautiful eyes, and I saw how he felt about me, and I knew that a million Poison Ivys couldn't make him stop loving me.

We kind of fell on each other, arms wrapped tight for a moment, just feeling each other breathe. Then there was kissing, and everything was okay again. Better than okay.

'I'm sorry about last night,' he murmured. 'I don't know what was wrong with me.' He pushed a stray lock of hair behind my ear, and stroked my cheek with his thumb. 'I know I was kind of ogling Storm. I'm a teenage boy – if you put boobs in front of me, it's hard not to look at them.'

'I looked at them too,' I said. 'It *was* hard not to. And she *does* have very nice ones.'

'Not as nice as yours,' said Hiro, then blushed. 'Er. I assume. Not that I'm trying to pressure you into anything. Obviously I'd love to see your breasts, but only if you're comfortable with it. I'm going to stop talking now.'

---

* 4WDs produce nearly three times as much CO_2 as a standard family sedan. How many times had Tyson's parents needed this ridiculously huge vehicle to travel off-road? I was betting zero. Zero times.

I laughed. 'I'm sorry I got so jealous,' I said. 'She just seems so . . . you know. Out there. Available. Adult. She makes me feel like a little kid.'

Hiro brushed his lips against mine. 'Trust me,' he said. 'You aren't a little kid. You are beautiful and sexy and brave and smart, and you are the only woman for me. You're amazing.'

'So are you.'

We kissed again, and my heart started to beat very fast. Hiro's hands slid under my shirt, and I moved in closer. This wasn't like our previous kisses. Usually things were slow, and sweet. But this was different. Everything felt raw and urgent after our fight. I didn't ever want to let him go. And after seeing Poison Ivy's topless dancing, I was feeling . . . braver. Ready to be a little more grown up. A little more ready for . . . more. I pressed myself up against Hiro and felt him groan in response. I slipped my hands under his shirt, and felt the smooth skin of his back. He bit my lower lip gently.

'Dude, what are you doing?'

It was Barney and Kyle, Hiro's stoner friends. We broke apart guiltily. I watched the colour drain from Hiro's cheeks, and he looked around, panicking, before affecting his usual glare. I tried to subtly straighten my shirt.

'You're dating one of the rich bitches?' said Barney, shaking his head. 'Man, you're such a hypocrite.'

Rich bitches? That was much worse than *Missolini*. I remembered how Hiro had called me a bitch the other day. Was that what he called me in front of his friends?

'We're not dating,' said Hiro, a little too quickly.

Kyle looked me up and down suggestively. 'Just a casual fling, then. Nice, man. She is kind of hot, I guess.'*

I waited for Hiro to defend me. I wasn't the type of girl who got . . . flung . . . in Tyson Okeke's garage!

But Hiro didn't say anything. At all. He just shrugged and ignored me. I stared at him, outraged.

'Astrid?'

Just when I thought it couldn't get any worse.

It was Dev and Paige. Paige looked furious. 'What's going on with you?' she asked. 'You just *left*.'

'Um,' I said. 'It's nothing.'

'Are you sure?' said Paige. 'What are you even doing back here?'

She gave Barney and Kyle a suspicious glance.

'Nothing,' I said. 'Really. Let's go back to the pool. Dev? You were going to tell me something.'

'Wait,' Dev stared at Hiro, then back at me with my rumpled hair and kiss-reddened lips. 'It's *him*, isn't it? Your mystery guy? It's Drug Dealer Guy from your garden!'

Barney frowned. 'Dude,' he said. 'You're dealing?'

'I'm not a *drug dealer*,' said Hiro with a scowl.

'No *way*.' Paige's mouth fell open. 'You're secretly dating *him*?'

'Do you have anything on you . . . you know, like, now?' Kyle asked Hiro.

I closed my eyes and took a breath. 'It's complicated,' I said.

'Is it?' asked Dev. 'Is he blackmailing you into dating him?

---

* Kyle didn't actually say 'fling'. The word he used did start with an f, though.

Does he have something you really want? Wait . . . is he selling you *drugs*?'

'What?' I said. 'No. Nothing like that.'

'Seriously, I'm not a drug dealer.' Hiro thrust his jaw out aggressively.

Dev raised an elegant eyebrow. 'You play the part well, regardless.'

'Astrid,' said Paige. 'We're worried about you. You've been so distracted and weird lately, and now we find out you're secretly dating . . .' She ran her eyes over Hiro with a disparaging toss of her head. '. . . *this guy*.'

'It's not like that,' I said. 'Hiro isn't like that.'

'Uh,' said Kyle. 'I think you'll find that Hiro is *totally* like that.'

He and Barney high-fived, and I glanced over at Hiro.

He was hunched over, glowering. In his skinny jeans and loose black hoodie, with his hair dangling into his eyes, he looked exactly the way Paige and Dev thought of him. Sullen, disengaged, resentful.

Dev made a face. 'Astrid, he's not the same number *or* the same colour as you. He's a *brown*, and a six at most.'

'Dude, you don't have to listen to this,' said Kyle. 'Let's go.'

Kyle and Barney wandered off, and after a moment, Hiro followed them.

He didn't even look at me.

'Okay,' said Paige after a pause. 'You're clearly in a very bad place right now. Maybe you need to meditate. Centre your *ki*. And then perhaps eat a tub of ice-cream and watch a few episodes of *Psychic Clutter of the Stars*.'

'Seriously, guys,' I said, 'Hiro really *isn't* like that. He's all prickly on the outside, but inside he's wonderful. He reads and he thinks and he cares about stuff. I never would have started bewildering if it wasn't for him.'

'Astrid,' Dev put a hand on his heart. 'Nobody knows better than me how easily the heart can be led astray. Remember when I fell in love with that guy who caught my train? I was convinced that he must be a poet, or an artist. I felt like I could see into his soul, even though we'd never spoken. Then when I finally mustered up the courage to go talk to him, it turned out he was a car salesman obsessed with football.'

'That's different,' I said. 'I thought Hiro was a loser at first too. But then I got to know him, and he isn't. People aren't always what they seem.'

'Sometimes they are.'

I was trying not to cry. 'You know he feels exactly the same way about you guys? Thinks you're totally shallow and brainless.'

Dev scoffed. 'Um, did he notice that we are the smartest people in Valentine?'

'He thinks all you care about is popularity.'

'Well, that just goes to show how little attention he pays to what's going on around him.'

I felt myself growing irrationally angry. 'Do you know what he calls us? *Missolinis*.'

Dev blinked. 'What? That sounds like a cocktail.'

Paige rolled her eyes. 'He *named* us? Like we're in some kind of teen movie clique? How incredibly original. And shouldn't it at least be *Msolini*?'

'Look,' said Dev. 'So this guy doesn't like us. Big deal. We're popular, and people get jealous of us. But you know what? I don't care. Just because we're popular doesn't mean we don't work hard. Being universally liked takes *work*. So does being an outstanding student, and a kickass musician. Heaven knows there aren't a lot of gay Indian boys who've found adolescence as enjoyable as I have. So I'm not going to feel guilty about it.'

'I wish you'd take the time to get to know him,' I said. 'I'm sure you'd change your mind.'

Dev looked around. 'I'd love to,' he said. 'But I don't see him anywhere.'

'Yeah, where exactly did he go?' asked Paige. 'If this guy is so amazing, why didn't he defend you against Barney and Kyle? Why didn't he try and convince us that he's worthy of you?'

I swallowed. Why *hadn't* Hiro said anything?

'To be honest,' said Paige with a toss of her head. 'Maybe he *is* worthy of you. Because lately you haven't been a particularly good friend. Dev spent all of last night crying on my shoulder. Where were *you*?'

I swallowed and remembered the look on Poison Ivy's face as I'd checked my text messages. 'I'm sorry I wasn't there,' I said. 'But this is bigger than that. We're helping people. We're changing the world.'

'Who *are* these people you're helping?' asked Paige, her forehead creased in a frown. 'And why do you care more about them than about your friends?'

I spread my hands. 'It's complicated,' I said again. Why couldn't she understand that what I was doing was important?

Paige stared at me. I didn't know what she wanted me to say. Finally, she shook her head sadly. 'It doesn't seem very complicated to me,' she said, and walked off.

Dev hesitated for a moment, then followed her.

I stood there, surrounded by shelves of paint tins and old suitcases, breathing in petrol fumes and feeling like I wanted to sink into the ground and become worm food.

Instead, I slunk out the garage door and headed for Tyson's side gate. It was hometime for Lobstergirl.

Music was thumping in the living room, and from the whoops and squeals coming from inside, I guessed that the general level of drunkenness had gone up a notch. I glanced back towards the pool, but didn't see Dev or Paige.

'Hey, Astrid. Did you find your friends?' It was Strawberry Guy.

I blinked up at him. He was quite good-looking, in a jock kind of way. He looked . . . uncomplicated. And he was smiling at me, and I really needed someone to like me.

'Do you want to dance?' I asked, grabbing his hand.

Then there was music. And dancing. And some sort of sticky, fizzy drink in a plastic cup. Then more dancing. Sweat rolled down my back and I turned my face up to Strawberry Guy, who grinned at me. I swung my hips. I remembered Poison Ivy and how *sexy* she'd seemed, dancing with Revolution without her top on. She'd seemed so . . . *powerful*. I wanted to feel like that.

'Do you want to get out of here?' I said into Strawberry Guy's ear, yelling to be heard over the music.

He looked down at me, and he didn't seem to be smiling as much as he had been before. 'I think maybe you should head home.'

I made a scornful noise and accidentally spat on him a little bit. '*Home?*' I said. 'Home is for losers.'

Strawberry Guy took my arm and gently led me away from the dancing into the kitchen. He took my plastic cup away, tipped the fizzy stuff down the sink and refilled the cup with water from the tap.

'Here,' he said. 'Drink this.'

I didn't want water. I wanted more of the fizzy stuff. I pushed the plastic cup away and it sloshed over Strawberry Guy's shirt. I giggled.

'Okay,' said Strawberry Guy. 'I'm going to call a cab. It's time for you to go home.'

He pulled out his phone and tapped at the screen.

'No,' I said. 'I'm having a *good time*. I don't want to go home. *You* go home.'

'Trust me,' said Strawberry Guy. 'You'll thank me in the morning.'

'*Thank you?*' I pushed him away. 'Who do you think you are? I'm not going to *thank you*. I don't even know your *name*.'

Strawberry Guy took a step back. He looked hurt.

Tyson came into the kitchen and looked at me with raised eyebrows. 'Astrid,' he said. 'You're embarrassing yourself. Go home.'

'I ordered a cab,' said Strawberry Guy. 'Can you make sure she gets in it?'

Tyson nodded. 'Cheers,' he said to Strawberry Guy, who was heading back into the living room.

Before he reached the door, Strawberry Guy turned.

'Damien,' he said, looking back at me. 'My name's Damien.'

I was going to open my mouth and say something devastatingly cutting, but a sudden wave of nausea sent me staggering to the bathroom, where I remained, curled around the cool white porcelain of the toilet, until Tyson came in to tell me that the taxi had arrived.

16

I woke up at about eleven the next morning, the sun streaming in through my bedroom window like daggers made of lightning. I wanted to die. The inside of my mouth tasted like old socks, and my head was throbbing so hard that I was afraid my skull would crack.

There was no possible way I could feel any worse.

Until.

Memories started returning. Dancing with Strawberry Guy – Damien. Falling over. Breaking something – a lamp or a vase. People looking at me with narrowed eyes and whispering. Dev and Paige being distant, then angry. And Hiro.

Hiro.

He'd walked off with Barney and Kyle as if I didn't mean anything to him. I felt a wave of nausea rise up inside me. He didn't want me. He'd just left.

I shut my eyes and the thumping in my head grew worse.

At least he hadn't seen me afterwards, drunk and ridiculous.

Unless.

I pulled out my phone, dread creeping over me.

I'd sent twelve texts to Hiro last night.

9:45   That was intense. I guess we should talk?

10:30   Are you mad at me?

11:26   I should be mad at YOU. You're the one who just walked off.

12:09   what the hell would you know I'm too good for you anyway

12:46   I found a new superhero his name is strawberry guy

1:13   why aren't you replying

1:15   are you with poison ivy

1:22   I miss you so much

1:38   I'm in love with you

1:42   please reply

1:43   please

1:44   please

I'd had zero replies. I moped on my bed for as long as I could, but was eventually driven downstairs in the search for tea and toast.

Mum and Dad were sitting at the kitchen table.

Together.

That was when I knew things were serious.

'Your principal called us earlier,' said Mum. 'He must be very concerned about you, to call on a Sunday.'

I sighed. 'Doesn't he have a life of his own?'

'I know things have been difficult for you lately,' said Mum. 'With your dad and I separating.'

'*Temporarily* separating,' Dad corrected, and Mum winced a little.

I considered playing the angsty teen card. Maybe I should blame it all on their separation*, tell them how upset and confused I was by it all. I'd always been the perfect daughter – surely I had a few get-out-of-gaol free cards up my sleeve.

'Look,' I said. 'You guys know me. You know I'm not doing anything stupid. You trust me, right?'

Mum and Dad exchanged a glance. Mum looked uncomfortable. 'Mr Webber says you've been seeing someone. An unsuitable boy.'

I felt my jaw drop. They didn't trust me. They thought I was sneaking around at night with some scruffy no-good boy, making out in dark alleyways.

I swallowed. That *was* what I'd been doing.

'Is that where you've been going at night?' asked Mum. 'When you say you're jogging?'

Dad turned to look at her. 'You've been letting her out at night? On her own?'

'She said she was jogging,' said Mum. 'I didn't have any reason to suspect she was lying.'

'What were you thinking?' asked Dad, his voice getting louder. 'She's a *teenage girl*, of course she's lying.'

'Oh and you'd know all about teenage girls, wouldn't you? You're dating one.'

'Very mature.'

Mum snorted.

'I'm not surprised, really,' said Dad. 'That you're neglecting our daughter. You're off every night doing who knows

---

* Dad could say what he liked, but I knew what was going on.

what, while she's sneaking out to sleep with her drug-dealing boyfriend.'

'He's not a *drug dealer*,' I said. 'And we're not sleeping together. Calm down, both of you!'

Mum and Dad looked taken aback. It was clear I was going to have to play the grown-up in this discussion.

'You know me,' I said. 'You know I'm not going to do anything stupid. I'm not out every night drinking or taking drugs or doing inappropriate things with boys. I'm *gardening*.'

Dad blinked. 'Is that what the kids are doing now?' he asked. 'Is it like chroming or dogging?'

'Shut up, Greg,' said Mum. 'She means the night-time gardening.' She looked at me. 'That's right, isn't it? It's you, doing all that.'

I hesitated, then nodded.

Dad went a funny colour. 'You're the eco-terrorist?'

Mum rolled her eyes.

'We call it *bewildering*,' I explained. 'We wanted people to realise that Valentine can be beautiful, we just need to bring a little nature in. And it's working, Dad. People are really paying attention. Did you see someone has started a petition to get the supermarket to stock more organic produce? A petition! Started by someone other than me!'

'You're breaking the law. I won't have it under my roof.'

He said it before he realised that I didn't live under his roof. I saw his stern expression falter a little. 'You're not old enough to understand the implications of what you're doing.'

I wanted to scream. *He* was the one who didn't understand. 'I'm doing something *important*, and you're treating me like a child!'

'You *are* a child.'

I made a frustrated noise. 'You're not *listening*.'

What was going on? I was acting like a teenager, and my parents were treating me like one. Why had they suddenly stopped trusting me? Why was I yelling instead of calmly explaining the situation? What was going to happen next, was I going to storm off to my room and slam the door?

'You're grounded,' said Dad.

I stared at him. I waited for Mum to say he was wrong. But she looked down at her mug of tea and nodded slightly.

Fine.

If they wanted a typical, hormonal, unmanageable teenage daughter, they could have one.

'I *hate* you,' I said, bursting into tears. I fled to my room, slamming the door so hard that a framed picture of me, Paige and Dev fell off my dressing table. It was the best feeling I'd had all day.

I sat down on my bed and fumed. They couldn't really ground me. Once Dad left, Mum would come and laugh about it all, and everything would be okay. Maybe.

My phone chimed.

Hiro: Come outside.

I snuck out of my bedroom and down the stairs. Mum and Dad were still in the kitchen, talking quietly. I headed out the back door and round the side of the house, and saw a hunched figure standing by the front gate. My heart leapt into my throat, and I felt like I might explode from the sheer joy of just *seeing* him again. He'd come back. He'd come back to apologise. He'd just needed to cool down.

I knew I probably shouldn't forgive him.

But I also knew that I would.

Because he was Hiro. He was *my* Hiro, and I hated the shape of my life without him.

'Hey,' I said.

Hiro moved his head in a fraction of a nod, but didn't look up at me. Why wasn't he apologising yet?

'Last night was intense,' I said, giving him an opening.

A flicker of an eyebrow raise. 'That's one word for it,' said Hiro.

A long, awkward pause.

'Sorry about the texts,' I said, squirming on the inside.

'Seemed like you had a good night.'

I wanted to grab him by the shirt and tell him it had been the worst night of my life. But I couldn't.

'So what can I do for you?' I said, trying to sound like I wasn't falling to pieces.

'I thought we should . . . you know.' Hiro managed to look even more uncomfortable. 'State where we stand.'

'Which is where?'

Another pause.

'This can't work,' said Hiro. 'You and me. It's fine when we're alone, but we can't go sneaking around forever. And now everyone knows anyway. Nobody'll understand. You're a perfect Missolini princess and I'm a stonery loser.'

'You're not a loser,' I said quickly.

'I'm not a stoner either, but that's hardly the point.'

'Is this because your friends know about us?' I asked.

Hiro shrugged. 'Partly,' he said. 'They think I'm a hypocrite, and they're probably right. I've spent my whole life hating people like you.'

'And you were wrong. This isn't *Romeo and Juliet*, you know. We have options besides breaking up or death. You changed your mind about me. I changed my mind about you. If we can become more open-minded, so can our friends.'

Hiro shook his head. 'I'm sorry.'

I didn't know what to say. I felt like I was made out of string that was slowly unravelling and being blown in different directions by the wind. Once all the string was unwound, what was left of me would tumble out and shatter on the footpath.

'So that's it?' I asked, my voice shaking. 'You're embarrassed that your friends know about me, so you want to break up?'

Hiro sighed. 'Look, Astrid, you know how I feel about you. But we both know it's not going to work out.'

'We don't know *anything*,' I said. 'You're chickening out because you're scared I'll affect your street cred.'

'It's not all about *me*, you know,' said Hiro.

'What do you mean?'

'You want me to fit into your life. You want me to improve my marks, and start thinking about going to university. You want me to be the kind of guy you can show off to your friends and bring home to meet your parents.'

'No, I don't.'

I totally did.

'And that's not who I am. I'm not that kind of guy. I'm not going to go to uni. I'm not going to take you to the school formal. Your friends will never like me.'

'They will! They just need to get to know you. The real you.'

'This *is* the real me. And your friends know it.'

'They *don't*!'

'What did Dev mean last night?'

I pretended not to know what he was talking about.

'He said I was a brown six. What does that mean?'

Hesitantly, I explained Dev's dating system. 'Brown is for emos and stoners. They're not *bad*. They're just . . . not very good at . . . stuff. Disengaged.'

'And I'm a brown.'

'I didn't say that.'

'You didn't exactly leap to my defence. What about the six part?'

I shifted uncomfortably. 'It's a ranking. How much status you have within your colour.'

Hiro closed his eyes.

'So let me get this straight. I can date other people who are brown. Or any other colour as long as they're a six as well.'

'I didn't make up the system,' I said. 'I don't even necessarily agree with it.'

'*Necessarily*?'

'Fine. I don't agree with it at all. It's a dumb system. There, are you happy?'

Hiro shook his head in disbelief. 'No, I'm not happy. You think you're this amazing crusader saving the planet. But you're not. You're not the solution, you're the problem.'

'That's not fair.'

'You have *no idea* how you appear to other people. You're snobby and aloof and you think you're better than everyone else. Just because you're pretty and popular, doesn't mean you're *right*. It doesn't mean you're *better* than anyone else.

Trying to save the planet doesn't give you free rein to treat people like shit.'

'Do you think I don't know that?'

He gave me a flat look, and all of a sudden he was the angry Hiro who had skulked into the kitchen garden all those weeks ago. I had a flashback to the look on Strawberry Guy's face when I'd told him I didn't know his name. I heard Paige.

Who are these people you're helping? And why do you care more about them than about your friends?

'What colour are you?'

I blinked. 'What?'

'What colour are you? And what number?'

I didn't say anything.

'Tell me.'

'It's not important.'

'Tell me.'

I sighed. 'I'm a gold ten.'

Hiro looked disgusted. 'And thus you prove my point.'

'No!' I said. 'I didn't mean that— I don't even believe in Dev's stupid system!'

My eyes filled with tears, and I squeezed them shut, trying to shake them off. When I opened my eyes again, Hiro was gone.

Numbly, I made my way back inside, through the front door. Mum and Dad were still sitting at the kitchen table.

'Astrid,' said Mum. 'Your father and I have talked it over, and while we appreciate your civic spirit, and your desire to do good, we're not sure that sneaking around at night is safe—'

'Don't bother,' I told them, my voice hollow. 'It's over anyway.'

I could tell they wanted more, but I didn't have anything to give them. I trudged upstairs to my bedroom and shut the door behind me.

What happened now? Was I supposed to cry?

I sat on my bed, feeling totally empty.

I'd never been dumped before. It was a new experience for me, and I didn't like it. Usually I gently told the guy that it wasn't going to work out. Most guys didn't seem to mind too much, it was all part of the high-school dating cycle.

I didn't realise it would feel like this. Like a part of me had been cut out.

I heard a car pull up outside, and my heart nearly leapt into my mouth. Maybe it was Hiro. Maybe he'd changed his mind, and asked Michi to drive him over so he could tell me straight away. I ran to my bedroom window and looked out. An unfamiliar red car was parked at the end of our driveway. I tried to peer in through the windscreen, but couldn't make out the driver's face. Nobody got out. After a moment I heard our front door close, and saw Dad walk to the car. As he opened the passenger door, the internal light came on and I saw the driver.

It was the Whippet.

The Whippet had come to pick up Dad. They were still together. He leaned over to kiss her, and I shut my eyes. I didn't need to see that.

I wondered if this was how Mum had felt when she first found out that Dad was cheating on her. This kind of hollow, bare emptiness. Like nothing would ever feel right again. But Mum was okay now. She was moving on with her life. She was *better* than okay. Better than she'd been in years.

Maybe that would happen to me. Clearly I was better off without Hiro. He was right, it was never going to work out. And it was better to find out earlier, instead of doing what Mum had done and throwing away seventeen years of my life.

And it wasn't like *he* cared. As soon as our friends found out about us, he'd bolted. He was ashamed of me.

I crawled into bed and pulled the covers over my head.

He was probably already over it. He was probably off with Poison Ivy, being edgy and disaffected and breaking laws.

I pictured them together, graffitiing a wall and smashing a window. Her eyes would be bright with adrenalin. She'd lean forward and press into him. He'd get his hands tangled in her dreadlocks, and he'd taste the metal of her lip stud.

Hiro and Storm. Storm and Hiro. They even *sounded* like they were meant to be together. Like two crusading superheroes. I was just a schoolkid, playing along.

I wanted to break something. I knew I was torturing myself, but I couldn't stop. I played the scene of the two of them over and over in my head, until all I could see were red dreadlocks against Hiro's olive skin.

I lay there all night, still fully dressed, wide awake. Night-time was the worst. The night had been my favourite time – the velvety darkness so safe and comforting, the chill of the night air exciting, promising new adventures and Hiro. Him and me, the only people awake. It felt like we'd been the only people in the world. But now there was no Hiro. Only me, all alone. The darkness was a thick, suffocating blanket. I thought the morning would never come.

But it did, and somehow I dragged myself out of bed and ended up at school. I felt like a ghost. I wasn't wearing any make-up. I hadn't even brushed my hair. Or my teeth. People avoided my gaze and whispered to each other. Everybody knew. I was a fallen dictator. All around the school people would be pulling down statues of me and cheering. I'd been exposed for who I really was – not a great leader, not a wonderful person, but a failure.

I avoided Paige and Dev – I couldn't bear to see their disappointed faces. I'd let them down, in the most horrible way. I wouldn't want to be friends with me either, if I was in their shoes.

My only consolation was that I didn't see Hiro. I saw Kyle and Barney, but he wasn't with them. When Kyle saw me, he made a rude gesture and Barney guffawed.

There were only four days of school left. Four days, and then I could hide my face for the whole summer holidays.

I stumbled into English, and Ms Manitas looked up. 'Astrid,' she said. 'Mr Webber would like to see you.'

Again? What was it this time? I dragged myself into Mr Webber's office and slumped into a chair. There was nothing he could say that would make me feel any worse than I already did.

'Astrid, Hiro Silvestri was arrested last night, trying to break into the Green Valentine Display Centre. The police believe he's part of a radical environmental group that's responsible for a series of illegal acts, including vandalism and arson.'

I stared at him.

'Is he okay? Did they let him go? Did they arrest anyone else?'

Mr Webber shook his head. 'It seems as if the others abandoned Hiro and let him take the flak. The police have released him to his parents.'

I swallowed. 'So what does this have to do with me?'

Mr Webber sighed. 'We know that you were involved too. The police have filmed you and Hiro on security cameras a number of times over the past month or so. They have footage of you destroying council property.'

'What? We never destroyed council property.'

Mr Webber raised his eyebrows, and I realised I'd just given him a confession of sorts. 'There is footage of you destroying a council garden bed.'

'Those plants were already dead! And we replaced them with fresh, healthy ones!'

'Nevertheless,' said Mr Webber, 'you broke the law. I've spoken to the police, and as you are both minors and this is your first criminal offence, they have agreed to waive any charges. However, there must be consequences for your actions. You are suspended for the rest of the week, and forbidden to enter the school grounds during the holidays. You're not to come back onto school property until the beginning of term next year.'

'But what about the kitchen garden?'

'You knew this was coming. In three months it'll be a building site.'

'Over my dead body it will.'

Mr Webber shrugged. 'It isn't *your* land, Astrid. It's the

school's. And as the school principal, I will decide how it will be best used. You have shown me that you're not up to this level of responsibility. I'm very disappointed.'

I tried to interrupt, but Mr Webber continued. 'You should know, Astrid, that my intervention was largely because of you. If this had just been Hiro, I would have been more inclined to let the police deal with the matter entirely. That young man is trouble, and I know that I'm partially responsible for putting you in his sphere of influence.'

'I'm not in his *sphere of influence*,' I said. 'I knew exactly what I was doing.'

'I'm sorry I threw you two together,' said Mr Webber. 'That's why I intervened. Because I know you have a great deal to offer at this school, and I hate to see you waste your potential.'

I stared at him. Was I supposed to be . . . grateful?

'Astrid, I'm sure you'll come to understand—'

I'd heard enough. Mr Webber wanted to suspend me? Fine. I stood up and walked out of his office, to his indignant astonishment. I didn't stop. I kept going, out the front door of the school and straight out of the school grounds. I was done, for this year at least.

17

Even though Mum and I had agreed we weren't doing Christmas, I still woke up at five am with a tingly, vibrating feeling inside my chest. It was as though sixteen years of Christmas-morning excitement had conditioned me, so every twenty-fifth of December I would wake up in this state, like Pavlov's dogs drooling at the ringing of a bell.

I heard Mum moving around in the kitchen and went to investigate. Even though I *knew* there was no Christmas this year, I still half-expected to see a Christmas tree twinkling in the corner of the living room, over an enormous mound of cheerfully wrapped presents. The little kid inside me shrivelled up at this final, unequivocal evidence that *Santa hadn't come.*

'Merry Christmas, darling,' said Mum, giving me a big hug.

'Merry Christmas, Mum.'

Mum handed me a cup of tea, and an envelope.

'What's this?' I asked.

'I know you said you didn't want to do Christmas,' she

said, looking guilty. 'But I thought this might come in handy.'

I opened the envelope. It was an annual subscription to The Diggers Club, a local heirloom-seed bank. I felt a stab of unhappiness. Where could I possibly plant seeds now that I was banned from the kitchen garden, and the police thought that the Victory Garden was some kind of eco-terrorist front?

'Thanks, Mum,' I said, giving her a smile that I hoped looked genuine. 'I didn't get you anything.'

'Not having to cook a turkey is the best gift you could have given me,' she said. 'I'm looking forward to spending a lazy day with my daughter.'

We ate crumpets with honey for breakfast, and instant noodles for lunch, and didn't get out of our pyjamas all day. We sat in front of the TV and watched the Queen's Message and that cartoon about the little boy and the snowman.

'Isn't this great?' said Mum.

'It sure is,' I said, but I was faking it a little.

I imagined Hiro and Michi sitting down to Maria's dinner table, which would be groaning with Christmas food, and felt a throb of miserable jealousy. What were Mum and I going to eat for dinner? Probably just toasted sandwiches or something.

I thought about last Christmas. Before the Whippet. Before Hiro. We'd gone to stay with my grandparents in Adelaide and eaten the turkey and the ham, and everyone had lovingly eye-rolled when I'd told them about how wrapping paper was ruining the planet. We'd eaten mince pies and pulled crackers and read out the stupid jokes. It had been corny, and clichéd, and entirely unremarkable. But it had been *Christmas*. This year, it was just a day like any other. Except it was a day where I couldn't call any of my friends, and every single program on TV reminded me of what I didn't have.

As the credits rolled on the *Vicar of Dibley* Christmas special, Mum hauled herself to her feet. 'I've been putting something off for ages,' she said. 'But I think I'd better get it over and done with.'

I looked at her curiously as she went into the kitchen and opened a drawer, pulling out a thick stack of white and red envelopes.

'Christmas cards,' she said. 'I haven't opened a single one. Most of them are from people who don't know . . . about your father and me.'

'Why don't you throw them away?'

'I don't know,' said Mum. 'I suppose it seems rude. And I'm going to have to get in touch with all of them eventually and tell them. But how am I supposed to do it? Call every single one? Take out an ad in the paper announcing that my husband slept with a twenty-five-year-old dental nurse and now my marriage is over?'

I shrugged. 'Surely you just change your Facebook status and everyone figures it out.'

Mum winced. 'I've been putting that off, too.'

'Let me do it,' I said. 'I'll change your Facebook status, *and* open all these cards and tell you if there's any juicy news or important messages.'

Mum looked relieved. 'Thank you.'

I opened all the cards, earning myself a nasty paper cut in the process. The jingling bells, cheerful reindeer and slightly creepy illustrations of the baby Jesus revealed no gossip or personal messages.

Dear Greg, Ellen and Astrid,

Hoping you have a Merry Christmas and a Happy New Year.

Love, People Who Pretend to Care About Your Lives.

What a waste of paper.

At the bottom of the pile there was an envelope, addressed to me, that I'd somehow missed. The letterhead announced it was from the Valentine City Council Mayor's Office. I held it for a moment, thinking. Maybe it was a letter from the mayor explaining that she'd accidentally forgotten to include any green features in the Green Valentine Scheme/Scam, and that she was rectifying this error immediately.

I opened the envelope. It wasn't a letter. It was a Christmas card, with Mayor Tanaka and her family standing in front of a glitzy fake Christmas tree. I opened the card.

Merry Christmas from the City of Valentine

That was it. No personal message. Not even a signature. I was about to toss it in the bin along with all the others, when something made me stop and look at the photo again. My hands started to tremble.

It was a standard family photo. The mayor. Her husband. Their daughter, who looked about nineteen. And their teen-age son. Their son who clearly didn't want to be there. Their son who wore a scowling, sullen expression that I knew all too well.

It was Hiro.

Mayor Tanaka was Hiro's mum.

He must have known about Green Valentine all along, and was just humouring me. Why didn't he tell me? How could I have been so stupid? Why hadn't I googled the mayor more obsessively? Surely there'd been other photos. Other mentions of her family. But I'd seen nothing. Maybe I hadn't found out before because I hadn't wanted to. Because I had to face facts now – I was all alone. I thought I'd found new allies this year – the new mayor, Hiro. But none of it was real. It was just me, and I was sick of trying.

I did the only sensible thing, and went to bed.

I woke up to the sound of something breaking outside. Were we being burgled? I sat bolt upright, my heart hammering. My bedside clock read 3:24 am. I suddenly felt hyper-aware that Dad didn't live here anymore. There was no man in the house to protect us.

A male voice shouted from outside. I frowned, listening, and then realised that it was the man who used to protect us doing the shouting. Dad was outside, and he sounded *really* drunk.

I crept downstairs, listening. I couldn't make out any words, but it sounded like Dad was . . . crying? And saying my mum's name over and over.

Mum was in the living room, wearing a dressing-gown and looking tired and angry.

'Oh honey, did he wake you?' She came over and gave me a hug. 'I'm so sorry.'

'What's going on?'

'It's Christmas. He's drunk. And . . .' She sighed. 'Last week I told him I want a divorce.' I heard Dad let out a choked sob. 'He isn't taking it very well.'

A divorce.

Not that I'd been expecting them to get back together. I didn't even really *want* them to get back together. But a divorce. It felt so . . . violent. So final.

Dad moaned outside. 'Ellen, please. It's Christmas.'

On the other hand, I wouldn't want to be married to that drunk guy in the front yard breaking our pot plants either.

'Greg,' said Mum through the door. 'You have to leave. Go home and we'll talk about this tomorrow.'

Dad pounded his fists on the door and mumbled something about mince pies.

'Seriously, Greg,' said Mum. 'I'm going to make one of two phone calls right now. One is for a cab to take you home. The other is to the police. You can choose which one.'

There was a pause outside. 'You promise I can come back tomorrow? And we can talk?'

Mum sighed again. 'Okay.'

Dad went quiet. Mum picked up the phone and dialled for a taxi. Then she put on the kettle.

'Herbal tea?' she asked.

I shook my head. 'No, thanks.'

'I'm so sorry, honey,' said Mum, fishing in the cupboard for a teabag. 'You shouldn't have to witness this. Your father should know better.'

I nodded. 'He's upset,' I said, and then felt like a rat for taking his side.

'I know, but being your dad should always be his first priority, and he doesn't seem to be doing a very good job of it at the moment.'

I picked at a chipped corner of the kitchen benchtop.

'And it's my fault too,' said Mum. 'I mean, he's upset because of me. And I know things are harder being a kid from a broken home. But I can't be married to your father anymore.'

'Mum,' I said. 'This is definitely not your fault. Dad cheated on you. He betrayed both of us. And now he's being a dick. He'll always be my dad, so I'll always love him. But I can totally see why you want a divorce. I don't blame you for anything.'

It was true. Mum seemed so much happier since Dad had left. It sucked to be Dad, but he should have thought of that before he hooked up with the Whippet.

Mum smiled weakly. 'This hasn't been a very good Christmas, has it?'

'I've had better ones.'

'We'll do better next year. I promise.'

I nodded. 'Next year.'

I went back to bed, but couldn't get to sleep. I kept seeing Hiro's face scowling out at me from the Christmas card. Hearing Dad's slurring voice shouting to my mum. And in the back of my mind, Valentine was already being transformed into a soulless, corporate wasteland, complete with designer shrubbery and genetically engineered deluxe lawn. I'd thought Valentine was bad before, but it was nothing compared with what it was going to turn into.

As soon as the first greyish light of morning crept between my curtains, I clambered out of bed and pulled on a light summer dress and a pair of thongs. I had to get out of the house. Had to clear my head. I needed to think. I needed a plan. The Victory Garden always made me feel better. Surely I could get away with it – it was Boxing Day and everything would be quiet. I'd breathe in the scent of summer earth. It was like what Paige said about meditation – it really did help to open up the mind and calm the spirit.

What if Hiro was there?

My heart leapt at the thought, full of swirling joy and terror. Maybe he would have realised that Poison Ivy and her goons were part of the problem. Maybe he was sorry. Maybe he'd want me back.

But he was the mayor's son. Even if he was there, I wouldn't want to talk to him. I was just going for the garden. To find some peace. I'd pull up weeds, and figure out a plan to stop the kitchen garden from turning into a heated swimming pool. I was Astrid Katy Smythe, and damned if I was going to let Mayor Tanaka bulldoze my capsicums.

Everything would be okay.

I turned the corner by the abandoned factory into the little side street where the Victory Garden was, and instantly knew something was wrong. A trail of dirt had been crushed into the road by heavy tyres. I looked up, and what was left of my spirit was crushed. The garden was gone. Every tomato, bean and pumpkin plant had been torn out of the ground and taken away, leaving bare dirt covered in footprints. The apple tree had been ripped out. The shopping trolley overflowing with potato plants was gone. Someone had even left an empty soft drink can on the ground. The lot had already started to revert to its previous state of decay. I took a few steps forward.

A single pink poppy lay on the footpath, its roots still crusted with earth. I picked it up and it drooped forlornly in my hands.

Who would do this?

My first thought was Poison Ivy. She clearly hated me and what I was trying to do. She was destructive and chaotic.

What if it was Hiro? said a nasty voice inside my brain.

No. It couldn't have been Hiro. Not after all the work we did.

Really? Are you sure?

Whoever it was, I was going to find them. I'd call the police. They'd be arrested for vandalism.

There was a sign attached to the chain-link fence. I walked over to look at it.

CITY OF VALENTINE
NO ENTRY
TRESSPASSERS WILL BE PROSECUTED

I stared at the sign, and went numb. It wasn't Poison Ivy. It wasn't Hiro. It was Mayor Tanaka. She thwarted my every move. In the comic book of my life, she was the supervillain. The big bad. But this wasn't a comic book, because I'd failed. I'd tried to save the world, and I'd failed. The Victory Garden was now an empty plot of crushing defeat.

Tanaka had won.

I couldn't call the police and report vandalism, because

I'd been the vandal. The council had taken back their land, and with it they'd shut down the only thing that made Valentine beautiful, and the only thing I had left.

What was the point anyway? Nobody cared about the Margaret River Hairy Marron. The Victory Garden was gone, and the kitchen garden was destined to become an indoor swimming pool. My friends hated me. Everyone hated the Invisible Garden Army and thought we were eco-terrorists. I hadn't managed to change the world even slightly. If anything, I'd made it worse.

Well, I was done. The planet was going to have to find another superhero to save it.

It was time to put on my pyjamas, turn on some truly depressing music and eat my feelings.

On New Year's Day, Mum tried to coax me out of bed. She offered me food, a shopping spree, and finally, out of desperation, told me that she'd donate a hundred dollars to the charity of my choice, as long as I got up.

Which was cheating, because then I had to. But Mum didn't specify how far I had to go, or how long I had to stay out of bed for. I went downstairs and watched *Maximum Midwifery* with her for half an hour and ate four muesli bars. Then I went back to my room and dragged the covers over my head.

'You have to get up,' said Mum. 'Do something. Go out.'

'Make me.'

'I'll call your father.'

I snorted. 'As if.'

Mum sighed. 'I didn't want to do this,' she said. 'But sometimes a mother has to be tough. Astrid Katy Smythe, if you do not leave the house tomorrow, I will donate five thousand dollars to Freeheart Citizens Alliance.'

I pushed the covers back. 'You wouldn't.'

The FCA was an anti-environmental group funded by some of the world's biggest polluters. They dominated the media, arguing for 'balanced views' on issues like climate change, and flooding the press with totally unscientific 'research' and made-up statistics.

Mum folded her arms. 'Try me.'

I scowled at her. 'You're evil.'

'I'm evil because I care. Are you getting up?'

'No.' I pulled the covers back over my head.

Mum came and perched on the end of my bed. 'I know it hurts now,' she said. 'I know you feel like everyone's against you. The first time you get your heart broken is bad, really bad. I know how you're feeling, and believe me when I tell you it will get better. You'll get over it, and everything will go back to normal.'

I didn't even know what normal was anymore.

'Honey.' Mum patted the doona. 'I know you liked this boy. But you've only known him a few months. It's not the end of the world.'

'What would you know?' I said through the doona. 'You don't know about love. Your marriage has ended, and you're not even sad. You don't feel anything. You're just a robot.'

I knew it wasn't true, even as I said it. But some stupid part of me figured, if I could make someone else hurt, then maybe I'd feel better. Maybe some of my hurt would be transferred.

Mum was silent and still for a moment. Then I felt the bed shift slightly as she stood up, and heard the click of my bedroom door and her footsteps down the stairs to the living room.

It hadn't worked. I felt worse than ever.

I was a terrible person. I'd spent so long trying to save the world, and hadn't paid any attention to the people around me.

A few hours later there was a knock on my bedroom door.

'Go away.'

'Happy New Year to you too,' said Paige, letting herself in. Dev followed close behind.

'Wow,' he said, looking around. 'You really are wallowing, aren't you?'

He went over and opened a window, while Paige perched on the end of my bed. I rolled over to face the wall. I couldn't face them. Not after what I'd done. I'd been a terrible friend. I'd said terrible things. I'd tried to act like I was better than them, and all for what? Nothing had worked. Nothing had changed. If anything I'd made the world a worse place to be in, not a better one. I couldn't imagine why Dev and Paige could *possibly* be in my bedroom, except maybe to tell me that our friendship was finally, utterly over.

'Seriously?' said Paige. 'That's how you're going to beg for our forgiveness? Instead of grovelling and admitting that you've been a terrible friend, you're going to sulk and mope?'

Forgiveness? I had a chance at forgiveness? I rolled back over to look at her. 'I don't know what I can say to make it right. I really screwed up.'

'Don't tell me,' said Paige. 'Tell him.'

I raised myself up onto my elbows so I could see Dev. 'I'm sorry,' I said. 'I wasn't there for you. That was terrible. You absolutely shouldn't forgive me.'

Dev looked quiet and sad. I'd really hurt him. 'You never even asked what happened, or whether I was okay.'

I blinked. 'I'm sorry,' I said again, and I meant it. 'I just got so wrapped up in my own stuff. Can you tell me now?'

Paige and Dev exchanged a glance. Dev shrugged. 'Okay.'

I sat up. 'Please,' I said. 'I want to know everything I missed out on.'

Dev sat down on my desk chair. 'Well,' he said, 'I followed Paige's advice and made a medium-sized romantic gesture in order to win Sanasar's heart.'

I remembered turning up at Hiro's house with my faux olive branch and felt a stab of grief, but squashed it down. For once, this wasn't about me. 'What did you do?'

'I wrote him a song.'

Wow. That *was* romantic. 'Did he like it?'

Dev tilted his head to the side. 'Ye-es,' he said. 'Sort of.'

'Just tell her already,' said Paige.

Dev winced. 'Okay,' he said. 'Well, after my lesson, I told Sanasar that I'd composed something that I'd like him to hear. So I sang the song. And . . . I mean, it's pretty clear what it's about. And I was nervous, but I think that made me sing *better*. So anyway, afterwards, he didn't say anything for a long time. And then he said, *I'm sure whoever you wrote it for will love it*, and then suggested I pitch it a bit lower and add a bridge before the final chorus.'

'So, did you tell him? That it was meant for him?' I asked.

'No,' Dev shook his head. 'He said it in this pointed way. He totally knew it was for him, he was just sparing my feelings.'

'Are you sure?'

Dev smiled weakly. 'He then proceeded to tell me about how he proposed to his fiancée with a song.'

'He has a *fiancée*?'

Dev looked sheepish. 'I guess my gaydar isn't as reliable as I thought.'

'Are you okay?' I asked.

Dev nodded. 'I will be.'

'I'm sorry things didn't work out with Hiro,' said Paige. 'But you must have known they wouldn't. I mean, he's . . .' She shrugged. 'He's definitely cute, in a kind of bad-boy way. But you know that's not really your thing.'

I picked at the stitching on my pillowcase. Hiro had definitely, unequivocally been *my thing*. But not anymore.

'I've never felt like this before,' I said. 'Like my heart's been ripped out and stomped on. I feel sad and hurt and used.'

'Welcome to my world,' said Dev.

'At least you're used to it,' I said. 'I have, like, six years of adolescent heartbreak to catch up on. I feel as if it's all come at once.'

'It sucks,' said Dev with a wry smile. 'But I've decided to make some changes. I went out for a coffee with Aaron Matthews yesterday.'

My jaw dropped. Aaron was in our year. He was one of the many guys who was constantly asking Dev out. Dev had *never* dated a high school guy before. In fact, to my knowledge, Dev had never dated *anyone* before.

'Really?' I said.

He nodded. 'Because you have been totally AWOL, Paige forced me to watch a whole season of *Extreme Horse Makeover.*'

'And you *loved it*,' Paige reminded him.

'*Love* is perhaps too strong a word. Anyway, I realised that I was like one of those horses. Maybe instead of endlessly searching for perfection in the form of unattainable guys, I should be paying more attention to myself. And maybe I was scared, like that one horse who wouldn't wear a saddle because it only had one eye. Maybe I need to see out of both eyes, and realise that I'm just too scared to commit to a relationship.'

Paige nodded. '*Extreme Horse Makeover* is so wise.'

'And that's no way to live,' said Dev. 'Sometimes you have to do something a bit scary, you know? You have to wear the saddle.'

I did know. I felt like everything I'd been doing for the past few months had been scary. I was sick of scary. I just wanted to be normal again.

'So . . . Aaron Matthews?' I said.

Dev shrugged. 'He's cute,' he said. 'And smart. And he has nice hands. Have you ever noticed his hands?'

I had not.

'Well, they're very nice.'

I nodded. 'Good for you,' I said. 'I hope it works out.'

It wouldn't. These things never did. We were all doomed to the same humiliating cycle of love and heartbreak, over and over again. This must be what books meant when they talked about *the human condition*. We had a disease. But I didn't say any of that to Dev. He'd find out soon enough.

'Wait,' said Paige. 'Aaron is what, a green seven?'

Dev tilted his head to the side. 'I'd say an eight.'

'But doesn't that mean you can't date him? He's not the same colour or number as you.'

Dev looked confused. 'Paige, you know the system isn't real, right? We made it up. This isn't *Brave New World*.'

Paige frowned. 'But you said Astrid couldn't be with Hiro because he was a brown six.'

Dev shrugged. 'That was shorthand for saying she's too good for him.'

Was I too good for him? Was he too good for me? I knew one thing – I was better than feral, grungy Poison Ivy. I sighed.

'Maybe you're right,' I said. 'Maybe it isn't meant to be. Maybe I fell for him because he was unattainable, because I knew it would never work out. And I guess the mature thing is to recognise that, instead of going the *Romeo and Juliet* route that will only end in tragedy.'

Dev's face twisted in a weird way.

'What?' I said.

'It's just—' He shook his head. 'Don't worry.'

'Tell me.'

Dev raised an eyebrow. 'To be perfectly frank,' he said, 'the problems that you and Hiro have aren't *Romeo and Juliet*-style problems. This whole situation is much more like *Pride and Prejudice*.'

'What's that supposed to mean?'

'The reason you kept fighting with each other is because he thinks you're an enormous snob and that you consider him to be socially inferior to you. And you do.'

'So you're saying that Hiro is Mr Darcy?'

Dev snorted. 'No, *you're* Mr Darcy.'

'What does that mean?' I asked.

'Lizzie thinks that Darcy is an enormous snob, right? That's her prejudice. And she's right. Darcy does think he's superior to her and her people. That's his pride. They're both right about each other.'

'So you're saying I'm an enormous snob?'

'I'm saying there's a reason why Hiro felt like you were trying to make him into something he wasn't.'

I swallowed. Dev was right. I *was* Mr Darcy. I thought I knew what was best for Hiro. I thought he'd be better off if he was more like me – if he tried harder at school and went to uni.

'But . . .' I tried to sort my brain into some kind of order. 'But I was trying to make him better. Getting better marks and engaging with schoolwork is *better*. That's not me being a snob.'

'Sure it is,' said Paige. 'They're your values. Not his.'

'But . . .'

'Don't get me wrong,' Paige continued. 'They're my values too. In fact, they're the values of a *lot* of people. But they're still values, and if Hiro has different values, then sure, you're allowed to talk about it, and debate it. But you can't expect him to change just so he can be more like you.'

When did my friends get so wise?

I told them about Hiro being the mayor's son, and about the whole Green Valentine debacle. They nodded knowingly.

'Dad's cleaning business has lost the contract for all the council buildings,' said Paige. 'Apparently some big corporate something-or-other is taking over. And Mum has to reapply for her job at the leisure centre.'

'My parents are devastated,' said Dev. They ran the local teen drop-in centre, which offered counselling services as well as an all-ages live music venue. 'The council have cut all their funding, and the centre can't operate without it. We'll probably have to move.'

'Oh, and did you hear? Patchwork Rhubarb is closing down. Apparently that block of the shopping strip is where some big new mall carpark is going.'

I stared at them both, and something started to dawn on me. Something that had been right in front of me all along, but I'd been too self-absorbed to see it.

Dev and Paige stayed for another half hour or so, and made me promise I'd hang out with them in the next couple of days. I walked them to the front door and gave them each a long, heartfelt hug.

'See you soon,' said Dev.

'You've got a whole season of *Big Hair Academy* to catch up on,' said Paige. 'Um, but maybe shower before you come over to watch it.'

I shut the door behind them, feeling better than I had in days. Even though everything else had fallen in a heap, at least I still had my friends. That was something.

I wondered where Mum was. In her room, probably. Was she mad at me? I knew I should find her and apologise. But I felt exhausted. One step at a time. I was about to head back up to my room, when the doorbell rang. I went and opened the door, assuming Dev and Paige had forgotten something. A tiny spark inside me hoped it would be Hiro.

It was the Whippet.

I stared at her, shocked. I hadn't spoken to her since I'd found out about the affair. And even before then it wasn't like we'd ever had a proper conversation. She looked tired too, like Dad. I'd assumed that she would have been delighted that Mum and Dad had split up. She'd gotten what she wanted; she should have been glowing and happy.

I heard a noise behind me, and turned to see Mum, standing in the hallway. She didn't look at me, and I knew she was still hurt by what I'd said. Mum's eyes locked onto the Whippet, and for a moment I thought she was going to attack her, but then her gaze softened and she came to stand beside me.

'Jessica,' she said. 'This *is* a surprise. Come in.'

The Whippet crept into the living room, her shoulders hunched. She looked like she'd entered a military zone and was certain of execution. Her enormous eyes were even bulgier than usual, and her hands were shaking.

'What can we do for you?' asked Mum, her voice all calm politeness.

'I-I wanted to apologise for Greg's behaviour,' said the Whippet, not looking up. 'I didn't know that he came here on Christmas night.'

Mum's expression didn't crack.

'I—' The Whippet took a shaky breath. She looked like she might faint. 'I know that what I did – with him – was wrong, and terrible. I'll never really forgive myself for it. I have no excuses, and neither does he. You are absolutely right to kick him out, and I'm not just saying that because you kicking him out means I get to be with him.'

Mum blinked, looking slightly bewildered. She still hadn't looked at me.

'And Greg needs to respect your choice,' said the Whippet, her voice barely more than a whisper. 'I know he's struggling right now – especially with everything to do with the business. But coming over here on Christmas night—' She glanced at me and lowered her voice even more. '*Drunk.* That was terrible.'

And for the first time, I saw the whole thing from the Whippet's point of view. She'd fallen in love with her boss – a married man. She'd given in to temptation, and had destroyed a marriage. Now she had the man, but he wasn't strong and charming anymore. He was a shuddering wreck who, instead of embracing his new life and partner, was begging to be let back into his old marriage. That had to be hard for her.

I could see Mum was thinking the same thing. 'It's okay, Jessica,' she said. 'I understand. It's not your fault – not this part, anyway. Greg's grieving because he's learnt he can't have his cake and be married at the same time. But he's a grown man, and he doesn't need you to apologise for him.'

The Whippet ducked her head in acknowledgement.

'But I appreciate you coming,' said Mum. 'Thank you.'

'You're welcome – thank *you* – I'm sorry,' said the Whippet, all in a confused rush.

She turned to me as she headed back to the door. 'Greg told me that you're behind all the gardening. I think you're brave. It's all so beautiful. My grandmother used to grow roses and I loved them so much.'

I felt a little taken aback. 'Um,' I said. 'Thank you. What did you mean when you said Dad was struggling with the business?'

'It's the new council scheme,' said the Whippet, a flash of anger suddenly animating her pale face. 'There's a new rates system which makes it almost impossible for independent businesses to operate. Greg's under a lot of pressure to sell to a dentistry franchise that gets a big rates discount from the council.'

'Right,' I said. 'Thanks for letting us know.'

The Whippet almost curtseyed, then slunk out. Mum shut the door after her, and started back up the hallway.

'Mum?' I said.

She stopped.

'I'm sorry. I shouldn't have said any of those things to you earlier. I know you're hurting too.'

Mum turned around and smiled. 'It's okay,' she said. 'Sometimes it's easy to forget that you're a teenager.'

I heard the Whippet's car pull out of our driveway.

'Poor thing,' said Mum, heading into the kitchen and switching on the kettle. 'Greg is going to walk all over her. Can you imagine? I bet she lives in some tiny one-bedroom apartment, and he's mooching all over it while she waits on him hand and foot.'

'Maybe she'll learn to stand up for herself,' I said.

Mum looked dubious. 'Maybe,' she said. 'I hope so.'

Back in my room, I dug out the comic book that Hiro had made for me. *Lobstergirl and Shopping Trolley Guy, Vol 1: The Victory Garden.* I must have read it twice a day, when Hiro and I were still together. It didn't look like there'd be any other volumes.

I opened it to a random page. Shopping Trolley Guy's shopping trolley had been hurled off the roof of the abandoned factory by the book's supervillain – a power-hungry developer who had been poisoned by an oil spill and left a greasy trail of pollution everywhere she went. I should have figured it out earlier. Hiro had been trying to tell me about his mum all along.

Lobstergirl was holding Shopping Trolley Guy by the wrist with one of her red pincers. The other clutched an old electricity cable – the only thing stopping them both from tumbling off the cliff to their certain death.

Let me go! shouted Shopping Trolley Guy. *Save yourself!*

Don't you remember? Lobstergirl's expression was defiant. *I never let go.*

I never let go.

I pressed the comic to my face. Hiro had made this. His hands had been on it. I wanted to absorb him, and maybe absorb some of Lobstergirl's certainty and determination.

I felt like I was trapped in a cage. I had to get out, back out into the darkness, the soft velvety night where adventures could be had and things could grow. Not just green things, either. Other things had grown in the Victory Garden. Hiro and I had grown closer, and maybe I'd grown up, a little. I didn't belong here in this little girl's bedroom, papered with Greenpeace posters and academic achievement awards. I belonged out *there*. My hands itched to be deep in loamy earth.

But the Victory Garden was gone. My rage crackled alight again, burning hot and deep in my belly.

I remembered something Hiro had said.

Sometimes it feels good just to break stuff.

I put the comic down carefully. My hands were shaking.

I was going to break something alright.

I pulled on a hoodie, a pair of jeans and comfortable sneakers, before looking at myself in the mirror.

'My name is Lobstergirl,' I told my reflection. 'I never let go. And tonight I'm going to break some *rules*.'

19

I stood on Hiro's front doorstep, clutching the Lobstergirl and Shopping Trolley Guy comic in my hand, rehearsing my speech. I didn't care if he was ashamed of me. I didn't care if he didn't want to be my boyfriend. I didn't care if he thought I was a ginormous snob and he never wanted to speak to me again. I had started this with him, and I wanted him to be there when we finished it. One more night, and then we could go our separate ways.

Behind me, a streetlight pinged on as the sun sank below the horizon. A breeze stirred the immaculate lawn in Hiro's front yard, and I shivered. I had no idea how Hiro would react when he saw me. What if he slammed the door in my face?

I raised my hand to knock, but before I could, the door opened, revealing Michi wearing sneakers, shorts and a David Bowie T-shirt, clearly heading out for a run. She blinked at me in surprise.

'Is Hiro home?' I asked.

Michi frowned. 'I thought he was with you.'

'No. How is he? I heard he got arrested.'

'Yeah,' said Michi. 'He's fine. Our parents went mental, of course. But that was two weeks ago. You haven't seen him since then?'

I shook my head. 'We . . . He broke up with me.' Saying it out loud felt like one of the most difficult things I'd ever done.

'Wait,' said Michi. '*He* broke up with *you*? Is he insane? Has he *seen* you?'

I felt myself go red. Of course he wasn't here. I knew exactly where he was.

'I-I think he's with Poison Ivy.'

Michi raised an eyebrow.

'Storm,' I explained. 'You know. The ferals from the other day.'

'Oh,' said Michi, a dark look on her face. 'I'm going to kill him. *Then* I'm going to kill her.'

I remembered Michi's reaction when I'd mentioned Storm in Maria's garden.

'Do you know her?'

Michi paused, then took a step back into the house, holding the door open for me. 'You'd better come inside,' she said.

We went into the kitchen. There was no sign of Hiro's parents. I perched on a stool, and Michi leaned against the counter.

'Storm was my high school best friend,' she said.

I blinked. 'She's from Valentine?'

'Back when her name was Alison Bainbridge.'

I *knew* her name wasn't really Storm.

'We became friends on the first day of Year Seven, and were totally inseparable. We were both very idealistic about making the world a better place. We organised a fundraiser to save this all-ages music festival we used to have, and a petition to protest the sexist restrictions Valentine High used to have on uniform, and what sports girls were allowed to play.'

Sounded familiar.

'But halfway through Year Twelve, something happened. She started hanging out with these radical environmentalists. You know, the ones who actually kind of *are* terrorists. I never wanted things to get violent. That's not the way forward. We had a massive fight about it, and we stopped speaking. Then before I knew it, she was all dreadlocks and hemp and calling herself Storm or . . . What did you call her?'

'Poison Ivy.'

Michi chuckled. 'Poison Ivy. I like that.'

I frowned. 'Does Hiro know her then? He never mentioned that they'd met before, but they must have if you two were friends.'

'I doubt he realises,' said Michi. 'She's unrecognisable. In high school she was a straight-A student. She ruled the school. She was one of those girls everybody loved. Everything was easy for her, you know?'

I knew. Poison Ivy had been a Missolini.

'I bet *she* realises, though,' I said. 'Who Hiro is. Who his mum is.'

Michi looked at me in surprise. 'Mum?'

I nodded. 'I think that's why Poison Ivy wants him. She knows that if she can expose the mayor's son as being one of the vandals, it'll totally undo her campaign.' I paused for a moment of grudging respect for Poison Ivy. Then my seething hatred kicked in again. 'What a bitch.'

Michi's face was pale with worry. 'We can't let Hiro get into more trouble,' she said. 'What if Poison Ivy's got some devious plan to get Hiro arrested again?'

'If she does, she'll also have someone filming it to make sure that everyone sees.'

'I'm going to rip her dreadlocks out,' said Michi between gritted teeth.

'Not sure that would play so well on YouTube either,' I told her. 'Anyway, you should wait here in case Hiro comes home. You can try and talk some sense into him.'

Michi nodded. 'But where will you go?'

I shrugged. 'If *you* wanted to stick it to the mayor, what would you have her son vandalise?'

I spotted them around the side of the Town Hall, hiding in a pool of darkness between streetlights. One of the dreadlocked goons tried to stop me as I approached, but then he saw my face and stepped aside.

Hiro was nowhere to be seen. I took a deep breath and marched up to Poison Ivy. She was wearing her usual low-slung fisherman's pants, and a skimpy singlet with Che Guevara's face on it.

'Hey,' I said.

She looked at me as if I was some kind of disgusting and irritating insect. 'What are *you* doing here?'

'Where is Hiro?'

'*Who*? Oh, your little friend. How the hell should I know?'

I narrowed my eyes. 'Stop playing games, *Alison*. I know your deal.' I glanced around the group of hippies, and noticed one of them swiftly conceal a video camera behind his back. 'Subtle,' I said. 'So I suppose you were planning to . . . what, leak it online? Sell it to a local news station? Imagine the headlines: *Mayor Disgraced by Terrorist Son*.'

Poison Ivy looked like she was going to deny it, but then her face spread in a smirk and she shrugged.

'You're an idiot,' I said. 'Have you *met* the mayor? She's ruthless. If she catches Hiro vandalising the Town Hall, she'll use it to her advantage. She'll tell everyone that not even her own family are exempt from her new anti-vandalism laws. It'll just make her stronger. People will respect her for taking a hard line, and you'll have just confirmed her argument that this suburb is full of eco-terrorists!'

Poison Ivy sneered. 'You'll say anything to get your boyfriend off the hook.'

That was when I realised. Hiro wasn't there. Poison Ivy had tried to lure him to the Town Hall, but he hadn't come. Something wild and roaring lit up inside me.

'You haven't seen him at all, have you?' I asked, just to be sure.

Poison Ivy gave me a withering look. 'No,' she said. 'I guess underneath all that badass attitude, he's just a goody-two-shoes like you.'

I was done. I had nothing else to say to her. I turned to leave.

'Wait,' said Poison Ivy. 'While you're here . . .' Her mouth curved in a smile. 'Do you want to be a little bit bad?'

I noticed for the first time that she was holding an egg carton. I felt a jolt of recognition, a flashback to when Hiro had first proffered me a seed bomb from an egg carton, back at the very beginning of all this.

Poison Ivy opened the carton. Instead of it being filled with seed bombs, it was filled with eggs.

'They're . . . *well aged*,' she said with a savage curl of her lip.

She lifted one out carefully, and then, in a smooth, sinuous movement, tossed it against one of the windows of the council building. The egg burst and splattered into bits of shell and yolk. It didn't take long before the smell hit us. It was almost overpowering.

Poison Ivy looked at me speculatively. 'Do you want a go?' she asked, proffering the egg carton.

Sometimes it feels good to break things.

I felt myself reach out.

It would feel so good to *break* something. To be bad. To break the rules and show the cretins in the council what I really thought of them. To inconvenience them just a tiny bit, so they would know how much they'd inconvenienced me. To destroy something.

'Or perhaps you'd like to do something a little more *extreme*,' said Poison Ivy, and she nodded towards the trolley. I peered inside. It was full of bricks and chunks of masonry. I blinked. They were going to throw rocks at the Town Hall. And it was only nine pm. There could be people in there. Late meetings. People could get hurt. Valuable property might get damaged or destroyed.

I took a step back, withdrawing my hand from the carton.

The eggs weren't even free range.

'I didn't think so,' said Poison Ivy. 'People like you, you're all talk.'

I knew I should walk away and forget about Poison Ivy and her feral minions. But I wasn't the kind of person who could turn the other cheek and walk away from a fight. People like her gave people like me a bad name. All I wanted to do was make people think more. And I knew that if people thought more, then they'd care more, and together we could make the world more beautiful. But Poison Ivy didn't want that. She wasn't trying to recruit people to her way of thinking, she was trying to make enemies. She wanted to destroy the system, not fix it.

'I'm not,' I said quietly. 'I'm not all talk. I do things to help, not to hurt, and I will continue to do them no matter how many people tell me I can't.'

'Yeah,' said Poison Ivy, her voice heavy with sarcasm. 'You're a regular little revolutionary.'

I'd had enough. 'Don't patronise me. You're the one wearing a Che Guevara top,' I snapped. 'Do you even know who he is?'

'Of course I do,' she said sneeringly. 'He deposed Fidel Castro in the Cuban Revolution.'

I shook my head in disbelief. 'No, he didn't,' I said. 'Let me tell you something about the Cuban Revolution. The Cuban *Garden* Revolution.'

Poison Ivy adopted a bored, superior expression but one or two of her goons seemed to be genuinely interested.

'Okay,' I said. 'In the 1960s Cuba spent most of their agricultural space growing lucrative export crops – mostly tobacco and sugar. Because they had these massive mono-cultural crops, they needed a whole heap of pesticides and synthetic fertilisers. They couldn't get them from the US, because of the trade embargo. Instead, the Soviet Union was Cuba's biggest source of trade. When the Soviet Union collapsed in 1989, Cuba's trade collapsed too. Food, medicine and gasoline became scarce, and their enormous crops of tobacco and sugar became worthless and impossible to harvest and transport. They also lost all their access to synthetic fertilisers and pesticides. The people of Cuba started to starve – their calorie intake dropped by a third. All of a sudden, Cuba had to produce twice as much food, using half the amount of synthetic fertilisers.'

'Oh my God, who *cares*,' groaned Poison Ivy. 'Why are you still *here*?'

'Shh,' said one of Poison Ivy's goons. 'Let her finish.'

Poison Ivy seemed so utterly taken aback that someone had dared stand up to her, that she fell silent. The goon gestured at me to continue.

'So the Cubans changed. In Havana, they converted vacant lots, plazas and rooftops into intensive gardens. Schools and businesses had their own kitchen gardens. They threw out all their petrol-guzzling farming machinery and started using humans, wheelbarrows and oxen. Because they were growing so many kinds of crops all together, the city's biodiversity levels increased so they didn't need to use pesticides anymore. They practised crop rotation and companion planting. They created their own fertiliser using animal manure and compost. And today, nearly all the seasonal produce consumed in Havana is grown within a thirty-mile radius. They produce their own eggs, honey, chickens and rabbits. They're a world leader in worms and worm farm technology. And everything is organic.'

Poison Ivy opened her mouth to make what I was sure would be a snide remark, but I kept talking.

'That's a *real* revolution,' I said. 'Our body converts food into energy, right? And energy is a kind of power. By growing our own food, we're taking that power into our own hands. Taking it away from ginormous corporations that chop down forests and drench our food in toxic chemicals and over-process and over-package everything. Growing our own food makes us powerful. It's transformative. It's therapeutic. And at the end, you get strawberries. So you can keep your rocks, and your carcinogenic fire-twirling, and your battery-farmed eggs. I'm off to change the world.'

The goons burst into applause. Poison Ivy snapped at them to shut up, but I didn't care about her any more. I had better things to do.

It was nearly ten o'clock when I reached school. The night was clear and cool. I slipped in through the front gate of the school, and headed across the footy oval to the kitchen garden.

Orange light spilled from the nearly streetlights, illuminating the garden gate. Open. I felt a chill run through me. I was sure I'd closed it when I left . . . how long ago was it? It felt like forever since Mr Webber had suspended me and school had ended. I hoped the seedlings would be alright. It hadn't rained for a few days – I'd need to water.

I saw a shadow move over by the tomatoes and snapped back to reality. Someone was in my garden. Was it one of Poison Ivy's goons, come to teach me a lesson? Or was it someone from the council, ripping up plants like they had done at the vacant lot? Either way, they weren't going to be too pleased to see me.

I could leave. I could run home and hop into bed and pull the covers over my head. I'd stay away from school – I didn't need to see them bulldoze my garden. Who had I been kidding anyway? I was too young to make a difference. I should just put my head down, study hard, get into a good university and find a job where I could make a difference. It'd only take, what, ten or fifteen years?

In fifteen years' time, it might be too late.

I thought about Lobstergirl in Hiro's comic book.

'I never let go,' I whispered to myself, and strode into the garden.

'Show yourself,' I demanded of the shadowy figure, which jumped slightly, then went very still.

'Jesus, Astrid! You scared the *crap* out of me.'

It was Hiro. Hiro was here in the garden. My garden. *Our* garden.

'What are you doing here?' I asked, moving forward so I could see him properly in the dim light reflecting off Valentine's dark orange clouds.

Hiro gave me a long look that I didn't understand. It was somewhere between sad and angry and defiant. 'I'm gardening,' he said at last.

'There's no point,' I said. 'It's going to become an indoor swimming pool.'

'I know,' he said.

We watched one another for a moment, each of us trying to read the other.

Hiro took a half step towards me. 'What are *you* doing here?'

I swallowed. 'I-I don't know. I was angry and I wanted to *do* something. I went to the Town Hall. But I can't do it. I can't be like you. Like them.'

I saw Hiro frown. 'Was Storm there?'

I nodded. 'I thought you would be too.'

'Me?' Hiro asked. 'After they abandoned me and let me get picked up by the cops? They planned it all along, you know.'

'It's because of your mum,' I told him. 'Poison Ivy knows who she is. She wanted to frame you, to discredit the whole Green Valentine campaign.'

Hiro winced. '*You* know about my mum.'

'She sent me a Christmas card.'

'I should have told you. But at first you were all rah-rah on her team, and I was so angry with her. And then you were angry with her too, and I was afraid you'd be angry with me. I . . . I didn't want to complicate things.'

'I get it,' I said. 'All superheroes have secrets.'

'I don't think I can be a very good superhero in this particular story,' said Hiro ruefully. 'I'm pretty sure I'm the son of the archvillain.'

I shrugged. 'A superhero with a supervillain mother? Seems legit to me. Like Luke Skywalker and Darth Vader, if Darth Vader was female, and instead of the Death Star there was a multilevel deluxe shopping centre.'

Hiro smiled a sad little smile. 'I wish I could pull off her helmet and redeem her. I'd even let her chop my hand off.'

I felt something flicker inside me. Something warm and bright. It started to burn away at my cold, hard rage. 'We don't get to choose our families.'

'We had a big fight tonight. That's why I'm here. She told me the council were voting on the Green Valentine Scheme next week, and I told her that the whole thing was corporate bullshit and she was going to destroy people's lives. She got all upset and cried, and then *I* felt bad, even though I'm supposed to be the good guy here.' Hiro's face twisted miserably.

'Tonight . . . ' I rubbed a basil leaf between my finger and thumb, inhaling the scent. 'Why didn't you go? I thought . . . You and Pois— You and Storm—'

Hiro snorted. 'What? After what they did to me at the display centre? Also, Storm is insane.'

'But . . . you thought she had all the answers.'

'I was wrong. You were right. People like her are never going to change the world. People like you are.'

The tiny warm, bright thing flared up.

'Astrid,' Hiro took another step forward. 'I'm sorry. About everything. About Storm, and about the way I treated you in front of my friends. I felt like you wanted me to be something I wasn't. It . . . it was like my mum, all over again.'

'It's okay,' I said. 'I'm sorry too. I *did* want you to be something you weren't. I thought I knew better, but that's not fair. You get to make your own choices, even if I think they're bad ones.'

Hiro looked down at the ground. 'I felt so *angry*. You made me angry that the world is broken. And that I couldn't fix it. I wanted to break things.'

I nodded. 'I feel like that too.'

He smiled at me. 'Can we just garden for a while? I've had enough of breaking stuff. I want to be productive.'

Despite having had no attention for over a fortnight, the kitchen garden was doing surprisingly well. We pulled weeds and thinned seedlings and added compost. A bumper crop of tomatoes and eggplant was appearing, and I wondered if they'd ripen before getting bulldozed and turned into a swimming pool.

As we worked side by side, I felt my heavy sadness lift. I realised that we could do this, Hiro and I. We could be friends. We could work together. No kissing, no torment, no angry words or overblown expectations. This – the two of us, digging and planting and mulching – it was good. It was enough.

Until.

As he reached for a trowel, Hiro's hand brushed mine, and I felt my knees buckle.

It was a wave of emotion, so strong and powerful that it washed away all my calm satisfaction. I felt drenched – my cheeks burned and I shuddered as my breathing grew shallow. I put out a hand to steady myself on the edge of the garden bed.

This was insane.

I'd been kidding myself that I was over him, and that we could just be friends. He made me weak at the knees. *Literally.* I thought that was something that only happened in books.

Hiro moved away from me – a few centimetres – but I noticed. Did he not want to touch me? Or was he feeling the same way I was, but trying to hide it?

I snuck a glance at him out of the corner of my eye. Did I notice a faint pink flush on his cheeks? Was the frown that creased his forehead one of concentration or displeasure?

His eyes met mine suddenly, briefly, for the tiniest fraction of a second. We both looked back to the garden. I repositioned a bamboo stake. Hiro scratched a fingernail into the dirt.

Blood roared in my ears, and I could hear myself breathing, loud as thunder.

Hiro leaned across me again, reaching for the packet of twist-ties we used to secure plants to their wooden stakes or trellises. For a moment, he leaned against me, his side against mine, and I held my breath.

That wasn't an accident. That lean. That moment. I waited for an agonising ten seconds, waited for him to say something or do something. To give me another sign.

Then I stopped waiting.

I deliberately put my hand on his. He froze, and I felt his whole body tense up beside me. My heart hammered. Had I been reading all the signs wrong? Was he going to reject me again?

We stood there in silence. I didn't know what to do. I'd been certain that Hiro would have reacted, one way or another. Either pulled away or moved closer. But he just stood there, like a vegetable. I felt like an idiot. Should I remove my hand?

I never let go.

I gritted my teeth and stayed put, my hand lightly resting on Hiro's. I felt his skin on my skin, and despite the tension, I thrilled to be touching him again.

'It'll never work,' he said at last, his voice low and husky. 'You and me.'

'I don't care.'

'Your friends will never accept me.'

'I don't care.'

'I don't want to go to university.'

'I don't care.'

'You're going to do all this amazing stuff with your life. You'll go to uni and you'll make all these new friends and you'll find big, exciting ways to change the world. And you'll leave me behind.'

'I won't.'

He finally met my eyes, and I felt dizzy. I *saw him*, deep inside, and I could tell he could see me too. All my doubt and anxiety washed away under his gaze. I knew he wanted me. I knew he felt exactly the same way I did.

And then suddenly we had our arms around each other, and were kissing like we'd never kissed before. Everything was urgent and desperate, but still *achingly* sweet. I was never going to let him go. Never. He pulled me in closer, and my hands slipped under his shirt to rest on the small of his back.

Our feet got tangled up together, and we fell, still clutching each other, into one of the raised garden beds. For a split second I mourned for the wombok cabbage that we were squashing, but then I was overwhelmed by the aroma of fresh earth and sugarcane mulch and *Hiro*. I felt myself sink a little into the soft garden bed, and my hands touched dirt and green growing things.

Hiro's hand sought mine, and our fingers entwined in

the soil as we kissed and kissed and my head grew light from lack of oxygen.

A cool breeze made the leaves around us sigh and shift, and the dark orange smog that usually covered Valentine lifted, and I saw the faint twinkling of stars overhead. I felt the garden all around us – breathing and living, full of wriggling, pushing, growing *life*. I felt calm and safe, cradled in the soft earth and Hiro's arms, our breath perfectly matched, our heartbeats in sync. Everything was as it should be, in this one perfect moment.

And I knew that I would never, never let go.

'So what's the plan?' murmured Hiro at last.

I tilted my face up to his so I could see him properly. His hair stuck up in all directions, and was littered with sugarcane mulch. He'd never looked so adorable, and I had to kiss him again. I felt his lips smile under mine.

'I meant,' he said, when we stopped for air. 'I meant what *else* is the plan. Apart from . . . *that*.'

I didn't want to get up. I didn't want to disturb our perfect little ecosystem of stars and earth and green tendrils, buds and leaves. But there would be no growing things unless we fought for them. So I sat up, and my head spun for a moment. Hiro smiled up at me.

'You're so beautiful,' he said. 'Inside and out. Beautiful and fierce.'

I trailed a finger along his cheek.

'The plan,' I said slowly, thinking it through. 'The plan. I don't know.'

'There must be something we can do,' said Hiro, hoisting himself up from the garden bed and brushing dirt and mulch from his clothes. 'We're not going to let Mum win. Right?'

'Right.' I scrambled up too, thinking hard.

But what could we do? Two teenagers and a few tomato plants.

'The council meets on Monday morning,' said Hiro. 'From what Mum said earlier, she's managed to get three of the nine councillors on board. She gets a vote too, which means she only needs to persuade two more in order to pass the Green Valentine Scheme.'

I nodded. 'So we need to make sure the remaining six councillors don't vote with her,' I said. 'How do we do that?'

Hiro shrugged. 'If only we really were an Invisible Garden Army, instead of just two people,' he said with a sigh. 'Then we could make a difference.'

I glanced down at the imprint in the earth where our bodies had lain. The wombok cabbage was definitely not going to recover. I felt a warm glow inside. We were still lying there, sort of. A part of us was, anyway. A part of us would always be lying there.

I wanted to recapture the excitement of those first few weeks with Hiro. The incredible highs we'd felt, as things started to sprout and unfurl. How could we make other people feel that way? That heady mix of ambition and passion and satisfaction?

'What if we were?' I asked, slowly.

'Were what?'

'What if we had an army? A real, non-invisible garden army?'

Hiro frowned 'We don't. This is Valentine, remember?

You can't get people to sign a petition, let alone attend a demonstration.'

I felt a smile spread over my face. 'I've been going about this all the wrong way. And I think I know what we need to do.'

20

The council vote was at nine-thirty am. At nine-fifteen, I stood on the steps to the Town Hall, feeling like the earth might open up and swallow me at any moment. The sun was high and hot overhead, spreading searing white light over everything. But I didn't dread the daylight anymore. It was time to stop hiding under the cover of darkness. I knew what was coming, and I wasn't giving in without a fight.

Hiro and I had been up all night, transplanting the flowers and vegies from the school kitchen garden into the empty beds around the Town Hall. I caught a glimpse of my reflection in the grand set of glass doors. I looked like a wild creature, my hair tangled and matted with mulch, my face and hands smeared with dirt. I smiled at myself, a fierce, wolfish smile. White teeth and piercing eyes glinted back at me. I'd never felt so free.

Our little plants were digging their roots down into their new homes, and turning their faces up to the morning sun. I could feel them settling in around me, taking root and starting to grow. Something was growing inside me, too. Something strong.

'Astrid.' It was Bryce Walker, Paige's dad, wearing his cleaning overalls. He didn't look overwhelmed with joy to see me.

I took a step towards him. 'Thanks so much for this,' I said. 'I really owe you one.'

Bryce's eyebrows drew together in concern. 'Are you sure you know what you're doing, Astrid? I could get into a lot of trouble for this.'

'I know. And I really appreciate it. But you understand, right? Why it's important?'

Bryce hesitated, then nodded. 'I suppose they're going to take the keys off me in a few days anyway, when the new cleaning company moves in.'

I smiled and tried to look braver than I felt. 'Trust me.'

He pulled a heavy bunch of keys from his pocket and let me through a door to one side of the Town Hall steps. Inside everything was quiet and cool, save for the wheeze of an air conditioner. Bryce led me down a corridor lined with framed portraits of previous councillors. They looked like an entirely shifty lot.

'So,' I said, trying to ease the awkward silence as we walked. 'How are those organic cleaning products I recommended going?'

'Great,' said Bryce over his shoulder. 'Until I lost the council cleaning contract. I now have a garage full of tea tree oil and orange extract.'

'Right,' I said. 'Well, hopefully we'll be able to do something about that today.'

Bryce didn't reply. I didn't exactly feel waves of confidence radiating from him.

A bored-looking security guard stood in front of an unremarkable door at the end of the corridor. Bryce nodded to him, and the security guard turned and opened the door. We walked through, and I couldn't quite believe that had been so easy.

The Town Hall was quite a grand space that had once held concerts and markets and seminars. Nowadays it was only used for council meetings, and everything was shabby and faded. The councillors sat around a long wooden table on a raised platform at one end, in front of the stage. There were a handful of uncomfortable plastic chairs set out in wonky rows, in case the council needed to consult with any community groups. Which of course they didn't.

Eight councillors sat around the table. I recognised a few of them – a couple of local business owners. Some I'd never seen before, and I suspected that Mayor Tanaka had squirrelled them in to be her cronies. She sat at the head of the table, wearing a neat business suit, her face a mask of cold, businesslike efficiency.

'. . . implementing our key deliverables according to the proposed timeline . . .' Mayor Tanaka broke off and looked up as we entered. Eight heads turned to follow her gaze.

'See?' the Mayor said to the councillors, indicating me and Bryce with a tilt of her head. 'This is why we need the services of a reputable, accountable cleaning firm, and not just some random local who can bring in *anything* off the street.'

Her eyes flicked to me as she said *anything* with a look

of polite distaste, as if I were some kind of feral animal, or an overflowing rubbish bin.

Bryce looked terrified. 'You're on your own, kid,' he muttered, and scurried away out the door. I swallowed, and then walked across the scratched parquetry floor until I stood before the wooden table.

'Hi, Mayor Tanaka,' I said. 'My name's Astrid Katy Smythe. I'm Hiro's girlfriend.'

Mayor Tanaka raised her eyebrows. 'Yes,' she said. 'I know who you are. Are you looking for Hiro?'

I shook my head. 'Actually, I was looking for you. I have something I want to say.'

'I'm sure you have some big speech planned,' said Mayor Tanaka, holding up a hand. 'But we really don't need to hear it. The vote will be going ahead. I'm sorry if you're disappointed.'

I felt the old rage-monster rise up inside me, but it was trampled down by the green, growing calmness. I didn't need rage. I had *certainty* instead.

I smiled at her. She didn't smile back. I wasn't sure she could. The door behind me opened again, and Mr Webber stepped into the council chamber room. I blinked. He scowled at me, walked across the room and sat next to the mayor.

'*You're* on local council?' I asked, and then wondered why I was surprised. Of course he was. Mayor Tanaka had probably promised him a nice cushy job as principal of the evil new Valentine Business College.

I shook my head. 'I always knew you hated my kitchen garden,' I said. 'But really, a heated pool?'

Mr Webber shrugged. 'All the best schools have a pool. It attracts the right sort of parent. Unlike your little garden, which, as I understand it, is just hazardous waste.'

Hazardous waste. That's what he called the garden. He was a hazardous waste of a human being.

'You know this is wrong,' I said to Mr Webber. 'You know it isn't fair.'

Mr Webber's face twisted. 'You know what, Astrid?' he said. 'Life isn't fair. You get to swan around school as if you own it. You get to skip class whenever you feel like it. Everybody likes you and listens to you. You have privileges at Valentine High that nobody else does – teacher or student. Is that fair?'

I felt as if he'd slapped me in the face. It wasn't fair. I was a Missolini, and it wasn't fair, any more than it was fair that Superman had super strength. But Superman's strength was also a burden and a responsibility.

'You're right,' I said to him. 'Fair doesn't come into it. There's no such thing as fair. There's no cosmic judge handing out compensation packages to people who have been treated unfairly. But that doesn't mean I'm not going to fight for what I think is right.'

Mayor Tanaka let out a derisive snort. 'Honestly,' she said, her voice heavy with sarcasm. Her eyes narrowed, and for a moment I could see Hiro in her face, resentful and full of anger. 'You and whose army?'

I heard a rumble coming from outside. 'My army,' I said. 'My Invisible Garden Army.'

The rumble got louder, a low thumping tramp, clapping, and music.

Mayor Tanaka glared at me. 'Enough of this bullshit,' she said, and turned to the notes in front of her. 'First order of business is the approval of the Green Valentine scheme. All in favour—'

I heard footsteps in the corridor outside, and the raised voice of the security guard.

'Mayor Tanaka,' I said. 'You can grow some pretty awesome stuff in bullshit.'

The doors behind me burst open, and my army flooded in.

They were dressed in all the colours of the rainbow, carrying placards and shovels and pots overflowing with green life. Paige was wearing a long, elaborate gown that seemed to be entirely made of leaves. She wore a crown of flowers, and trailed ivy tendrils behind her. She was surrounded by an adoring crowd of fans, who carried placards that read RESISTANCE IS FERTILE. Michi and Cara wore twin crowns of woven flowers. Hiro's nonna pushed a wheelbarrow full of vegetables and seedlings. Dev's parents led a troupe of singing teenagers carrying a banner saying DON'T LET OUR DROP-INS DROP OUT. Paige's mum and the rest of the leisure centre staff waved pool noodles like flags of victory. At the front was my mum and some people from her art class, carrying an enormous banner that just read VALENTINE, where every letter was decorated with the different things that brought our community together – library books, meals-on-wheels, soccer clubs and working bees. I saw my dad and the Whippet, both carrying enormous white boxes with the logo of Dad's dentistry practice on the sides.

They crammed in, filling the hall with noise and colour. Just when I thought we were at capacity, more people would squeeze in through the door. People from school with their friends and parents. The staff of Patchwork Rhubarb handing out iced coffees and juices. Teachers from school. I spotted a couple of Poison Ivy's goons, and didn't even feel annoyed that one of them was banging on a djembe, because it was drowned out by our *entire school marching band*, who managed to elbow their way up onto the stage behind the council, playing a very up-tempo version of 'Rockin' in the Free World', being led by Dev, who was dancing in front of them with his flute like the Pied Piper of Hamelin.

And up the very, very front was Hiro, waving a foam lobster claw and looking *extremely* pleased with himself. I loved him so much, in that moment, that I thought I might fall apart.

Mayor Tanaka pulled out her BlackBerry and began speaking urgently into it, yelling to be heard over the din.

Mr Webber turned to me, his face dark with rage. 'You,' he shouted. '*You* did this.'

I shook my head. 'No, Mr Webber. Valentine did this. We may live in the ugliest suburb on the planet, but that doesn't mean we don't care about it.'

Hiro and I had worked all weekend. We'd called in Paige and Dev and harnessed the vast social networking powers of the Missolinis. We'd doorknocked and texted and tweeted and Facebooked. We hadn't tried to convince anyone of anything – we hadn't needed to. Everyone had heard about Green Valentine, and everyone was angry that they hadn't been consulted. I looked out over the sea of people. Not a single one of them had signed my Hairy Marron petition. But that didn't mean they didn't care about anything.

Hiro scrambled up onto the councillors' table, motioning for silence. His mum looked utterly horrified. The marching band stopped playing, and everyone turned towards Hiro.

'Hi,' said Hiro, his voice sounding out clear and loud, so different from his usual mumbling. 'So, a lot of you don't know me. And most of you who do know me probably don't like me. But that's okay, because I don't know you either. And you *do* know this girl here.' He gestured towards me. 'Everyone knows Astrid Katy Smythe. Whether she raised money for your soccer team, or helped you with your science homework, or pestered you into signing a petition about some random endangered crustacean, you've all met Astrid, and undoubtedly been charmed by her cheerful determination. So I'm going to stop talking, and let her do all the hard work.'

He reached down and pulled me up onto the table. Everyone cheered, and the marching band played a little fanfare. I felt like I was in a dream. I glanced down at Mr Webber and Mayor Tanaka. They were both furious. The Mayor was jabbing savagely at her BlackBerry while Mr Webber seemed to be muttering apologies and excuses into her ear.

Then I looked out over the crowd. It was the strangest group of people I'd ever seen. There were plants and musical instruments and gardening implements and pool noodles. They were shoulder-to-shoulder, taking up every inch of the hall, crammed in together like one giant, swirling mass of colour and weirdness.

I cleared my throat. What on earth was I supposed to say? In the crowd, I saw Dev grin and give me a thumbs up. I didn't have anything prepared. I hadn't thought this far ahead.

'Um,' I said. 'Thanks for coming . . .'

'Enough,' said Mayor Tanaka. 'This has to end. You think you can storm in here, interrupting official business, and everything will go your way like in a movie? It doesn't work that way. You can't save the world by planting a bloody tomato.'

I stared down at her, and suddenly I knew *exactly* what to say.

'Yeah, I can,' I said. 'Because you know what I can do with that one tomato? I can get about fifty viable seeds. And I can grow those seeds, or give them to other people to grow. And that makes fifty tomato plants. And we can harvest around twenty tomatoes from a tomato plant. And if we collected the seeds from just one tomato per plant, and grew those as well, we'd have twenty thousand tomatoes. And you can feed a lot of people with twenty thousand tomatoes.'

A ripple of applause went through the crowd.

'Mayor Tanaka thinks that Valentine needs to change, and she's right. But she's like I used to be. She's trying to force Valentine into the mould of what she thinks a successful suburb should look like. But she hasn't *listened*.'

I looked out over the sea of people. I saw small business owners and students and children and pensioners and retail employees and musicians and teachers. I saw a community.

'I learnt something this week,' I told them. 'I've spent years trying to get you all to care about the things I care about. But I've gone about it totally the wrong way. I've been telling everyone around me that they're wrong, that the way they do things is bad, that they should be ashamed. But I've been a total hypocrite, because I never listened to any of you, when you tried to tell me what *you* cared about. You all have passions and dreams. Everyone cares about something, whether it's your house, your family, your job, your pet. I thought that just because Valentine doesn't look like the happy, friendly, white-picket-fence suburbs you see on TV, it meant we had no community. I was wrong. We have a community, and all we needed was for someone to listen.'

The crowd burst into applause.

'I believe Valentine can be better,' I continued. 'I believe it can be beautiful. And I know you all believe that too. And every single one of us will have a different idea of *how* it can be better. We should share those ideas. Because a truly great community can't be built with just one idea. It's built with hundreds and hundreds of little ones.'

I thought about the sneering remarks Poison Ivy had made about my tomatoes. 'A high school kitchen garden might not be much,' I said. 'But it's a seed. And seeds can grow into amazing, beautiful things. One seed can end up feeding thousands. People think of gardening as being relaxing. It's something that we do to get away from all the terrible stuff going on in the world. It's something little old ladies do.'

I heard Maria let out a whoop.

'And although gardening *is* relaxing, it can also be radical. It can be political. When all our food is grown from genetically modified seeds, created in laboratories that are owned by just five companies worldwide, growing our own vegetables is an *act of resistance*. And it's not a negative resistance like a boycott or a strike. It's *positive*. We're *creating other options*, opening up new pathways to live and be.'

I glanced over at Hiro and he grinned at me.

'When I started the school kitchen garden, I did it because it was good for the environment. Seventy-five per cent of the energy needed to produce our food is used *after* it's left the farm. Home-grown food uses less energy, fewer pesticides and up to eighty-nine per cent less water. And I've realised this summer that growing your own vegies is about more than just the environment. Gardening is about *people*. It's about sharing your excess lemons and tomatoes with a neighbours and friends. It's about getting together to install new garden beds. It's about sitting down at a table full of food that *you* grew, that only had to travel a few steps to your kitchen. It's about sharing that food with the people you love. It's about talking, and listening. Food brings us together. And we're not going to save Valentine unless we're all in it together.'

I had them. The crowd were with me, hanging on my every word. I felt like I could float off the table, through the ceiling and into the sky.

'The word *radical* comes from the Latin word *radix*, which means *root*. Gardening is radical. Growth is radical. It's built into our *language*. So let's be radical. All it takes is one seed. Just one seed, one idea, and then you're on your way to growth, and change, and community. So let's get our hands dirty!'

The crowd erupted into applause, and things went crazy

for a while. The brass band started up again and everyone whistled and cheered and sang along.

The councillors were talking urgently with each other around my ankles. Mayor Tanaka was banging her hands on the table, struggling to be heard. Mr Webber's face was purple with rage.

I took a deep breath, and hoped that I'd said enough. That we'd shown them. I held up my hand and the noise died down.

'I'm sorry we interrupted your meeting,' I said, looking down at the councillors around the table. 'I think you were about to put the Green Valentine Scheme to a vote. Please continue. I promise we won't interrupt again. You won't even know we're here.'

I clambered down from the table.

Mayor Tanaka picked up her papers and shuffled them, and I could see that her hands were shaking. She looked down at her notes, as if they could provide her with a way of delaying the vote, so she could get control back.

The hall fell completely silent. Everyone's eyes turned to the Mayor, waiting.

She sighed. 'All in favour of the Green Valentine Scheme, say *aye*.'

I held my breath.

'Aye.' One of the anonymous councillors.

'Aye.' Another anonymous councillor.

'Aye.' Mr Webber narrowed his eyes at me.

Mayor Tanaka raised a hand. 'Aye.'

I waited, my heart pounding in my chest. My eyes darted from councillor to councillor. They were all looking at their folded hands, or at their notes, trying to appear as small and unnoticeable as possible. The silence stretched on. Four votes. The Mayor needed two more.

We waited.

Finally, Mayor Takana closed her eyes in defeat. 'All against.'

There was a chorus of *nays*.

'The *nays* have it,' said Mayor Tanaka, standing up so quickly that she knocked her chair over. 'The Green Valentine Scheme will not proceed.'

She pushed through the crowd and headed out the door as everyone filled the room with whoops and cheers. Mr Webber followed her, shooting me a look that implied my Missolini privileges had been revoked.

The council chamber was getting very hot and stuffy, so we all trooped out as well, spilling out onto the street and into the blinding, baking sun.

People pressed forward to hug me or congratulate me. Everyone was sharing questions and ideas – one man suggested starting a Valentine seed co-op, where we would all share and swap the seeds we saved from our gardens. Someone from Mum's art class was talking to the owner of Patchwork Rhubarb about setting up an Art and Coffee club. Paige's mum and Dev's parents were discussing the possibility of a festival of dance. Mr Gerakis gave me a hearty handshake, and told me that, council be damned – he was going to use all our fresh produce in his Home Ec classes.

'Astrid.' It was Mum.

I gave her an enormous hug, and she hugged me back. 'I'm so proud of you,' she said. 'How did I ever produce such a wonderful daughter?'

I grinned at her. 'I guess you must have been an excellent parent.'

Mum's eyes grew serious. 'It wasn't just me, you know,' she said, and jerked her head over to Dad.

I nodded, and gave her another hug.

Dad and the Whippet were at the centre of a tight cluster of people. It turned out that the giant white boxes they'd been carrying were full of cupcakes. Green cupcakes. With creamy yellow icing.

'They're made using spinach,' she explained to me. 'Don't worry, they taste good.'

I tried one, and she was right. They really did taste good. I barely even noticed the spinach.

'Organic spinach,' the Whippet – Jessica – added hurriedly. 'I bought organic spinach.'

'It must have taken you ages to make all these,' I said, through a mouthful of green crumbs. I reached for a second cupcake, realising how *hungry* I was.

Jessica smiled. 'Your dad helped,' she said shyly. 'He's actually a very good cook.'

I stared at Dad. I'd never seen him so much as boil water. He shrugged.

'I'm trying,' he said. 'Trying to learn new things. To be better. That's all we can do, right?'

I gave him a hug. 'Right.'

Hiro came up and slipped his hand into mine. I squeezed it. 'I'm sorry about your mum,' I said.

'Me too,' he said. 'She'll get over it, though.'

'Maybe we've inspired her to be more engaged with community values,' I suggested hopefully.

'I sincerely doubt it,' said Hiro.

'Well,' I said. 'We'll just keep fighting. Until someone comes along who listens.'

'About that,' said Michi, coming up behind us. 'I'm about to climb up on Mum's BMW over there and announce through this megaphone that I'm running for local council.'

Hiro stared at her. 'Seriously?' he asked. 'But what about moving to the city?'

Michi shrugged. 'Rent here is cheaper,' she said. 'And Cara's suddenly developed a passion for gardening.' She turned to me. 'I'll need your help, of course.'

I blinked. 'Um, yes, of course. Anything.'

Local government. Grassroots politics. Getting involved with the community. Changing the world from the bottom up. That was something I could get behind. The fight wasn't over, but we'd won this battle, and I was totally up for more.

'This is certainly going to make our family dinners more interesting,' said Hiro with a grin.

I looked around at all the wonderful people in my life. Now Mum was talking to Dev's parents. Maria was admiring Paige's leaf gown. Even Barney and Kyle were there, munching on spinach cupcakes and trying to look like they weren't involved. Poison Ivy's goons were examining a rubbish bin planted with geraniums. Strawberry Guy was holding his strawberry pot and talking to Tyson. I saw Dev in the distance, holding hands with Aaron Matthews, and I felt so ridiculously happy that I had to stop myself from running over and flinging my arms around them both. I saw people planting things they'd brought with them in the Town Hall's garden beds. Everywhere, things were growing. People were talking, eating, sharing. We were a *community*.

Hiro put his arm around my shoulder.

'This whole saving-the-world business,' he said. 'It feels pretty good, doesn't it?'

I nodded. It did. It was the best feeling ever. I felt happy and alive and as though at last, after all my petitions and letters and speeches, I was finally making a difference. I took that feeling and held it inside me, so it burned with a bright, joyful flame. I held it gently, letting its warmth spread through me.

And I knew I would never, ever let it go.

Acknowledgements

Thanks first of all to my mum, who made some very helpful suggestions at the very beginning of this process, when I was wondering out loud whether it was possible to write a novel about gardening that wouldn't be totally boring. Mum also took me on a tour of the guerrilla gardens of Clifton Hill, which was awesome and inspiring.

Thanks as always to everyone at Allen & Unwin, especially Jodie Webster and Hilary Reynolds – a girl couldn't ask for better publishers and editors.

Thanks to two amazing writers and friends: Paul Gartside, for reading an early draft and pointing out that the story needed a villain; and Penni Russon for suggesting the book's title.

This book was written as the creative component of my PhD in Creative Writing at the University of Melbourne. Massive thanks must go to my supervisors, Pam Macintyre and Kevin Brophy, for their patience, advice and understanding.

Thanks to all the guerrilla gardeners, permaculturalists and environmental activists that inspired the book – you do amazing work to remind us to be better people, and to look after our planet.

And finally, thanks to my beautiful family. To Michael who is always on hand to help me nut out a plot tangle, and to Banjo for napping so I could get some work done. I love you both.

About the Author

Lili Wilkinson was first published at age twelve in *Voiceworks* magazine. After studying Creative Arts at Melbourne University and teaching English in Japan, Lili worked on insideadog.com.au (a books website for teen readers), the Inky Awards and the Inkys Creative Reading Prize at the Centre for Youth Literature, State Library of Victoria. She is completing a PhD in Creative Writing and spends as much time as possible reading and writing books for teenagers.